‘

"There's nothing you could ever tell me that would change the way..." He took a deep breath. "...the way I love you." He'd said it. He'd wanted to say it before, but the time was never right. He waited, suspended. He knew how she felt, but he needed the words.

Time stopped as Jesse released him. They faced each other. She found his eyes, her hair falling away. "I love you, too. I had no idea what love was until I met you." She studied him in the soft, special way he dreamt of. "From that first morning, I've thought about you so much. You're part of me."

She grabbed him with unexpected force. Then, she found his lips and kissed him. He was afraid she'd devour him, and he loved it. He kissed her back, feeling the soft, tender warmth of her mouth and tongue as it sought his. Her fragrance surrounded them as his hands slipped inside her jeans, feeling the soft warmth as he caressed her. She followed his lead.

They stopped in unison, breathing heavily as they clung to each other. Searching desperately for a sanctuary, their eyes fell on the same thing. Parked a block away was Matt's Mustang convertible. He took her hand, but she was already pulling him toward it.

"You're sure…" He never finished.

"Yes, Matthew, *yes!*"

They ran toward his car. Matt fumbled for the keys and opened her door. He looked around. She touched his hand, sending strange, new sensations through him. He wanted to touch every inch of her rich body and more than anything he'd ever wanted in his life, he wanted to be with her.

Praise for Kevin V. Symmons

"A riveting saga of one woman's journey through triumph and adversity. *Solo* paints an unforgettable portrait of Jesse, a singer whose beauty, talent, and drive propel her toward an uncertain destiny. Part romance, part suspense, this engrossing tale will keep its readers guessing."

~Arlene Kay, Best-selling author

"In my years working at a center serving survivors of domestic violence and sexual assault, it can be frustrating to see these issues sensationalized or misrepresented in the popular media. Symmons did his research. *Solo* communicates the lifelong effects of such trauma in a very poignant and authentic way."

~Caitlyn Slowe, Violence Intervention and Prevention Person at Health Imperatives

"In *Solo*, Kevin Symmons captures the essence of a young starlet caught between the purity of her craft and the tumultuous road to success. ...poignantly accurate in the midst of a heroine's quest for love."

~Kirstie Wheeler, Asst. Prof., Berklee College of Music

"A thrilling story of romance, jealousy, ambition and betrayal. ...The ending will make your hair stand up. Don't miss this exciting novel."

~Steven Marini, Best-selling author

"Solo takes the reader on a breakneck journey through struggle and hope as they search for what is most important: their love."

~Virginia Young, Best-selling author

Solo

by

Kevin V. Symmons

Solo

Cover Art by *Debbie Taylor*

The Wild Rose Press, Inc.
PO Box 708
Adams Basin, NY 14410-0708
Visit us at www.thewildrosepress.com

Publishing History
First Mainstream Women Edition, 2014
Print ISBN 978-1-62830-302-5
Digital ISBN 978-1-62830-303-2

Published in the United States of America

Dedication

To all those who toil against
violence, fear, and loneliness...
to my fellow musicians and writers everywhere.

PART I

Chapter One

June 1988

It was sweltering Sunday afternoon. But Sundays had no special meaning for Jessica Long. Just another crowded space on the calendar. Moving deliberately through the moist air that hovered over Boylston Street, the heat rising from the sidewalk penetrated the worn souls of her loafers. Perspiration grew thick on her skin, darkening her thin cotton blouse.

A massive steel skeleton stood nearby. Having grown to a height of thirty stories, it guarded Copley Square's busy expanse. Halfway up the I-beams that comprised its brick-red frame an electronic sign flashed ninety-three degrees.

Many residents hid, sheltered inside, letting their fans or air conditioners battle the early heat-wave while they lolled away this June afternoon watching the Red Sox or movie reruns. The more adventurous, young, or athletic populated the banks of the Charles River or sought the cool breezes of South Boston's Carson Beach.

Jesse found the summer heat in Boston unwelcome and unexpected. She could never remember any semblance of a spring, just a cool damp season that one day surrendered as the unrelenting damp heat emerged like a chrysalis. Thanks to the onshore breeze from Casco Bay, it was never this hot in Portland. But Portland held more demons than she could exorcise in one lifetime. Jesse was glad to be rid of it.

She swallowed deeply, clenching her fists. This job could mean the difference between continuing her career or returning to the bleak life she'd left in Maine. Now that her mother and daughter Alexis had appeared, she had to find more work to support them while she finished her training at New England Conservatory.

She studied the brightly decorated windows of the cafes and boutiques, ignoring the glances of the men she passed. Young couples, stylishly dressed in their lightweight summer clothes stepped aside as she moved on her mission toward the address on the slip of paper Mario had given her.

Jesse peered through the murky glass. She scanned the adjacent shops, hesitating. Whatever it was, Martel's Coffee Shop and Bakery played counterpoint to Boylston Street's more fashionable establishments.

Her dim reflection showed a tall, slender young woman who favored her father. Or so they'd told her. She'd worn her best cotton slacks and a dark blouse. Jeans or shorts would send the wrong message, and Jesse couldn't afford a bad first impression. Her thick black hair hung loose, framing her face. She took a deep breath to help her relax. Checking her image in the dirty glass, she wiped the perspiration from her forehead and neck, drying her palms on her pants.

Taking another deep breath, she opened the door. Prayer was not on Jesse's agenda, but it crossed her mind. She knew the city was flooded with pretty co-eds and single mothers willing to work for almost nothing. Mario's influence might be worth something, but she was taking no chances. She wasn't given to fits of superstition, but she closed her eyes tightly and crossed her fingers. Anything that might give her an edge was worth a try.

"Please, Mr. Martel," she whispered, looking around self-consciously. "I need this job."

The door's glass was so grimy she couldn't see inside. Could Mario have been wrong? Was this place really open for business?

Inside the air was cooler, but not much. It held a stale, damp odor. If Martel's was air conditioned, someone should apply for a refund. She froze as she searched the shadows, trying to understand why anyone would use such a gloomy color. Her throat tightened. She squeezed the doorknob as she thought about leaving. A few fluorescents lit the front, but the rear was hidden in shadow.

"It was my mother," said a man's voice from the shadows. Despite the quiet, almost soothing quality of the voice, Jesse jumped.

"I beg your pardon," she said, scanning the darkness. "Did you say 'It was my mother'?"

"Yes," said the man with the soft voice, still out of sight. "You're Jesse?"

"How did you...?"

"Mario called to say you'd be coming by. He described you. He didn't exaggerate."

Jesse felt her face flush.

"My mother had a condition called photophobia, a sensitivity to light. Since she spent her life here, she wanted it to be dark, I'm too busy to repaint it. People ask about it. I took a guess when I saw you looking around." As he finished speaking, the man moved down the counter. He was small and thin, almost frail, but his face was kind, his smile warm. He approached, offering his hand.

"It's nice to meet you. I'm Gerry Martel. It's Gerry with a G."

Looking around, Jesse saw a thin counter running the length of the restaurant and disappearing into the dark. Like everything else, it was old and worn—red Formica, aged to a soft pink, hinting at warmth. She saw cake trays, napkin holders, and other hardware.

"Would you like to know where I've worked?" Jesse wanted to get on with the interview. She was a lyric soprano, not a psychologist.

"Mario said you'd been a waitress. He also said you were a good kid and needed the work." He paused. "Have you worked in a place like this?"

Jesse looked around, questioning.

"Our main business is in the morning. We get hundreds of customers in here between six and ten. Some office types, but right now a lot of construction guys. They're okay, but they can be tough, especially on someone who...who looks like you." He gestured in her direction.

Jesse answered the challenge. Desperation was a great motivator. "I'll tell you what. Give me a week. I'm good. Really good." Her adrenaline surged. "I'll work for tips. If you're not satisfied, just tell me. But if I can do the work, pay me four bucks an hour, plus my share of the tips."

Gerry held up his hand. "Calm down. Mario recommended you. That's good enough for me. But

4

four bucks an hour, that's a lot. I don't know. It wouldn't be fair to the other girls."

"Watch me and see. You can't lose. Either I work for nothing, or you'll see I'm worth the money. Come on. What do you say?"

"Okay. You're right. I can't lose." Gerry put his hand to his chin. "I'll bet you're a lot tougher than you look."

"I can handle anything this place can throw at me." She smiled.

He returned her smile and nodded, holding out his hand. She shook it. "I think we've got a deal."

"We have." Relief swept over Jesse. "I'll be here Monday morning. Is 5:30 okay?"

He nodded again.

"Oh, there's one more thing. It's about the air."

Gerry looked puzzled. Jesse rephrased her question.

"Sorry." She shook her head. "Does it get very smoky in here?"

"Not really. Our air conditioning keeps it pretty clean. And we don't let anyone smoke in here." He seemed poised to ask another question, but she looked at her watch and turned.

"Great." She sighed, heading toward the door. She had what she wanted. Jesse had no time for idle conversation. She walked out the door and back onto Boylston Street. She knew what Gerry thought—the same thing they all did. She hated it, and them for thinking it.

She exhaled. "Thank you, Gerry with a G!" she said, catching the attention of a passing jogger. He turned, sucking in his generous gut.

Jesse headed for the MBTA station to catch the train to Symphony. She had work to do at the Conservatory.

She turned, glaring at the jogger. "What do you want?" she yelled as she headed to the subway.

Chapter Two

The phone rang in the large, immaculate apartment overlooking West Springfield Street in Boston's South End. Mario Altieri shifted his ample frame in the recliner, crushing out his cigarette as he picked up the receiver. "Gerry?" he asked, knowing who was on the other end.

"Hello." Mario heard him breathing.

"Relax, my friend. We *are* friends, aren't we?"

"Of course. Our families go back to the old country… and the old ways."

"Good," Mario said softly. "Jessica came to see you today?"

"Yes." Gerry paused. "She's quite a young woman. Wouldn't take no for an answer."

"Good. I've explained how important this is to me."

"Yes, I won't let you down. You have my word."

"I know you won't." Mario's tone left no doubt as to the serious nature of the task. "If there's anything else you can do to help her, you'll have my undying gratitude and my financial support if—"

"Please don't insult me. I'm grateful for this opportunity to repay you."

"I want reports every day." Mario hung up the phone.

A slim, silver-haired woman stood in the bedroom

doorway. She listened to the conversation, the trace of a smile on her face when Mario replaced the receiver. "So, my love, after forty-five years it's begun."

Mario got up, crossed the room, and hugged her tightly. "Yes, God has smiled on me. I have to tell them before Jessica arrives," he said thoughtfully. "Some of these locals are such amateurs." He opened his mouth. She anticipated his question.

"You know I'll help you. We're in this together." She held him close. "You're right. These locals are amateurs. We wouldn't have survived." She pushed him away and took his hand. "We've waited too long for this chance, Mario. Believe me, we won't miss our chance."

****

Martel's had the stale bouquet of humanity masked poorly by Right Guard and Aqua Velva. But Matthew Sullivan paid no attention. He stood hypnotized, his attention on something new behind the counter.

"Matt, *hey, Matt,* are you with me?" It was David Jenkins, a friend from the construction site, and another recent graduate of Boston University. Matt ignored him. His gaze was fixed on the new waitress. Now, as he waited in line, he tried not to be obvious. "Huh…what'd you say, Dave?" Matt mumbled.

"Yeah." Dave grinned and gave his friend a shove. Matt stood waiting patiently as the beauty glided behind the counter.

As he got closer, he read her nametag—Jesse. He liked it. She was tall and filled out her worn jeans. Her thick, dark hair was short and tied in a ponytail. Her smile was dazzling, but what drew his attention were her eyes. They were light blue, with just a hint of green—the color of the sky on a warm summer day and so large Matt was sure he could walk right into them.

Reaching the counter, Matt took a deep breath as she approached showing a smile. Suddenly Ellen, one of the other waitresses, asked, "What'd ya want, kid? There's a hundred guys waiting. You want something or are you just window-shopping?" she asked, chewing a wad of gum. nodding in Jesse's direction.

"Sure…ah, a regular coffee with c-cream and one sugar," he stammered, eyes fixed on Jesse. "Please," he added to impress.

Ellen got his coffee as Matt fumbled with some change. He left a generous tip, hoping the new girl would notice. As he was leaving, Ellen mouthed, "Better luck tomorrow!" She clicked her gum and nodded toward Jesse again.

Matt stumbled out of Martel's trying to find the new girl in the tight jeans and the shortie apron one last time. As he reached the door she smiled. Ellen nodded in his direction and said something to Jesse. They giggled, then Jesse gave him a soft, special look Matt would never forget. He walked through the door, held open by the long line of customers, then staggered onto Boylston Street, laughing.

"What's with you?" asked Dave again. "Is this the guy who scored two short-handed goals to win the Beanpot?"

Matt ignored his old teammate. He grinned all the way to the construction site. He couldn't wait until tomorrow.

Chapter Three

Gerry stood in the kitchen on the Saturday afternoon of Jesse's first week. "That's almost $700 for the week, ladies." The kitchen was in sharp contrast to the restaurant side of Martel's—modern, well equipped and brightly lit. Jesse enjoyed her frequent trips back there. It was more inviting than the crowded counter space out front and always filled with the fragrance of Gerry's homemade pastries.

The three women surrounded him as he counted the generous pile of tips. The two older women stood at attention. They looked at each other then at Jesse. There was the Gilbert construction job across the square and a new exhibit at the Boston Public Library, but everyone knew she was responsible for a lot of those tips.

Ellen, the senior counter person, spoke first. "Best damn week we ever had."

"Sure is!" added Marie, a tiny woman whose eyes gleamed when she spoke.

"Come on." Gerry pointed to the three piles on his stainless steel prep table. Counting out each woman's share, he seemed as excited as they were. "There's $210 for each of you and $74 for the slush fund." The slush fund was part of the weekly tip pool that he put away for emergencies.

"Thanks, G." Marie stuffed her money into her pocketbook as she left. "Not bad, kid, not bad at all."

She nodded at Jesse.

"Thanks, Gerry." Ellen walked to the door. She turned toward Jesse. "I didn't think a little princess like you would last a day. Shit, was *I* wrong! You're okay, Jess." She left the kitchen, lighting a cigarette as the outer door slammed.

Gerry stood appraising his newest employee. "You were right. It's the best week we've ever had. You did great this week, Jess. I've never seen anyone handle those guys the way you did."

"Thanks, Gerry. I've had plenty of practice." Jesse stuffed the money in her backpack and headed for the door.

"Oh, I wanted to ask you. I'm ready to start cleaning the place up. You know, scrubbing and painting. If you can give me a hand, I'll pay you overtime."

Jesse stopped. Was this the come-on she'd grown to expect? She turned slowly.

He seemed to read her mind. "Jesse, when I say clean-up, I mean *clean-up*. Marie's got three kids and nobody to watch them. Ellen doesn't want the overtime. I need someone. You'll work that nice butt of yours off and go home tired. That's all you'll do." He raised his voice. "If you don't want to, I'll find someone else."

She'd overreacted. "Okay, Gerry. I could use the cash. Just tell me when. I have to check my schedule and talk to my mother." She smiled weakly. "And thanks." She felt ashamed for jumping to conclusions.

Gerry softened his expression. "Jess, what happened to you before is none of my business, but I'm not like that." He turned away.

She wanted to say something, to explain, but he

went to the sink and began washing pastry trays. She knew he was right. But Jesse hated feeling guilty.

Jesse had a knack for finding people like Gerry and her grandfather's old friend, Mario. Not that her life had been easy. It had rained misery on her in buckets. But since the day Pauline Richards had discovered her, she'd managed to deal with the obstacles life had thrown in her path—at least most of them. Pauline recognized Jesse's talent at their first meeting, giving her young disciple hope as she opened the world of music to her. It was a world of beauty, passion, and purity, a world far removed from the threadbare existence Jesse had known. A world she'd grown to love and cling to like a life buoy.

With her most critical year at Boston's prestigious New England Conservatory beginning in the fall, Jesse would do anything to get by, especially since the arrival of her mother and daughter. Somehow her tiny family would survive. They just had to, for at least one more year.

Jesse avoided men. Perhaps it was her brutal stepfather, or because she was so busy chasing success. More likely it resulted from the night she was drugged and attacked—the night when Ali was conceived. Since then she'd ignored the male sex

Then, on her first day at Martel's, when everything seemed in place, she saw *him*. And now he possessed her. He was tall, with a thin tanned face, a dimpled chin and steel blue eyes that could see inside her. He looked athletic, but he tripped all over himself whenever he saw her. In spite of that, perhaps because of it, she couldn't stop thinking about him.

His name was Matthew—Matthew Sullivan. Jesse had asked some of the other men about him. He was bright and young, working construction to get money for graduate school. She couldn't find out too much without being obvious, and she didn't want to be. She didn't *want* to be anything to him, but she couldn't help it. Every time she saw his strong, kind face, felt his eyes look into her soul and watched his easy, casual way with everyone, the blood rushed to her face. And there was the way he looked at her—like some sweet, adorable animal, needing to be cuddled.

There was no place in her endless days for him. She had to work, train, study, find time for Ali and her mother. There's no time for you, Matthew, get out of my head!

She felt like a character in one of those syrupy Rodgers and Hammerstein shows she'd done in summer stock. But each time she saw him, she cared less about what she *had* to do and more about what she *wanted* to do. Jesse's rational side was losing. She had never wanted anyone like she wanted Matthew Sullivan.

Chapter Four

July 1988

Early July saw no relief. By 7 a.m. the sign in Copley Square flashed eighty-six degrees. The crowd in Martel's had grown. It could be the service or something else. It wasn't the air conditioning, the pastries, or their coffee. For Matt, it was Jesse.

Each morning he maneuvered back and forth, working the line to make sure she'd wait on him. Maybe it was his imagination, but he thought she did the same thing behind the counter. Jesse balanced three cups of coffee and two toasted bagels. She put them down, smiling cheerfully at the grizzled worker she was waiting on.

"All yours, Ike." She placed the cups in a cardboard tray.

"Here you go, beautiful, keep the change." He left a ten-dollar bill.

She looked embarrassed, thanking him quietly. He asked what time she got off.

"I don't, Ike. They keep me chained here day and night." She laughed and everyone chuckled. But before he could say anything, the chorus of jeers told him the men in line were getting impatient with his flirtation.

"Okay, okay, I'm *going*." He disappeared into the heat.

Matt didn't mind the wait. It was cooler inside, and he could watch her float back and forth, maneuvering like an exquisite ballerina as she filled orders. He was always fantasizing about her—the way she smiled at him, her magnificent eyes, the way she moved in the faded jeans that fit as if they were tailored just for her...

"The usual, Matt?" Her question brought him out of his trance.

"Sure, Jess…ah, the usual. Thanks," he stumbled with his words. *What a doofus*, he thought.

Matt was so excited the first time she'd said his name. He could hardly wait to hear her say it every day. He stood, trying to think of something, anything to spend a few extra minutes with her.

"I didn't eat breakfast this morning. How about a bagel?"

"Sure. You want it toasted?"

Matt considered that. "Why not?"

Waiting for the toaster, she showed the soft expression that haunted him. "How come *you* don't ever ask what time I get off?" she asked with a warm smile.

He froze. Was she serious? She continued looking, eyebrows raised. The toaster popped. Jesse came back, her face flushed, putting the bagel in a bag.

"Jam or jelly, Matt? You don't look like a cream cheese guy to me." She tilted her head again.

"No…thanks. That'll be it for today." He wanted to kick himself. This incredible woman had just invited him to ask her out, and all he could do was mumble, *Thanks!*

"That'll be a dollar thirty," she said, looking at the endless line behind him.

Matt put two dollars on the counter. "Keep the change," he said softly.

"See you Monday, Matt. Have a nice weekend."

He headed for the door, still angry with himself. When he got there, he turned, stealing a look in her direction. She was waiting on another customer, but looked straight at him. She smiled, giving him a nod. His grin broadened into a smile as he flew across the square.

Chapter Five

The front door slammed. Jesse heard coughing and heavy footsteps on the stairs. She could hear her mother whimpering through the thin walls.

The bedroom door opened, and her brother Ryan stood there looking terrified, clutching a baseball bat in his hand. "Nothing's going to happen tonight, Jess, I'm not going to let him near you...ever again!" He was always trying to protect her and her mother from Alton.

"Let's sneak out the back way. Maybe he'll fall asleep," she begged. "Please don't do anything. You could get hurt." Alton was in a mean mood tonight. She could tell from the way he was breathing.

"No. Then what happens to Mom? I'm not leaving her here, and there's no way we can get to her and get out. This has got to stop, Jess...Jess...Jesse..."

Suddenly, she was awake.

She'd heard Ryan say her name, his voice echoing through her mind as she lay there sweating. It was always the same. The night when Ryan and her stepfather Alton had died. She lay there, listening to the air conditioner, her sheets moistened with sweat.

The clock on the small table that served as a nightstand said it was 3:45 a.m. Sometimes sleep would come again, sometimes it wouldn't. She had to try, because she had to get up in an hour, and she needed the rest. Then she remembered. It was Sunday, her weekly reprieve, an oasis in the desert of endless activity—work, training, being a mother, a daughter...and suddenly, *he* was there again.

Damn you, Matthew, she thought as the sweat dried on her body. She turned on her side, curling into the fetal position, reveling in the sensation. Jesse imagined his piercing blue eyes and the subtle way his muscles seemed to push on his T-shirt. She remembered how she felt the first time he looked at her in the special way that everyone had noticed.

A smile crossed her face as the terror of her dream faded. She pictured Matt standing in line, maneuvering so she'd wait on him and knowing that the other counter people would step back and let her.

"Why don't you just get a room?" Ellen had asked. "I'm getting horny just watching you two."

The thought was tempting. Jesse wondered what it would feel like to have him hold her and say all the things she wanted him to. But no one had penetrated Jesse's armor long enough for that. After that terrible night four years ago, she thought no one ever would. She reached under her T-shirt, feeling the scar tissue that served as a constant reminder of her humiliation and pain.

No, this was her year. The Thanksgiving recital was her big chance to showcase her talent. That night, influential people would flood Jordan Hall. No way. No hunky guy in a tight T-shirt was going to interfere with the dream—no matter how weak her knees felt or how many times her stomach did flips.

So why had she asked him that question? "Why don't you ever ask me what time I get off, Matt?" She was possessed. That must be it.

"Damn you, Matthew. *Stay out of my fucking life!"*

Maybe he'd forget about it. There were probably a dozen girls waiting to be with him. But there was the way he looked and acted when he was around her. No, Jesse couldn't fool herself. It might take time to work up his courage, but he wouldn't let the invitation pass.

What would it feel like to have him hold her and feel his lips touching her ears and neck and mouth? She closed her eyes, getting drowsy as she imagined him…and suddenly, it was 8:15. Jesse lay there, letting consciousness creep into her body. She got up, putting on her robe. She pulled up the shade. Last night's warm, soaking rain had passed. She pushed open the cranky window that overlooked the alley. Feeling the cool, fresh breeze, she turned off the air conditioner. It was the one small luxury she allowed herself. Jesse needed her sleep, so the few extra dollars were worth it. Mario had given her two window units—one for her room, another to help her mother's emphysema.

Jesse walked into the living room. The central area was about fifteen feet square, with a small kitchen to the right. The furnishings consisted of an old couch covered with the tattered afghan her mother had made for Jesse, a chair in the corner and a small table that served as a dining room, an office and a place for Ali to play with her toys. A nineteen-inch TV sat across from the couch on the mate to her nightstand. The apartment wouldn't be mistaken for a luxury condo on Beacon Hill, but it was clean, cheap, and cozy. More importantly, their street was safe and Ali had found a few nice playmates, so Jesse was happy with it.

Ali, as she called her daughter Alexis, sat on the sofa watching cartoons and playing with a little kitten

19

Kevin V. Symmons

they'd adopted. Her mother said that Ali looked so much like she had as a child—tall, thin and exceptionally pretty. Ali had Jesse's thick, dark hair and the aquamarine eyes that drew everyone's attention. Jesse hoped that fate, or God—who or whatever force controlled the universe—would give her daughter an easier path to follow.

"Hi, Mommy." Alexis smiled at her. "Can we go to the park today?" The park was the Public Garden, Metropolitan Boston's crown jewel. It was an open area in the heart of the city surrounded by trees and flowers, chosen for their color, beauty, and diversity. On what promised to be a spectacular, midsummer afternoon, there was nowhere better to be.

Despite the extra sleep, Jesse felt drained. She'd gone for weeks without a break. But looking at Alexis, she smiled, knowing there was only one answer she could give.

"Sure. Would you like to ride those boats that look like giant swans?" Jesse asked.

The swan boats were a major attraction of the Public Gardens. They consisted of six, foot-powered vessels that patrolled a three-acre lake known as the Lagoon. Each swan boat was made of two pontoons about thirty feet long and had benches for twenty. Gerry was a buff on local history, and he'd given Jesse all the details. While she'd only been once, it was all Alexis could talk about.

"Can we please...*please*?" Ali looked like a bubble about to burst. "Can Grandma come, too?" she asked as Jesse's mother, Alice, came out of her bedroom, punctuating her slow movements with a steady cough. Alice was a tiny, frail woman with thick gray hair and the same sparkling blue-green eyes that graced her daughter and granddaughter.

"Maybe you and Mommy could spend some time together without me tagging along," she suggested.

"Let us talk for a minute, okay?" Jesse pulled her mother aside. "Mom, if you really want to rest, I understand. I made some great tips this week, and we could take a cab over and back so you wouldn't have to walk."

"I could use the rest, but if we can afford it, I'd love to spend the time with Ali and you." She coughed. "I hardly ever see you, honey."

"I've got an even better idea. Let's get cleaned up, because we're taking a cab and riding the swan boats." Jesse strutted around while Ali giggled. "But…before we do *that,* we're going out for breakfast." She grinned. "When was the last time we did that?" Ali ran over and hugged her legs, squealing with excitement.

Alice sat on the couch to catch her breath. Mornings were the most difficult for her. She looked up at Jesse, her eyes moist.

"That's wonderful. Sunday with my two best girls. You've made my week," she managed.

"You're a great mother, and you've been so good to Alexis. If it wasn't for you, I could never have gone to the Conservatory."

"Nonsense, its Pauline's help and you working like a slave that made it possible. Someday soon it's gonna pay off. I know it is."

There was some truth in what she said, but Jesse wouldn't hear of it. "Don't *ever s*ay that. After all you sacrificed, living on nothing so I could sing. Pauline was good to me, but you're my mother. Besides, today I feel wonderful. I haven't felt this good in a long time."

Jesse thought of Matt, wondering what he was doing on this Sunday morning, how long it would be before he asked what time she did get through work and more importantly, what she'd say when he did.

Chapter Six

Across the city in South Boston, on the first floor of a well-maintained three-family home, Matt Sullivan slept peacefully. The house was on East 8th Street, between K and L Streets, in one of South Boston's better neighborhoods. Matt had spent his entire life in South Boston. The area was a white, working-class community, populated largely by Irish-American families and their descendants. Matt's neighborhood, like most, tended to be very close knit, almost insular, inhabited by families spanning several generations.

Growing up, Matt saw the area's social life center on the bars and clubs sprinkled along South Boston's two main streets, Broadway and Dorchester Avenue. But the community's reservoir of strength was its three Catholic Churches; St. Augustine's on West Broadway; Gate of Heaven on East 4th Street; and the Sullivan's church, St. Bridgid's, between N and O Streets on East Broadway.

"Time to get up, Matt." It was his father, Daniel.

Matt groaned. Attending Sunday morning mass was a ritual that was never broken short of disability or death. Matt appreciated that his father had adapted to the times, however. Recognizing his son's active social life, he allowed Matt to sleep until nine o'clock most Sundays.

"C'mon, Dad, it's the middle of the night. Have a

heart," Matt pleaded, having slipped into bed only a few hours before.

"I do have a heart, Matt, that's why I let you sleep until the middle of the day. Now get out of bed and get cleaned up." But Matt imagined him smiling as he listened by the door, waiting to hear the floor creak so he'd know that Matt was headed to the shower.

Matthew was the third generation of Sullivans to live in South Boston. His grandfather Seamus had come to Boston in 1925. Matt had been weaned on stories of his exploits in the Irish rebellions.

The Sullivans weren't community leaders in the political sense. His father said politics was a profession for those of questionable morals and motives. The Sullivans led by example. When a problem or need arose, they were always first with a helping hand or a kind word.

Matt shared the first floor with his father, while Jeanne, her husband Allen, and their two daughters lived on the second. It was accepted that when Matt married, he and his bride would occupy the top floor.

In June, Matt had graduated with honors from Boston University. He majored in history, with a minor in English. Matt hoped to get a Master's Degree in history, but he wouldn't pursue it until he'd saved the tuition. That was another of the Sullivan family tenets—if you couldn't pay for it, you didn't buy it. His grandfather told them of his native Ireland, where friends and family had been burdened with debt, becoming slaves to their wealthy landlords. Seamus swore that would never happen to him or his.

As he grew, Matt read voraciously. He was never without a book or his journal—one of many small notebooks he carried to write down everything he saw or felt. His special love was historical novels—reality-based fiction that weaved reality with romance and adventure.

For someone else growing up in such a tough, robust environment, his love of the ethereal and the romantic might have posed a problem. But Matt had another love, one far removed from the fairytale world of books and imagination. Matt was an outstanding high-school hockey player. The program at Boston University was thought to be the finest in the nation, so when its coach, Jack Parker, became a frequent visitor to Matt's games, everyone thought he was headed for collegiate stardom.

Matt had been an all-state defenseman in high school, but wasn't sure he had the speed or size the professional game demanded. So after a disabling injury to his left knee one snowy night in February of 1986, he was forced to accept that his career was over.

The orthopedic surgeons operated to give him some use of his shattered knee, but playing hockey again was out of the question. Since the Sullivans world had revolved around Matt's hockey career for years, it was a devastating loss to Matt and his family. But the Sullivans provided him with the love and support he needed. His anger and frustration at his misfortune subsided very slowly at first.

"I'm sorry about what happened to you," his father said as Matt sat with his leg iced downing his third Budweiser, "but sitting here drinking isn't going to change anything, son."

Matt studied his beer as he flipped through the channels.

"You've got to think about what's ahead," Daniel told him. "Hockey's been part of your life—part of all our lives for as long as I can remember, but it's over."

Matt continued playing with the remote.

"Hockey was great, *but you don't need it!* You have so much going for you, Mattie," Daniel Sullivan continued. "You're smart and you love history and writing. Use those talents. Make the best of them and stop thinking about what might have been. It's time to move on."

Matt looked up at his father. "I know, Dad. You're right." He felt a smile cross his face. "Believe me. I'm trying."

"I know you are, son." Daniel approached him, giving him a gentle slap on the knee. "Here." Daniel put several ragged notebooks on the coffee table. "I promised your grandfather that someday I'd give these to someone who'd make sense of 'em." He smiled warmly. "Here's your chance. It may take your mind off hockey."

"Thanks, I'll look them over." And as his recovery progressed, he did. Matt was fascinated. The most fascinating part was that they were true. Before his return to BU he'd begun an outline, making detailed notes on how to use the journals.

Now, as he stood in the shower, Matt hoped the water would wash away the Budweiser lingering in his system. The Minnesota North Stars had drafted his friend Evan Lassiter, and last night Matt and his old teammates had been celebrating Evan's good fortune. Matt's life had changed, but there was no one better at having a good time than his old hockey buddies.

As he stood there, letting the water work its magic,

he could see *her* face. It was happening more and more in the month since he'd met Jesse.

"Jesse...*Jesse...Jessica.*" He said her name slowly and smiled.

And now this thing on Friday.

Why don't you ever ask me what time I get off, Matt? There was something in the way she asked. She wasn't teasing or flirting. Women were always flirting with him. This was different. It was almost like she *had* to ask him...

Don't get carried away, he thought, pondering her question.

He got out of the shower, feeling better. After dressing, Matt ran onto the front porch where his father, sister Jeanne, and her family were waiting. They headed toward Broadway and the short trip to St. Bridgid's.

Walking along, they saw several neighbors. Some returning from eight thirty mass, others just out enjoying this dazzling Sunday morning.

Jeanne's two little girls, Theresa and Caitlyn, did their best to tease and poke Matt. He felt better and picked up Theresa, twirling her around. She was the youngest and his favorite. "Uncle Matt, you smell funny this morning."

They all looked at Matt, knowing he'd been celebrating into the early morning. Jeanne's husband Allen and Matt had become good friends since he'd lived at the Sullivan home. He tried not to smile.

"Uncle Matt had a good time last night, honey. Sometimes, when you have a good time you drink something that makes you smell funny," he explained.

"I don't understand, Daddy." Theresa looked at Matt then back at her father.

They arrived at St. Bridgid's and headed up the steps.

"Uncle Matt got hammered last night," offered Caitlyn who was turning eight in a month. They all looked at each other, and Jeanne shook her head as the family broke into laughter.

Chapter Seven

"Did you like that, Ali?" Jesse asked after treating her family to breakfast.

"Loved it, Mommy." Alexis took Jesse's hand.

They headed for the Public Gardens. The day was spectacular, offering a brief escape from a brutal summer. That afternoon, strong northwest winds chased the humidity from the city, replacing it with a deep blue sky and a touch of fluffy, white clouds. As Jesse and her family headed down the path toward the Lagoon, yellow day lilies, red geraniums, and purple and white petunias surrounded them, shining as they reflected the bright sunlight.

Alexis beamed, perhaps because today was an exception. In her daughter's four years, life had been difficult. For much of that time, Jesse had been absent—ninety miles from their Portland home. But thanks to her hard work and the generosity of her grandfather's friend, Mario Altieri, their tiny family had been reunited.

Despite her love for Ali and her mother, their arrival meant adding long hours at Martel's to the singing and piano jobs she worked at night. Her extensive portfolio of scholarships, grant money, and financial aid were already stretched paper-thin, so there was little left for a sick mother and young daughter.

But on that sparkling July afternoon, Jesse decided

for a few hours she was going to laugh and enjoy her family. As they waited for Alice to catch up, Jesse couldn't help herself. She laughed out loud, picking Ali up. Twirling her around, Jesse hugged her daughter so tightly, she squealed with joy.

****

It was ten forty-five when the Sullivan family left St. Bridgid's heading home.

"Do you remember your promise, Uncle Matt?" Caitlyn danced around him. He had no idea, but Matt was in no mood to play the devoted uncle this afternoon. He wanted to go home, lie on the hammock, and listen to the Red Sox game.

"No, I don't."

She looked up with disappointment. "You promised the next Sunday it was nice you'd take us to ride on those boats that look like swans, *remember*?" Her voice held such conviction that Matt hid his smile.

He remembered. They were watching a special about the Public Gardens. The girls enjoyed it so much that Matt volunteered to take them some Sunday afternoon. He could never have guessed the adventure might be preceded by a Saturday night spent drinking Faneuil Hall dry. But he was devoted to his nieces, so reluctantly, Matt agreed.

He walked along, the girls dancing around him. As they approached the house, Matt thought of someone who could help him.

"Would you guys mind if we brought along a friend?" he asked.

They shook their heads.

"You know Donna Flaherty? Remember how much fun you had with her at Jimmy Walsh's First

Communion?"

Donna and Matt had grown up together. They'd been close since grammar school, but the fall she left for the University of Vermont, Matt found Gretchen, a flighty figure skater. When he called Donna, she agreed to share the adventure. At 1:00 p.m., they were on an MBTA bus, heading toward the Public Gardens.

By early afternoon, Matt had recovered. He and the girls laughed and sang their way around Boston Common. When they turned onto the path leading toward the swan boats, Matt stopped at the drinking fountain. He hoisted Caitlyn, then put her down to give Terry a chance.

He grinned at them, yelling, "Last one to the swan boats is a rotten egg!" As they darted off toward the Lagoon, Matt bumped into someone.

"Excuse me," he said, following the girls with his eyes.

"It's all right, Matt," Jesse said. There was a little girl and an older woman behind her. She didn't introduce them; her attention was on Donna and his nieces. They stopped and ran back.

"I didn't recognize you, Jesse, you're…out of uniform," Matt said self-consciously.

"So are you." She continued with a noncommittal smile.

Matt's mind raced. Would she think he was married and had a family? The girls laughed and circled him, ignorant of the tension. After catching her breath, Caitlyn spoke. "Hi, I'm Cait McDonough. Do you know my uncle Matt?" she asked with a grin, adding, "Isn't he nice?"

The tension drained from Jesse's body at the sound

of the word uncle. Bending over, she put her hand on
Cait's shoulder and returned the grin. "Hi, Cait, I'm
Jesse. I see your uncle every morning. He comes to my
restaurant and buys coffee and donuts...*sometimes* even
a bagel." Jesse raised her eyebrows. She looked into
Matt's eyes. "And yes, he's very nice," she said,
blushing.

Matt watched her in a way he couldn't at Martel's.
Her lustrous black hair hung loosely, framing her face.
A hint of freckles worked their way around her nose
and those deep, wonderful eyes he could get lost in.

"This is my mother, Alice, and my daughter,
Alexis," Jesse continued.

"Hi." Matt smiled warmly at Alice then bent over.
"Hello, Alexis, my name is Matthew." He looked up at
Jesse as he spoke. "I'm a *friend* of your mommy's.
She's beautiful," he added, looking at Jesse.

"This is my other niece, Theresa." He smiled at his
younger niece. "And this is Donna Flaherty. She's—"

"Just an old *friend*, Jesse," Donna interrupted.

"Yes, an old *friend*," Matt emphasized.

"I get it, Matt. She's a friend." Jesse nodded in
Donna's direction.

"Well, now that we've met, would you guys like to
tag along and ride the swan boats?" Matt asked
hopefully.

Jesse looked at Alice and Alexis then at Matt. "I'm
really sorry. Maybe another time." She paused, raising
her eyes to meet his. "We can talk about it this week."
She took his hand and squeezed it gently.

He agreed. "I'd like that...very much."

They said good-bye. Jesse turned, following Matt
as she walked away. Matt did the same until she

disappeared behind the trees.

They sat on the swan boats, floating under the bridge and around the Lagoon. Matt smiled at the girls. He put his arms around them and squeezed until they squealed. Donna sat there with a curious smile on her face.

"What?" he asked.

"I'm just glad it wasn't fall," she answered.

He shrugged. "Why?"

"The way you two looked at each other," she continued.

"What are you taking about?"

She laughed out loud. "With all the dry leaves around, there would have been a terrible fire!"

Chapter Eight

"What a nice young man that Matt is. He couldn't take his eyes off you," Alice said as they got into a cab.

"I guess he's okay." Jesse ignored the comment then changed the subject. "Well, Ali, were the swan boats as much fun this week?"

"I had a real good time," Ali replied. "Who was that nice man, Mommy?"

Alice hid a grin.

"He's someone I know from work. Let's not get excited." She glared at her mother. When her mother used her full name it was serious. Jesse stared out the window to avoid any more debate about Matt. The afternoon had been special, but Jesse wanted to be left alone. She was fixating enough on him without any resident cheerleaders.

"If he asks me out, I'll think about it. Until then, I'm not going to worry," she lied, hoping the matter had been put to rest. He was the last thing she needed right now.

Jesse pulled Alice close, kissing her softly on the cheek. "Thanks, Mom." She took Ali's hand. As the three rode away from the Public Gardens, Jesse put her head back and closed her eyes, drifting into a restless sleep...

Suddenly, she could see his face, those piercing eyes that hypnotized her. Somehow, he knew everything about her—the sadness, the loneliness, the guilt, her need to be the best.

His strong hands found her, caressing her bare shoulders. She tried to speak, but he touched her lips and shook his head. "It's all right," he said softly, pulling her closer.

She could feel his chest hair as she surrendered. "It always will be...as long as we're together." And it would be. Somehow, she knew it. She'd known it since that first morning at Martel's.

"You don't have to be afraid anymore," he whispered.

His face grew close and his lips parted. She closed her eyes as his fragrance surrounded her. Their lips met and she felt their soft, moist warmth as they joined. A thrill went through her. He pushed closer. The excitement built, erupting within her. When it was over Jesse felt completely satisfied for the first time in her life.

****

Two hours later, Matt and his companions walked slowly to Park Street Station. His second wind was just a memory, and he had to get up at six a.m. for work.

Donna had been teasing him about his chance meeting with Jesse. He liked it. But then he liked anything to do with Jesse. Matt suspected there was another man in Donna's life. He wondered who it was. Donna deserved the best.

"Well, Romeo, what's your next move? Can your old sweetheart give you some pointers?" She grinned. "Every woman in Southie would cut her arm off to go out with you, but Jesse works in Copley Square. Maybe she hasn't gotten the word."

"I'm not gonna overanalyze this," Matt said, knowing he was doing *exactly* that. "I'll just go up and ask her out. She seems like a regular girl."

They rode along in silence. Matt wore a satisfied grin as he daydreamed about the surprising afternoon. They got off the bus across from the L Street Bathhouse. Matt walked Donna to her house with the girls following closely.

He kissed Donna on the cheek. "Thanks, beautiful. The girls love you. You made it a great afternoon." Matt faced her, resting his hands lightly on her shoulders. "Donna." He looked into her soft, brown eyes. "Are you seeing someone?"

She nodded. "Frank Kelly for about four months."

Matt studied her face. Her lustrous hair gathered the late afternoon sunlight.

"I know Frankie—the BC goalie. He's a good guy." Matt smiled. He still cared for Donna. "Good for you." They stood quietly, finding each other's eyes. For an instant a spark flickered, a distant reminder of their youthful moments spent together.

He touched her hair gently, turning to go. Donna took his arm. Her soft look changed. "Matt, what do you know about Jesse? I mean *really* know."

He thought about her question. "Practically nothing." He shook his head slowly. "But when I see her, touch her, it's like electricity going through me."

"Be careful, Matthew." She nodded, while the girls played with her neighbor's terrier. She hugged them. Matt kissed Donna on the cheek again.

When he reached the corner, Matt turned. Donna stood, following him with her eyes. He stopped, but she turned and headed toward her house.

"What's wrong, Uncle Matt?" Cait asked.

He shook his head.

"Nothing," he answered, hoping he was right, "nothing at all."

Chapter Nine

The Longs left the taxi at the corner of Mass Avenue and West Springfield Street. As they headed toward the brick façade of their building, Jesse saw Mario coming toward them.

Mario Altieri was a large, friendly man with a head full of thick gray hair. He appeared to be in his early sixties. No matter what he lent his substantial frame to, he was always well dressed and perfectly groomed.

Ali ran to meet him.

"Well, hello there, precious one." Mario beamed at Ali.

In the short time they'd lived in his building, Ali had grown very fond of him. His duties as their landlord still left ample time to spend as the informal mayor of this section of Boston's South End. Though his apartment was located some distance away, he always seemed to be nearby. On several occasions when her mother was having difficulty with her emphysema, Mario assumed the role of caregiver.

"Hi, Uncle Mario." He picked Ali up effortlessly, showing his toothy grin as he spun her around.

Jesse sat contentedly on the dark granite steps with her mother. When her mother experienced a shortness of breath Jesse put her arm around Alice's thin frame. Kissing Alice's forehead, it occurred to Jesse that intimacy was unlike her. Could the kindness of those surrounding her be tempering her stubborn independence? Could someone break through the walls she'd spent years constructing? As she thought about it, Mario and Ali came over and sat next to them.

"It's been a wonderful day, but I'm going to lie down for a while." Alice got up, coughing as she climbed the stairs to the front door.

"Get some rest. We'll be up soon." Jesse squeezed her hand.

Mario nodded.

Ali waved and planted a kiss on her grandmother's shallow cheek. "Bye, Grandma. I love you."

Jesse was always amazed at Ali's endless capacity for love. Jesse hugged her daughter. The afternoon had fulfilled the morning's promise as the sun peeked from behind a few fluffy clouds, warming them.

As Mario hypnotized Ali with one of his stories, his deep baritone mesmerized Jesse, too. She thought about their first meeting in May.

During her last year in high school, good fortune had befallen her family. Portland had bought their ramshackle home to make way for an urban renewal project. While the project never began, the settlement provided enough so they could relocate to a decent apartment in a better neighborhood. Perhaps more importantly, the windfall enabled Jesse to sustain her mother and daughter during her first two years at New England Conservatory.

Last winter, her mother's emphysema worsened. Their meager savings ran low and it was becoming difficult for Alice to care for Ali by herself.

Enter Mario. He'd called, inquiring about Alice's father, explaining they'd been in the army together.

When Alice said her father had died, Mario gave his phone number and address saying he owned apartment buildings in Boston. He offered to help if they ever needed it.

"We grew very close. I was a young soldier, an immigrant, and your grandfather took me under his wing," Mario had explained. He wore an odd, faraway look. "I told him if he ever needed anything—anything, Jessica—he need only call. He was a fine officer and a kind, caring man." He looked at Jesse, putting his hand on her shoulder. "I guess you're that call," he added with a warm smile.

"Well, Mr. Altieri…"

"Please call me Mario. When a beautiful young woman calls me 'Mr. Altieri', it makes me feel very old.

"Sure—*Mario.* My mother hoped you could help us. You see, I'm going to New England Conservatory and she's sick. She and my daughter need to come to Boston and well, we don't have a lot of—"

"Stop. I can do more than give advice. You can have a nice apartment in one of my buildings." He gestured toward the surrounding properties.

Jesse looked around. There were bad sections of the South End, but the buildings Mario owned looked clean and well-kept. She was excited about finding a place so quickly, but her concern was the price.

"It would be wonderful to live in one of these buildings…"

He interrupted again. "There's a nice park over there." He pointed up the street. "How old is your little girl?"

"Just turned four."

"She'd love that park. There are always kids to play with."

"Ali would love it here, but I don't think that we—"

"How about twelve hundred?"

Jesse looked at the sidewalk. "Thanks." She offered her hand. "But we could never afford that."

He waved her hand away. "All right, all right, let's not argue. I'll give you a two bedroom unit for a thousand dollars a quarter, but you've got to throw in a couple of tickets to one of your recitals."

Jesse's head dropped, disappointed that he couldn't help—"Wait…did you say a thousand a *quarter*? Three hundred and thirty-three dollars *a month*?"

She couldn't have heard him correctly. That price was ridiculous.

"All right, all right. You're just too tough for me. Make it an even three hundred a month." He looked stern as he spoke. "But not a penny cheaper. And I love classical music, so don't think you'll get away without those tickets." He shook his head.

Jesse closed the space between them and threw her arms around him. "God bless you, Mario." It had been a long time since she'd used the Lord's name except to curse. She released him as tears of gratitude rolled down her cheeks. But…something he said raised a question. "How did you know about the NEC recitals?"

"Jesse, you'd be surprised what this old man knows." His laughter was so infectious she joined him.

"As soon as your family arrives, call me. I have a couple of vacancies. You can have your pick. I'll get you the keys." His kind smile was replaced by a stern look. "Do you have a job?"

"Well, I'm looking around, but there's not much available. Don't worry about me, I'll make out," she said with a confidence she didn't feel.

"Well, I don't know if you've been a waitress, but I have a friend who's looking for someone." He handed her a card with Martel's name and address. "Gerry's a good man. Just in case your other prospects don't work out."

"Well, I have waitressed. Maybe I'll give him a call." It was another godsend. Other than a few singing jobs she had no work for the summer. "I mean, if nothing else works out."

"I'll let him know—just in case."

She nodded. "That'd be great, Mario. Thanks."

He came close and looked into her eyes. She had the uncomfortable feeling he could see right through her. "Jessica, I don't want to offend you. Would your family mind if I threw in a few things—you know—a rug, couch and...you said your mother was sick? I have a couple of old air conditioners lying around."

"I've never heard of a fairy *godfather*. If I do, I'll know who to think of." She hugged him again. As she did, a large black sedan pulled up in front of the building next door. Two large men got out.

"Gotta go. Call me when you're ready." He waved as she walked back toward Mass Avenue.

Jesse turned, concerned as Mario approached the two men. They were dressed in dark suits that did little to conceal their muscular physiques. She was worried. But her concern quickly vanished. The men had come to see Mario. But *he* was the one doing all the talking. They stood at attention, as he spoke. When he was done, they nodded respectfully, returning to the big

Lincoln. It sped off in the opposite direction. Jesse shook off a sudden chill. She couldn't believe her good fortune.

Since that May afternoon, she'd seen the big Lincoln and more men in dark suits. They always kept a discreet distance from passersby. Once, coming home late, she'd heard Mario's usually mellow voice raised. She hid behind a stairway until the men drove away. But Jesse had larger and more immediate concerns than the shadowy figures or Mario's meetings with them— her financial situation, her career, and Matthew Sullivan—not necessarily in that order.

Chapter Ten

Monday morning dawned clear and bright. The sparkling weather continued its hold on eastern Massachusetts. The smell of fresh baked goods filled Martel's as Jesse stood behind the counter. After her meeting with Matt on Sunday, she should have felt wonderful. She didn't.

Gerry brought some trays out of the kitchen. "Have a nice weekend, Jess?"

Jesse stood silently, eyes glued to the door.

"Jess?"

"I think Juliet is looking for Romeo," said Ellen.

"Sorry. Am I missing something?" Gerry asked.

"Shut up, Ellen, I'm not in the mood," Jesse said. "Get Bernie's coffee and stay out of my life."

"Everything all right in the world of arias and oratorios?" Gerry asked.

"Everything's fine, Gerry." She went back to her customers, filling orders, terrified of what to would do when Matt came to the counter. Several of her regulars asked if she was all right. She just went about filling their orders.

Jesse had lain awake half the night. Just holding his hand sent electricity surging though her. She needed to see him, to be with him. But there was no time for him. Her emotions and her practical side were at war!

Next time Jesse looked up, he stood, beaming at

her. When he approached the counter the other women backed away. But Jesse turned and ran toward the kitchen.

"Hi Jess...Jess...*Jesse*..." he called.

She hid, pressing against the door. Across the kitchen, Gerry put a new batch of muffins in one of the ovens. Jesse peered around the corner.

"What'll it be, Matt?" Ellen asked, looking over her shoulder to see where Jesse was. She stayed behind the door with no intention of returning. The intimacy she'd shown at the Public Gardens was a mistake. It would lead to one of two things—she'd let herself love him, and he'd break her heart, or she'd let herself love him, and he'd take her dream away. Neither was acceptable.

"Sorry, kid. Trouble in Paradise?" Ellen asked.

"I don't know," he said. "I didn't think so."

"Look, Matt," Ellen said, "I'm sorry if something's happened between you two. But there's a hundred guys waiting, so just tell me what you want." Jesse heard angry rumblings in the line.

He shook his head and glanced toward the kitchen. She thought he might see her, but instead he turned to leave.

She emerged from the kitchen. Ellen said nothing, but walked over and put her hand on Jesse's shoulder. Jesse moved away quickly, ducking the intimacy.

"Everything okay, kid?" Ellen asked.

Jesse gathered herself and rushed around filling orders and making conversation as if nothing had happened.

"Just perfect, Ellen." She turned and smiled at the man she was waiting on. "Everything is just the way I planned it!"

****

The rest of Matt's day dragged by. He hardly spoke. When he got home, he disappeared into his room, slamming the door without the usual banter he exchanged with his father.

He lay staring absently at the ceiling, trying to figure out what went wrong. On Friday she practically asked him out. Yesterday afternoon she'd held his hand. The way she looked at him wasn't something he imagined. Everyone saw it.

He got up, went out to the kitchen and searched for the phone book. There was no listing for Jessica Long.

He gave his father a nod, still avoiding conversation as he headed back to his bedroom. He picked up the phone and dialed Information. The operator came back with a listing for Jesse on West Springfield. He didn't know the street, but Matt was on a mission. He needed to talk to her and find out what happened.

He dialed the number. It rang four times before someone picked up. His stomach was doing gymnastics. He'd never felt this way about any woman. In spite of her reaction today, he was sure she felt the same.

"Hello. This is Ali, who is this?" said the little girl from the swan boats—Jesse's daughter.

"Hi, Ali, this is Matt. You may not remember me, but I'm the man from—"

"I know who you are. You're mommy's friend," she said enthusiastically.

Matt felt a surge of excitement.

He heard a cough as someone took the phone from

the little girl. "Hello, who is this, please?" It was Jesse's mother.

"Hi, this is Matt Sullivan. We met yesterday afternoon. Could I speak to Jesse?" he asked, hiding his impatience.

"Yes, Matt. It was nice to meet you. But she isn't here right now. Can I take a message?"

"Would it be all right if I called later, Mrs. Long?"

"She's at the Conservatory, and then she's going to the restaurant to help her boss. Maybe you could try another night. I'm sorry, I'm sure she'd like to talk to you."

After the way she'd acted that morning Matt wasn't sure, but he was determined. He took a chance. "Did you say the restaurant, Mrs. Long? Do you mean Martel's?" He tried to sound as casual possible.

"Yes, that's right, Martel's. The place she works."

"Thanks a lot. I'll leave my number? It's 617-426-7780. I hope to see you again."

"I hope to see you, too." She hung up the phone.

As he stared at the phone, an odd feeling came over him. He remembered Donna's question. "What do you really know about Jesse?"

Nothing, he thought. But there was only one way to fix that.

He got cleaned up, then told his father that he had an early date. Thirty minutes later he was on his way to get the train to Copley Square...and Jesse.

****

The phone rang in Martel's kitchen. "Gerry?"

"Hi, Mario."

"You haven't called in a couple of days."

"I'm sorry. I've been busy redoing the place—

cleaning it up and painting. Actually, Jesse's helping me. She's doing well, but there is one thing."

"What?"

"She has a crush on one of the customers—a kid. The girls tell me his name is Sullivan—Matt Sullivan. He's from South Boston. I asked around. He went to BU. Played hockey. He was a big deal till he blew out his knee." Gerry paused. "He's working for Gilbert on their new job."

"Thanks, Gerry. I appreciate it," Mario said, but his mind was already somewhere else. He had another call to make.

Chapter Eleven

It was seven forty-five when Jesse came out of Martel's.

Love. She heard the word so often. It was all around her. Yet she'd found so little evidence of it. She loved her mother, Ali, and Pauline. Damn you, Matthew, I have no more love to give. But Jesse thought about his smile and how he looked at her, and the wonderful easy way he had with his friends while he waited every day for their precious two minutes together. She remembered the open, affectionate way he'd played with his nieces, and she wondered—could there be room for him in her life?

She closed her eyes and sighed deeply. Her mouth had a dry, sour taste. She searched her backpack, finding a last piece of gum. Jesse reached into her jeans and pulled out a small vial, taking two tablets—five milligrams of Percocet and five of Valium. She popped them into her mouth and chewed them quickly so they'd go to work right away. Ever since that terrible night in Portland, she'd been using the drugs. She never abused them, taking them once or twice a day when she needed a lift. She had a prescription from the health center, but it wasn't hard to score in the circles she moved in.

It was a warm night, more humid than the morning, but a light breeze from the river worked its way between the buildings, giving the evening a comfortable feel. The Red Sox were at home, so the cheers from Fenway Park could be heard in the distance. Jesse looked at the darkening sky and sighed again. She was exhausted. She moved her neck and head from side to side, working out the soreness. She undid the tie that held her thick, damp hair in a ponytail and ran her hands through it, shaking it loose to let the cool air dry it.

She'd been up since five. All she wanted to do was to get on the train, go home, and take a long, hot shower then spend a few minutes with Ali and her mother. It seemed like days passed without seeing them. There were times she felt so guilty about her absence from Ali. She'd been such a bad mother, but she swore that when she became a success, she'd make it up to her and to Alice.

She'd been depressed all day. Her session at the Conservatory had been awful. She couldn't think about anything but Matt. She had no heart for scales and arpeggios when she remembered the hurt, empty look on his face.

"Please, just leave me alone," she said and headed toward the MBTA station.

"Who is it that you want to leave you alone?"

She jumped as a voice asked the question from somewhere nearby. It was Matt. For an instant she thought her fatigue and the drugs were conspiring to bring on hallucinations. Why would he be here?

He spoke again. "Jesse, who is it that's bothering you?" Before she could answer, he came out of the shadows and stood in front of her. "The guy who owns the restaurant?" he asked, looking angrily toward

Martel's.

"Matt, what are you...?" Then she realized what he'd said. "Oh no, it's nothing like that. I was just thinking out loud. There's no one bothering me—not the way you think." Jesse was still baffled by his presence, but as she looked at him a smile crossed her face. Whatever the reason, he was the answer to a prayer. She turned away, afraid that her happiness and exhaustion might bring tears.

"Really, I know some pretty tough guys, and if you need help, I can..."

She didn't let him finish. She approached him, putting her finger to his lips and told him, "Shhh. It's all right, Matt."

She hadn't expected it, but they came together, gently at first, then tighter. When he held her, it was like her dream in the taxi. His touch sent sensations of pleasure and warmth through her body she could never have imagined.

They clung to each other. Neither spoke. For a moment Jesse was lost in a safe, private world—a world she didn't want to leave. She sighed, knowing there was nowhere else she'd rather be and knowing he felt the same way. For an instant, she let her doubts evaporate, thinking there might be a time and a place for them. Just as quickly, reason returned, telling her this wasn't it. She backed away.

"What are you doing here?" she asked him.

"I called your house looking for you. Your mother said you might be here. So I came here to wait for you. After the way you acted this morning, I had to see you—to talk with you."

She understood, but didn't know how to react. She

needed him, wanted to be with him, but...

"Jesse, I see how you look at me, how you act around me. You must know the way I feel about you." He found her eyes and took her hand, whispering, "I've never felt this way before." She caressed it, not letting herself look at him. As they stood on the sidewalk holding hands, passers by smiled. "Don't play games, Jesse, please. I'm fall..."

She took her other hand and put it to his mouth, stopping the words she desperately wanted to hear. "Don't, Matt. Don't say it. You don't know me."

"I know everything I need to." He freed his hand and eased her face toward his. "I won't. But that doesn't change anything. I know you feel the same way."

He pulled her to him, but she jerked away, searching his face. "It's been a long, brutal day, and I have another tomorrow. All I have is long, brutal days. I'd like to spend a few minutes with my little girl before I go to bed." She hung her head.

"Could we walk to the subway...please?" No matter how she felt when he held her, she was exhausted and determined. She started down Boylston Street, then stopped and turned, waiting for him to follow. He stood motionless for a second and then ran to catch her. She put her arm around him tightly. She felt so safe—so much at home. The feeling was totally new. It was both magnificent and terrifying. But Jesse was being torn apart.

They walked along in silence, next to each another. Jesse refused to loosen her grip, frightened their magnificent but tenuous relationship might vanish in the damp evening air. They reached the entrance to the train and stopped, turning to face one other.

"We haven't solved anything," he whispered over the sound of the traffic.

"I don't think we can solve anything. A wise friend once told me to never forget my dreams. Dreams are what we cling to, where we take refuge. They're what we live for, Matt. I have a dream I've clung to since I was twelve, and it's all I have room for right now."

Jesse had made her decision.

"You were right, Matt," Jesse nodded. "I do feel the same way about you. But I haven't got time to run around the Public Gardens, hold hands, or doing any of those other things that you and I could do…should do if things were different."

Jesse sighed deeply and took a step back. "If you want me, it'll have to be on my terms and on my schedule. Both are killers. I've never felt like this before, Matt. I wish I had time for all of it. But I don't—at least not now. If you want me," she said, feeling the tears overflow onto her cheeks. "You know where to find me."

Jesse stepped toward him and kissed him softly on the lips. She headed toward the subway. Turning, she stopped. "You remember the question you asked me earlier? About who it was that I wanted to leave me alone?"

He nodded slowly.

"It was you. God help us both, Matthew. It was you…"

PART II

Chapter Twelve

Early August 1988

At five thirty a.m. Jesse sat on the subway, surrounded by a group of seedy companions. She headed toward Symphony Station and Martel's, ignoring the stale, rank odor in the car.

She'd been sure her feelings for Matt would pass like the hunger pangs she lived with as a child— remembering too late that they never went away. She told herself he'd call...run after her...accept her terms. She knew he loved her. But as the days became a week and the weeks a month, Jesse realized that she'd misjudged him. He was just as proud and stubborn as she was.

She retrieved a small, tattered pamphlet from her backpack, skipping to the last paragraph. It was her favorite part. *"Today, you incoming students will be taught by the brightest and best in the musical world..."* A smile crossed her face. *"NEC boasts a faculty of prestigious musicians of world renown. The Conservatory is the destination for anyone who has serious career aspirations in the world of classical music."*

Jesse closed her eyes. *"...the destination for*

anyone who has serious career aspirations in the world of classical music." She knew who that person was. The Conservatory had been waiting to give her the polish she needed to fulfill her destiny—that of being the finest lyric soprano in the world.

The subway rattled along, lights flickering. Jesse stared out the dirty window, shifting on the hard plastic seat as she studied the darkness. Once again, the long, painful journey leading to the Conservatory came to mind.

Her father died when Jesse was three. Her family lived in a run-down house in Munjoy Hill, on the outskirts of Portland, Maine. Jesse could see her street. The asphalt looked abandoned and cracked. The stark, lonely trees stood witness to the poverty and despair filling the houses in this forgotten section of Maine's largest city.

Their house was a two-story structure. Its dull, white sides lacked anything to distinguish it. Her mother tried bringing a trace of warmth to their desolate home. But after her father's death, she'd been forced to sell the better pieces of furniture, so the meager remnants did little to improve the interior.

The children in the neighborhood were tough and unruly. Her only friend was her brother. Ryan was five years older, a wiry, handsome boy whom she worshipped. But like her mother, he delivered newspapers, groceries, and anything else he could to help the Longs survive. He was seldom home. Jesse withdrew to a private world, using her father's old tape player and collection of classical music to escape. It seemed strange that a man without education or means could find refuge in Mozart, Verdi, and Puccini, but he had, and his passion was his sole legacy to his daughter.

Desperate and alone, Jesse's mother turned to Alton Eads—a devil masquerading as a decent man. He was given to violence and abuse when he drank—a pastime he practiced too often. He routinely tormented her family, most often Jesse, before dying one October night. His death should have been cause for celebration, but it was bittersweet. Sadly, on that same night, Jesse's brother died as well. Soon afterward, Jesse's mother was diagnosed with emphysema.

Despite the sadness she'd endured, as she grew, two things were certain: Jesse's talent was without equal, and she was as beautiful a young woman as Portland had ever produced.

Jesse lived for music, taking refuge in it. To truly excel, she needed a mentor and good luck. She got the first in the compact form of Pauline Richards—a retired vocal coach from Boston. When she and her husband returned to Maine, Pauline offered her services to an old friend, then head of music for the Portland Public Schools. Her old colleague accepted, offering Pauline a teaching position in one of the smaller schools. What happened changed both her life and Jesse's.

"On my first day in Portland," Pauline had said, "I met a sweet, beautiful child. She was tall and painfully thin, dressed in a threadbare dress. She seemed so shy. I put her in the back, away from the more outgoing children. But that girl had a surprise in store. When the class began to sing, one voice came through, strong and clear and true. It was a voice from the back row. Your voice, Jesse."

Pauline adopted her. Before that a shy and abandoned Jesse felt like the only person on earth. Her new mentor taught Jesse everything she could, drilling her endlessly, even teaching her protégé enough piano to earn a few extra dollars. As Pauline opened the world of music to her, Jesse felt special, someone of value, no longer the by-product of her mother's sad, short marriage.

Pauline made music come alive for Jesse. By her fourteenth birthday she was performing many of the most difficult arias. Throughout those formative years, Pauline imbued her protégé with every detail about music. But Jesse never waited for the good luck to come and find her. Instead she learned something else. As she blossomed into womanhood, she saw men watch her lithe figure, smile at her; sometimes they even touched her. Rather than protest Jesse understood and used the only assets she possessed—her talent and her nubile beauty. She learned ways to use her ample charms and guile to help gain advantages that her poverty and lackluster academic record might have kept out of reach. It was a dark side of Jesse that Pauline never saw, one she wasn't proud of and one that came back to pay her cruel dividends one damp night in July of 1983.

****

Ninety miles away, in the close-knit neighborhoods of South Boston, Matt Sullivan had experienced a different upbringing. He spent his formative years nurtured and happily surrounded by friends and family.

Matt had lived in the house on East Broadway for all of his twenty-three years. He'd grown up with all the brash self-confidence worthy of his good looks, athleticism, and superior intelligence. Like Jesse, Matt had lost a parent. His mother died of cancer when he was fourteen, and two years later his older brother James, a lieutenant in the Marine Corps, had died in a training accident. These two tragic and untimely losses had left their mark on Matt and his family, but they stubbornly refused to let tragedy defeat them.

His mother had been an integral part of Matt's life, but as he'd come to expect, his father had been there to help dull the pain, shuttling Matt to his hockey games and giving him pointers as he watched his son skating at the Castle Island Rink. And while Matt had many friends, it was common to see him, his brother, and his dad at the South Boston Boys and Girls Club, shooting baskets, working out or throwing a few friendly punches at each other. And there was something else that had been a part of his life since he was a boy—his writing. Whenever you saw Matt Sullivan, he was carrying a hockey stick and a notebook. Everyone who knew Matt accepted that when he wasn't shooting a puck, he was scribbling in his journal.

Matt's family had lived in their home for over five decades. Much of the last one had been stormy as South Boston was central in Boston's frustrated attempts to racially balance its schools. It was where they lived as his mother gave birth to their three children, and it was where they lived as his father's small retail business grew into something larger and more prosperous. Matt knew the family could easily afford a nice home in a quiet, more prestigious suburb, but the thought never crossed his mind. The Sullivans possessed an extensive circle of friends, were devoted members of St. Bridgid's parish and a strong influence within their tightly-knit community.

The Sullivans lived in the middle of a large, vibrant

city, with the growing collection of high-rise buildings in full view. The constant stream of planes headed to Logan Airport flew so low you could nearly touch them, but like their neighbors, Matt and his family knew that everything they needed was within the friendly, narrow streets of South Boston.

Chapter Thirteen

Late August 1988

"You're not mad I'm working on this while I'm on duty, are you?" Matt asked Walt Kellogg, his supervisor at the Boston Public Library. Walt stood over his shoulder at the papers scattered on the desk. Matt liked his weekend job at the BPL. It paid well, and he needed the money for graduate school.

He worked at the information desk of the Library's main branch in Copley Square. Outside the weather was warm and humid again, but inside the climate-controlled atmosphere was a comfortable seventy degrees. As Matt surveyed the expanse of volumes before him, the subdued lighting gave this intellectual cocoon a warm, almost cozy feeling.

"Of course not," Walt assured him. "No one wants to be here on a beautiful summer afternoon. You've got to do something or you'd go crazy. How many inquiries did you have this afternoon?"

"I'm not sure. It's in the log."

Walter turned and checked the book resting on the table next to Matt. "Seven. That's about what I thought." Walter smiled and shook his head. "You've got to do something," Walter repeated while he hovered behind Matt. "C'mon, Matt, let me have a look. I teach literature. Maybe I can help."

Reluctantly, Matt nodded and backed away. Walter leaned closer, studying the pages. Matt watched nervously as Walter read.

"You say you wrote this from some of your grandfather's old journals?"

Matt nodded. "Yeah, he was an officer in the I.R.A. during the early Twenties. He was right there with Michael Collins, de Valera, and all of the rest of them."

After an endless few minutes, Walter pronounced judgment. "This is good, Matt...*really* good." Walter kept reading.

"Well, I always loved history and writing, so I promised myself that I'd do something when I had the chance. This summer has been kind of slow—" He paused, an empty feeling grabbing him. "—so I decided I'd make a job of it. Weeknights, I go home and convert the stuff from the journals into this." He gestured toward the papers.

Walt turned toward Matt. "Look, I'm not a writer, but this looks really good. It could use some editing, but for a first draft, it's amazing. The way you write—your use of imagery, blending facts with fiction—is great. Would you mind if I copied it and showed it to someone who might be able to help you?"

"I guess it would be okay," Matt said, feeling proud. He knew Walter had a master's in English and his enthusiasm was encouraging.

His friend took the material and disappeared. Matt smiled to himself. Matt's thoughts were interrupted by an older couple who wanted to know where to find the ornithology section. He helped them and went back to the newspaper.

Matt's job here gave him more time to work on his novel. He could use the library computers to do research on things that the journals left unclear. Despite the tedious nature of the work, he enjoyed it. He'd gotten to the point that he couldn't wait to get home each night, add a few words or polish his work from the night before.

It was getting close to six, so he looked for Walter to thank him again. He was nowhere in sight, so Matt signed out, spent a couple of minutes talking with the security guard about the Red Sox and then headed off to catch the train.

The trip to the MBTA station was still painful since he walked by Martel's. He'd tried to forget about Jesse. He was in love with her, and he was sure she was in love with him. But Jesse was a new experience to him. He'd never known a woman who was so driven. He wanted to love her and be with her so badly that he was *almost* willing to accept her terms. But Matt was stubborn and proud. He just couldn't envision himself waiting to see her when *her* career or schedule allowed it—no matter how his passion worked to convince him otherwise.

He hadn't been to Martel's since their last meeting. He envisioned her moving gracefully behind the counter, smiling softly and nodding as she saw him in line… He shook his head and moved on, running down the stairs to the train as he thought about the night ahead. He was going out with David Jenkins and a couple of his old hockey buddies. They were good friends, and he was trying to adopt their attitude.

"Fuck it, Matt. The building may fall on us tomorrow, so screw around as much as you can and enjoy it!" He could just see the broad smile on Dave's face.

Matt couldn't forget Jesse, perhaps he never would. But he couldn't get enough of his new love—writing. And just maybe, if Walter was right, this one wouldn't leave him wanting.

Chapter Fourteen

Jesse dragged herself down West Springfield Street. She was exhausted. She'd spent four hours at the Conservatory after helping Gerry move and paint that morning. She was strong, but Jesse had been operating above capacity all summer. It was having its effect.

Even her vocal coach showed concern. Jesse's voice was unusually strong and resilient for a young soprano. That was one of the things that made her special. But recently, her voice would crack or become hoarse if she rehearsed more than thirty minutes. Even her range seemed to be shrinking. Jesse was frightened.

She'd ignored academics, using her musical and physical gifts as leverage in high school and later, to gain entrance to the Conservatory. But without her voice her only career choice would be someplace like Martel's.

Twice each year, once on the Tuesday before Thanksgiving and again just before Easter, there was a recital during which a few talented upper-class students were showcased. Last spring Jesse was sure her opportunity would come this fall, but that wouldn't happen if the problems with her voice continued. Jesse indulged her mother by making an appointment with a throat specialist, but what she needed was rest.

And then, of course there was *him*—his face, his eyes, his smile were specters that haunted her. Jesse had never known the joy or the pain of love before, but since that evening outside Martel's, she'd become an expert. Sometimes she thought Matt's loss was wearing her down more than her nonstop schedule. She was glad she'd be back at the Conservatory full-time in a couple of weeks. Maybe it would help her to be rid of him.

Jesse trudged up the front steps. This Saturday night she had nothing to do, thank God. Most weekend nights she played piano with some classmates from the Conservatory. There were three of them: a guitarist, a bass player and Jesse. They played at the Fallen Angel, an exclusive nightclub near the waterfront. She wasn't great, but thanks to Pauline she could play most of the standards and improvise quite well. Besides, when she wore her clingy low-cut dress, the male customers didn't care what she was playing and the tip jar filled to overflowing.

As she was about to go inside, Mario called from the alley. "What's a matter, no job tonight?" he asked with a warm smile.

"Actually, no, got a night off. I'm just going to put my feet up and enjoy my family." Tired as she was, she couldn't resist returning his smile.

Suddenly, his smile disappeared and for a moment they stood in awkward silence. A cold look came over Mario's face, and Jesse felt a chill. "It's good you're taking a night off. You look like you could use the rest. And you're right, my dear, you can never spend enough time with your family…" His words trailed off as he looked away.

She nodded, adding a "Thanks," and went inside, thinking she was being ridiculous. But suddenly she wondered how Mario knew she worked every Saturday night. She hadn't seen him when she left or came home. And in their casual conversations she'd never brought it up.

But at this point she didn't care about Mario and the mysteries surrounding him. All she wanted was to sit down and rest. Before she did, she wanted to look over the bills. She had enough to pay their rent through February, but after that, she wasn't sure what would happen. Mario had been so kind; she didn't want to impose on him.

She entered the living room, sat at their small table and pulled the stack of bills toward her. Jesse assumed Alexis and her mother were at the park.

As she went through the pile, adding up what they owed, she smiled. Things weren't as bad as she'd thought. They'd be all right as long as she kept the job at Martel's. Gerry was willing to let her come in at the normal time and leave when she had a class or a practice session, but she didn't know if her body and her voice could take it. She was *so tired*. She put her head on her arms for just a minute and closed her eyes...

She heard his loud rasping breath as he reached the top of the stairs. He stopped for a minute. She knew it was her imagination, but she thought she could smell his foul, alcoholic breath as he headed for her mother's room, banging the walls as he went.

"Where are you fucking people?" he demanded, his speech slurred. "When a man comes home his family should be there to greet him, shouldn't they?" he ended with a hoarse laugh.

He entered the room next to where she and Ryan huddled, still unsure what to do. Ryan clutched the baseball bat tightly as Jesse heard her mother crying in anticipation.

"What are you doing hiding in here, you skinny, useless bitch? Go get me something to eat...and make it something good!"

"Alton, just get out of here. We don't want you anymore!" Alice yelled at him, summoning her courage. "All you do is hurt us."

"Really. Well, who's going to pay the bills for you and those useless kids? I don't see you getting a job. If it weren't for me, you, Ryan and sweet little Jesse would be out on the street where you belong." When he finished, she and Ryan heard a vicious blow and Alice screamed. "Now go get me something to eat, while I pay my stepdaughter a visit. I'm sure she wants to kiss her daddy hello...don't you Jesse," he yelled, serving notice he was on his way to find her.

"You stay away from Jesse, you son of a bitch. If you touch her again, I swear I'll..." There was another hard slap, and Alice screamed again.

"You'll what, you lazy bitch?" he screamed back at her. Alton headed for the door to the hallway. Alice must have gotten to her feet because they heard her running to get to the door first...

"Jesse...*Jesse...Jesse*, honey." She thought it was Ryan, but it was her mother shaking her. "Are you all right? We could hear you from outside. You were crying and screaming. Mrs. Mendoza next door was worried.

"Mommy, are you okay?" Ali came over and grabbed Jesse around the neck, hugging her so tightly it hurt. Jesse wiped the tears from her cheeks. She took a couple of deep breaths and stood up, freeing herself from Ali's grip. The bad dreams always came at times when she was tired and vulnerable.

"I'm sorry. It was nothing," she said, brushing off their concerns. Alice looked at her. Jesse wondered if she knew about the dreams. Maybe she was haunted by them herself.

"Where were you guys? I missed you." She smiled at Alexis. Jesse squeezed her, still shaken by her dream, but hiding it well.

"We were over at the park off Washington Street. Ali has made a couple of little friends, and they were playing on the swings and the jungle gym. One of the girls has a grandma like me so we were just exchanging stories and complaining about our aches and pains," Alice offered with a tender look as she rubbed her daughter's arm. Jesse felt ashamed that she knew so little about her daughter's life.

"How about if I spring for pizza?" She was too tired to cook, and she didn't want her mother to do any more. "I want to catch up with what's been going on— new friends, new places. I can't wait to hear about it." She gave them her best smile, put her arms around them and gave each a kiss on the cheek.

"Wow, awesome, Mommy."

"Count me in." Alice coughed. "Do you want to walk down to Mass Avenue or have it delivered?"

"It's more fun and cheaper to go out. Let's go down there. We can rent a video. Maybe we three hot chicks can hook up with some good looking guys. What do you say, Ali?" Jesse was feeling better. In spite of the dream, the short nap had refreshed her. "You go get washed up. Then I'll take a quick shower," she told Ali. "I think Mommy needs one." She held her nose.

Ali laughed and headed for the bathroom.

"Are you all right?" Alice asked.

"What do you mean?"

"This isn't the first time you've had one of those dreams."

"It was nothing, just some stupid thing with monsters and ghosts. Kids stuff." She didn't want to talk about the nightmares. "Just some horror movie stuff, really," she insisted.

****

The three of them left the building heading toward the busy hum that was Saturday night on Massachusetts Avenue. It was one of the city's central conduits, running from South Boston over the Charles River, into Cambridge and beyond.

As they walked along, Jesse thought she'd forgotten her house key. She turned back in the direction of their building when she saw a bulky man about 50 feet behind them. The man stopped, looking around clumsily. He seemed familiar.

"What's the matter?" her mother asked.

"Did you see that man behind us? The one walking away."

"Well, my eyes aren't what they used to be, but it looks like one of the young men who come to visit Mario. They come around a couple of times a week," Alice offered casually. "They seem very nice."

Jesse looked at her mother, but her mind was elsewhere. She thought she recognized their shadow. He looked like one of the large men she'd seen talking to Mario near the Lincoln. She was sure he'd been following them.

"Mommy, are we going to get our pizza?" asked an impatient Ali.

Jesse dismissed her suspicions. She *really* did need some time off. "Yes, honey. But I've got to go back and lock our apartment."

"Its okay, Jesse. I did it while you and Ali were waiting downstairs." Her mother pulled the key out of her handbag.

They had pizza, and while Jesse and Ali inhaled a large pepperoni, Alice had a small cheese. Then, afterward, they stopped and rented an animated video that the three of them watched in their living room. Halfway through the movie, they all fell asleep.

Alice awoke when Jesse pulled out the sleep sofa where Ali slept. Very gently she put her daughter onto the small bed and pulled the sheet up over her. It was a beautiful summer evening, and she left the window open to let the light breeze in. Alice got up, but instead of heading into her room, she followed her daughter. When they got into Jesse's room, she closed the door.

"You know, Jessica, I've always minded my own business when it comes to your personal life, but…can I ask you something?" Jesse thought this *must* be serious, since her mother hardly ever used her full name. She nodded.

"Do you remember the Sunday we went to the swan boats?"

Jesse nodded again.

"What ever happened to that nice young man we met?"

Jesse was caught off guard. She stood silently.

"He seemed very nice. You know he called for you one night? I wrote it down—"

"It…didn't work out between us. He wanted too much. You know, with work and school and practice…"

She and Alice had never discussed Jesse's love life, perhaps because she'd avoided having one. Probing wasn't something her mother seemed comfortable with, especially after the night four years ago, but she continued.

"You can't spend your whole life alone. Sometime, somewhere, you're going to have to care for someone and let them care for you. I just thought he might be a good person to start with."

Jesse avoided her mother's eyes. Suddenly, the emotion she'd kept locked inside overflowed. "I know you're right, but it's too late. I was falling in love with Matt, but I wouldn't let him get close. I was sure of myself—so sure he'd want to be with me that I gave him an ultimatum." She stumbled through the words as the tears spilled onto her blouse. "He hasn't talked to me since that night. He doesn't even come to Martel's anymore." Jesse collapsed on the bed, crying herself to sleep in her mother's arms.

As Alice closed the door, she looked back toward her daughter's room. Smiling, she whispered as Jesse's eyelids closed, "It's never too late, Jesse, it's…never…too…late.

Chapter Fifteen

It had been a whirlwind courtship since Walter had asked his uncle Paul Kellogg to read Matt's manuscript. As the CEO of Baldwin Publishing, Kellogg had arranged a personal meeting. Paul explained the details of the publishing process, making Matt an offer for his work and assuring him it was extremely generous for someone who had never been published.

Matt felt like a rookie who'd just been elevated to the major leagues…excited but unsure of the implications. He knew nothing about the intricacies of publishing and even less about Paul Kellogg. He explained he needed time to think about the offer. Kellogg agreed, once again stressing the generosity he was displaying toward someone so young. Matt went home and gathered the Sullivan clan: his father, sister Jeanne and her husband, Allen. They listened as Matt discussed the Baldwin offer.

"Sounds like you'd better talk to a lawyer," Daniel said. "It's a great chance, but you have to be careful. You don't want to get tied up with these people if you could do better somewhere else."

"Dad's right," Jeanne agreed. "Don't you have someone who does your legal work?"

He nodded. "I'll call him tomorrow if Matt wants, but this isn't his specialty." Daniel smiled at Matt. "Do you mind if we read what you've written?"

"I guess not." Matt was still shy about letting people read his writing. He went to his room, returning with his manuscript. "Here it is." He pushed aside an ashtray and put a thick, loose-leaf notebook on the coffee table. "It's not finished, but you're welcome to read it."

"Thanks, son. I'll call my lawyer and ask him what he thinks. Now, if no one minds," he said, picking up Matt's notebook, "I'm going out on the porch and read the Sullivan family's first best seller." He slapped Matt on the back.

Matt went to his room. A few days ago, he was a construction worker, now he was an author. It still sounded strange when he said it. He was superstitious, so he wouldn't celebrate until he had a contract and some money in hand.

He flopped onto his bed and lay there thinking about all the exciting prospects—fame, travel, money. He thought how odd life was as he stared at the shelves overflowing with books, trophies and mementos of his hockey career. Not long ago he hoped to be a professional athlete. The injury that destroyed those dreams led him toward writing. He just had to tell someone, so he reached over and dialed a familiar number. The phone rang three times before she answered.

"Hi, it's me," Matt said.

"Hi, you, what's up on this gorgeous summer evening?" Donna asked.

"You up for a walk? I got something to tell somebody, and you're the first person that came to mind."

"Well, I'm not sure I believe that, but I'll meet you

halfway. How 'bout the corner of N Street in ten minutes?"

"See you there, beautiful."

It was almost seven p.m. As Matt approached her, Donna smiled warmly. It was a beautiful late-summer night. The darkening sky was clear, almost cloudless, and the light cool breeze blowing toward them delivered a taste of salt air from the beach. The setting sun shone orange on the L Street Bathhouse and the trees that guarded Carson Beach. Her pale complexion shone crimson around her freckled nose.

"Looks like you've been to the beach," Matt said, returning her smile.

"Yeah, we went to Wingersheek—up on the North Shore. But it was so cold I just lay in the sun while Frank played touch football with his buddies. I guess I got a little burn."

Matt wanted to tell her she looked terrific. She was dressed in a pair of faded jeans that fit her perfectly. Her pale-blue sweatshirt with the words "Southie Forever" on its front did little to hide her full breasts. The lustrous, shoulder-length, auburn hair that Donna took so much pride in seemed to shine as it picked up highlights from the fading sun.

He hugged her, took her hand and pulled her toward him. He looked into the large, soft brown eyes that were as warm and welcoming as ever. As he and Donna headed toward the beach, Matt squeezed her hand.

After dodging the evening traffic on Day Boulevard, they made some small talk while they sat on the low, stone wall in front of the beach. A few sailboats took advantage of the light breeze, heading home in the twilight, while the seagulls competed loudly for what the swimmers and sunbathers had left behind. The fragrance of the tide competed with the soft scent of Donna's perfume.

Finally, Matt couldn't wait any longer. "Donna, you're not going to believe what's happened!" he blurted out. For the next ten minutes they sat on the wall as the sun worked its way below the trees across the Boulevard. Once Matt started, he couldn't stop. Everything that had happened overflowed as he told her about his writing, Baldwin's offer, and meeting with the lawyer.

When he was done, she laughed and clapped. "Oh, God, Matt, I'm so happy for you. Your dad must be *so* proud of you."

They got up and walked along Carson Beach, discussing how Matt's life would change. In a while, without thinking he'd put his arm around her. Donna made no protest. Instead, she put her head on his shoulder, old friends walking back across the wide, tree-covered lanes of Day Boulevard toward home.

Matt took Donna to her door, thanking her for listening to his exciting news. He looked down at Donna, staring into her warm, inviting eyes. He bent and gave her a kiss on the cheek. "Okay, cowboy, back off," she said. "I've got a guy. And what about Jesse, the girl we met at the Public Gardens?" He'd been able to put her out of his mind for a while, but with the question the pain came flooding back.

"It-it didn't work out between us." He avoided Donna's eyes. "Why?"

"I just wondered." She'd been teasing, but Matt could see Donna knew she'd opened a wound. "I just thought you two seemed like the perfect couple. I'm sorry, Matt," she said with regret.

"It doesn't really matter." He sighed, suddenly feeling very tired.

"Of course it does. Everything that happens to you is important to me. It's the same with you. I care about you, and I always will." She looked up at him as she spoke softly.

"And how is Frank these days?" he asked.

"He's fine. Thanks," Donna said. "I'm sorry it didn't work out, Matthew. Honest to God, I am." She took his hand and squeezed it.

"No big deal. I mean who knows? We probably..."

She didn't let him finish. She put her fingers to his lips, the same way Jesse had in front of Martel's. "Matt. Don't put on a front for me. Don't cheapen what you felt, what you're still feeling." She pulled his face to hers and kissed his cheek again. "You know if you ever need somebody..."

"I know, thanks."

Matt backed away. "You better go. It's getting late."

She touched his arm "I'm so happy about your book, Matt." She gave him a broad grin and turned. "Just don't forget me when you win the Pulitzer and become the darling of the talk shows." He watched her walk away and thought how lucky he was to have a person like Donna. But then, he had so many good people in his life. He thought about Jesse, wondering who she could turn to, wishing he could ease her loneliness.

"I'd *never* forget you," he said, giving her a wink and a wave as he headed home.

"I know." She gave him a wave.

Matt walked the three blocks home, oblivious to his surroundings. He felt excitement, confusion and sadness in equal parts. When he got there, he sat down on the front porch, looking up at the muted stars, their light dimmed by the haze and lights of downtown Boston.

He heard a noise and saw his father standing in his worn, flannel bathrobe. It was the one his mother had given Daniel the Christmas before she died. He stubbornly refused to let anyone replace it.

Matt smiled. "I miss Mom too, Dad, but you've got to retire that robe before it walks away on its own."

"Nonsense, it just needs a good wash. I'll give it to Jeannie tomorrow." He smiled at Matt. "Anything I can help with? You look like you're carrying the weight of the world on your shoulders."

"No, I'm all right. It's just that every time I think I've got everything figured out, life seems to blindside me." Matt shook his head. He looked at his watch, knowing he had to be up early for work.

"Well, son, I don't know exactly what you're talking about, but I can tell you this. You're bright, talented and handsome. Life is funny, Matt. Sometimes the more you're given, the more difficult it becomes to sort it out." Daniel stepped out and sat next down.

Matt nodded.

"Everything new and wonderful we're given seems to have a price attached. Sometimes it gets so difficult you get to thinking it would be easier to give up." His father studied the hazy, night sky and shook his head. "But Matthew, I believe you have a destiny bigger than anything I ever imagined. I read what you wrote. You have a gift, son. Your words paint pictures. They bring out feelings."

"Thanks, Dad."

"When I finished reading your story, I knew you were meant for great things, but be careful, because having that kind of talent can be a blessing…or a curse. Use what God's given you to inspire people. We all have a purpose, and you've found yours."

Matt got up and hugged his father. It had been quite a day. As they looked up at the faded night tapestry, Matt said, "Thanks, Dad, I'll give it a try," as he went inside.

"Don't try, Matt. *Do it!*"

As he lay in his bed, drifting off to sleep, Matt replayed the day. He thought of Donna—how warm and exciting it felt to hold her again, of his meeting with Baldwin, of his father's sage advice. But as sleep overtook him, there was another vision, more vivid and compelling than any of the others. It was a vision of Jesse smiling at him the first time he'd seen her at Martel's….

****

"Hello."

"Well, well," the man answered. "To what do I owe the honor of this call, my old friend?"

"I know it's been a while, but I need some information. I want to check on someone and I hear you have some associates that might be able to help me in South Boston." Mario hadn't spoken to Frank in two years. There was a long silence.

"You *are* calling from a pay phone?" Frank asked.

"Of course," Mario said respectfully.

"What's the name?"

"Maybe we should meet in person—at our old spot. You know, just in case," Mario suggested.

"You're a wise man, my friend. I'll see you there on the day and time we used to meet." His friend hung up the phone.

Chapter Sixteen

Late August 1988

Ali played on the beach in front of the small cottage on Cape Cod's South Shore. She laughed, as she moved her hands up and down making sand angels. Jesse shaded her eyes as she watched her daughter and the little girl from next door. Gulls floated lazily on the updrafts, while in front of her the flat, gray expanse of the Atlantic extended south and east for two thousand miles.

The weather had been perfect during their short vacation. As Ali giggled, Jesse was disappointed that their Cape adventure would last only two more days. Then they'd pack up and head back to the city.

Alice sat next to Jesse under an umbrella. She slept away this crisp, late summer afternoon, covered by a blanket with a copy of *The Ladies Home Journal* resting on her chest. Jesse noted with contentment that her breathing seemed loud but regular.

So this is what it's like to have a family vacation, Jesse thought, grateful Mario had once again shown his ability to know exactly when the Long family needed something. His surprising offer to let them use this small beach house had come as welcome relief. But despite her gratitude, there were times when she wondered if there'd be a day of reckoning. She wanted to believe this man was what he appeared to be: kind, generous, perhaps a lonely soul who felt indebted to the Longs. But life had taught Jesse a bitter lesson—what people appeared was often in contrast with what they were.

As her little girl laughed and played, the sun's warmth and the murmur of the waves lulled her. But as she laid there, thoughts of that damp July night when Ali had been conceived, the dark, terrible night that had almost stolen her dream surfaced again… Billy Herbert and his friends, their smug looks and suggestive comments…then the soda laced with something to guarantee both her compliance and forgetfulness. Jesse shuddered and felt her eyes burn as she pictured those last few minutes before she passed out…

Jesse let her anger disperse, refusing to think about that night, determined not to give its cruel outcome any life. She looked around self-consciously, wiping the dampness from her eyes as she focused on her dream. Within two years she'd be in New York, Vienna, Milan...as far away as her talent could take her. The problems with her throat were disappearing. Each day her voice grew stronger and her range was returning. She'd been right. Rest was the cure.

There was barely any wind and the listless waves of Nantucket Sound lapped at the sand twenty feet away. Now, as she closed her eyes, she couldn't avoid thinking of *him*. She'd been right, of course. There'd been no time for him since the night when he'd come to find her. Still, she couldn't help smiling as she thought about his gesture. No one had ever done that before. Men had wanted her, propositioned her, even offered extravagant favors, but no one had ever really cared the way Matt had. That was why it hurt so much.

Jesse had hoped that after a few weeks, he would be a distant memory, but she'd been wrong. She found herself wanting him more than ever. As if the old dreams that haunted her weren't enough, new ones had grown to torment her.

Ali said good-bye to her new friend. Jesse opened her eyes, looking at her daughter. Someday very soon Jesse would make up for all the days and nights she'd left her daughter alone. She got up, walked to Alexis and grabbed her by the hand. This afternoon Jesse was determined to enjoy the sun, the water, and her little girl. As they ran splashing into Nantucket Sound, Jesse tried to put her bad memories and thoughts of Matt behind her.

And for a few precious minutes, she did.

Chapter Seventeen

September 1988

In his sixth floor office overlooking Times Square, Lawrence Webb was bored. He sighed, yawning loudly as he watched the tourists being assaulted by sidewalk vendors selling everything from T-shirts to counterfeit Rolexes.

For much of the spring and summer Lawrence had been on a quest for fresh talent for his new production. It had been twenty-five years since he boarded a bus in Chicago, leaving his adopted family in Illinois to seek his fortune, and now, at the age of forty-seven, he'd achieved almost everything he dreamed of when he headed for New York City in the summer of 1963.

Lawrence—only his sister dared call him Larry—was incredibly wealthy, had produced a successful show in each of the last dozen seasons and was the object of constant pursuit by writers, fans, and beautiful women. What still eluded him was the pure artistic success he craved. But Lawrence had made up his mind. No matter what the expense or effort, he was going to win the coveted Theatrical Guild Award for Best Musical before reaching the age of fifty.

He'd discussed it with his agent and his publicist, and the conclusion was that Lawrence needed new faces—fresh talent with voices that evoked the image of opera rather than musical comedy.

He'd held auditions, workshops in the Village, advertised in the trade papers and called on his extensive network of talent scouts. To date, they'd yielded limited results. Lawrence had seen dozens of young women, but not the one he wanted. She had to be perfect.

Now as summer waned, he realized that no new Webb production would grace his theater, but that was all right. He could not only live with the idea, he'd grown to like it.

The buzz surrounding his efforts to create an artistic success was gaining momentum, no doubt spurred by the articles his publicist had strategically placed in Variety and the Times' arts section: *"Lawrence Webb, the great impresario with the golden touch, had turned a deaf ear to the cash register and opened his heart and his pocketbook to produce something of lasting quality and value."* He smiled, thinking he couldn't have written it better.

He'd found the vehicle when he'd stumbled across *Gates of Paradise*—a work based on the early years of the Mormon Church. The play was written by a professor at Stanford.

When he'd read it for the first time, Lawrence smiled. It was just what he'd been looking for. It was exciting and mysterious with characters an actor or actress could get their arms around. But he wanted a musical, so Lawrence solicited the services of the finest songwriting team in the industry.

Within a month Oliver Donnelly and Jacob Weisman were on their way to writing fourteen beautiful pieces that would find their way into the minds and hearts of the theater-going public. Lawrence insisted on serious pieces, songs of substance that required range and strength to perform. His new production would have no fluff.

Their crowning achievement had been an unforgettable signature piece. He envisioned people across the country humming the haunting notes of *Gates of Paradise* as they showered, shopped, or waited for a cup of coffee.

His concerns about finding a director had evaporated when Ian DeStefano had come to him two weeks ago. There was no one better. Ian had already won two Tonys while working with another producer. He was also the most lecherous man Lawrence had ever met.

Ian had heard about Lawrence's quest for an artistic mega-hit, and he wanted to be involved. The two of them had worked together on several successful projects, and despite Ian's weakness for attractive young women, Lawrence had great respect for him. Lawrence detailed his progress to date and showed Ian the rough draft and the music. Ian signed on immediately.

Lawrence wanted his new talent signed by the time he went to his sister's for Thanksgiving. That would give him until New Years to round out the company with the extras *Gates of Paradise* would require.

All he needed to make the whole thing work was someone very special: a fresh face, a young woman new to Broadway, who was beautiful, talented, and willing to walk through a brick wall for him.

He smiled, pouring his favorite brandy as he lit a cigar and watched the tourists in Times Square. He savored the liquor and the strong, sweet smell of his expensive cigar.

No problem, Lawrence, he smiled, *no problem at all*.

Chapter Eighteen

"An *agent*? You mean like one of those people who represents athletes, Mr. Whitehead?" Matt asked.

"That's right, Matt. You've heard of people like Bob Woolf who represents a lot of our local sports stars. Well, we'll get you someone to do the same for you." Peter Whitehead, Daniel's lawyer, was speaking. He was an imposing gray-haired man with a booming voice that fit his stature.

He smiled as Matt sat next to his father in the well appointed but cluttered office in Boston's Federal Reserve Building.

"Think of it this way, Matt, you're now an artistic star…or you soon will be," he chuckled. "You'll need the services of an intellectual property attorney. I don't get into that, but I can recommend someone. The firm downstairs does a lot of that kind of work. They'll help you with copywriting and make suggestions as to the best agent. Since you've got a deal in hand, it shouldn't be a problem."

Matt was confused.

"It's really simple, Matt. You'll be up to speed in no time," Peter said.

"But I have to give Baldwin an answer by Monday."

"You can talk to Ron Stein at the firm downstairs, but from what you've told me, they're anxious to get your work. They'll give you an extension," Peter reassured Matt, who looked at his father.

"Can you give me Mr. Stein's number?"

"I'll do better than that. I'll see if he has a few minutes he can spend with you right now."

"That'd be great." Matt nodded. He was enjoying being courted by powerful businessmen and attorneys.

Peter picked up the phone and dialed his colleague. He winked at Matt as he was put on hold. He explained it was important and waited until his friend picked up the phone.

After some good-natured banter, Peter Whitehead related Matt's experience with Baldwin and then listened for a few minutes. He hung up the phone.

"He has a client meeting in about ten minutes, but he'd be glad to meet with you at one thirty. Tell you what, I'll buy you lunch at Lochober's. Then we can come back, and I'll introduce you to Ron. You're going to like him, Matt. He's the best this side of New York. You've heard of Robert B. Parker, the man who writes the Spencer Mysteries? Well, Ron's his guy, and Parker swears by him."

"What do you say, Matt?" Daniel looked at his son.

"Sounds great to me—especially the lunch part. I'm starved." Matt grinned.

Peter broke into one of his deep, throaty chuckles. "If your work is as good as I suspect, you can get used to this. Publishing is known for its long, elegant lunches."

They shook hands. Daniel slapped Matt on the back as they headed for the elevator. Last week, he'd been cleaning up construction debris for $3.50 an hour. Today he was on his way to being Boston's newest literary celebrity. It was a heady feeling.

His book could be a *significant literary work,* Paul Kellogg had said. As an author, you could change the world. He had a wonderful opportunity, but with that opportunity came great responsibility. For the first time in years he thought of his grandfather's words.

"Every man has a destiny, Matt, a purpose he's put on earth for. Some men never know their destiny, but for others—a special few—life has an important role in store. I think you're one of those."

The elevator stopped.

"What do you think about the LLC idea, Matt?" Peter asked.

Matt had no idea what he was talking about. He smiled at Matt, who stood embarrassed, caught at having been daydreaming.

"I was talking about forming something called a limited liability company. It's a new idea many professionals are using. It offers them the flexibility of a simple partnership with the protection of a corporation…" He stopped in mid-sentence.

"I-I really don't know, Mr. Whitehead. I thought that authors wrote books. I didn't know there were so many other things involved."

Peter put his large hand on Matt's shoulder as they headed toward Lochober's on Winter Street.

"You're right. That's what authors should do. For the next hour let's forget the details. We'll get one of their private rooms, have a drink and a meal to celebrate your success." Peter looked at the two of them as he spoke. "We'll get a bottle of their best champagne and drink a toast!"

"Yes," added his father, who'd been silent during

the exchange between Peter and Matt. "I want to drink a toast to the best son a man ever had!" And with that they turned into the elegant, wood paneled foyer of Boston's finest restaurant.

Chapter Nineteen

Jesse entered 295 Huntington Avenue. She headed right and followed tradition, tapping the Statue of Beethoven for luck as she ran up the stairs. The building was the main teaching location for New England Conservatory. The three upper floors housed the studios where students honed their craft. The building was also home to Jordan Hall: an eighty-five-year-old performance venue with impeccable acoustics and seating for 1100.

Jesse was late for her lesson with John Van Zandt. He wouldn't be happy. John was a superb vocal coach, perhaps the best at the Conservatory, but she knew her constant tardiness irritated him.

She ran down the hall, hearing the noise from the other studios. She stopped outside number 210, took a deep breath and knocked on the door. Nothing. She knocked again, a little louder this time. Still no response. She opened the door, looking inside. But the room was empty. The only activity was the large window fan blowing air into the room. She studied the empty studio, remembering their first meeting on the afternoon of her audition.

Pauline had talked to John before her tryout. As with all prospective students, Jesse had thirty minutes to impress selected members of the faculty. John introduced himself before her performance that March day in 1986. When she'd finished, he approached her.

At NEC and other good music schools, your teacher carried as much weight as your talent, perhaps more. Jesse knew there was no one better than John Van Zandt.

"Pauline didn't exaggerate, Jesse. If you join us at the Conservatory this fall, I hope we can work together."

All Jesse had managed was a meek, "Thank you."

Now, she stood, biting her lip. John had always been so nurturing, her biggest supporter and champion. Was he angry with her? She went outside to check the grease pad where he wrote his appointments. Her name was there. Concerned she'd been too late, she was about to check his office, when she heard footsteps on the hardwood floor. They turned the corner, and she saw John walking toward her.

He was usually very upbeat, but today he wore a sober, almost harsh expression. As he approached, he nodded slightly. When he got to the door, he managed a weak smile, patted her shoulder and ushered her inside. "Hello, Jessica. Please take a seat."

"John, I'm *so* sorry I was late again, it's just that with—"

"It's all right. I know your situation. That's not what I want to talk about." He faced her. "The recital committee met this afternoon to discuss the candidates." He looked into her eyes.

Jesse bit her lip. She'd hardened herself against the world, but the recital meant so much to her. She could hear her heart racing.

"I'm afraid we have a problem," he said.

Jesse looked away, feeling the tears growing. But

as she turned to face him again, he wore a grin. As he walked over to where she was sitting, his grin grew to a smile. "Now that you've been chosen, we have to pick *just* the right piece. I'm not sure which I like, the Puccini or that little French piece we were working on the other day," he said, laughing. "And of course there was that haunting thing from the play you sang for me last week." She sprang to her feet and hugged him, tears cascading down her cheeks.

"I'm sorry, I hope I didn't cause you any anguish." He hugged her. "I'd never do anything to hurt you."

"You had me going, John." She shook her head. "But I'll forgive you." She brushed away her tears.

"You got everyone's vote on the committee, even that old fart Heidelman. They all think you'd represent NEC wonderfully."

"I don't know how to thank you."

"You can thank Pauline. We both should. If it hadn't been for her, we might never have worked together, and that would have been a great loss for me."

"For me too, John." She squeezed his hand.

He looked at his watch. "Let's get to work! It's twelve forty-five. We've only got six weeks and you haven't sung a note yet!"

As she had on that afternoon in 1986, Jesse just offered a meek "Thank you."

Chapter Twenty

Matt sat in the outer office of Benjamin, Halloran, & Stein waiting for his ten a.m. appointment. His mind should have been on the business of the day—meeting a literary agent and signing the contract with his lawyer, but it wasn't.

He'd worked to forget about Jesse—until the call last night. Alice Long asked to meet him for lunch. She promised what she had to say was important. He didn't know why she'd called, but assuming it had to do with Jesse, he'd agreed to meet her.

"We're ready for you." It was Ronald Stein. He ushered Matt into his office. Stepping inside, Matt surveyed the room. He swallowed hard, hoping to calm the butterflies dancing in his stomach. There was Ron's secretary and a man Matt had never seen. And sitting in a large leather chair was a lovely young woman with short, bright red hair and almond shaped green eyes. Matt couldn't help but stare. She was breathtaking.

Ron cleared his throat.

"I'm sorry, I don't know some of these people," Matt apologized.

"I was just about to introduce you," Ron said, smiling. "This is Milton Aaronson, President of the William Coughlin Agency. We discussed their representing you." Ron nodded toward Milton. "They're one of the oldest and most respected talent agencies in the business."

"Hello, Matt, it's always a pleasure to meet someone with so much talent." Milton Aaronson shook Matt's hand. "I wanted to be here. Stephanie is our top literary agent. If you decide to sign with Coughlin, she'll be dealing with you on a personal basis."

"Matt..." Ron gestured toward the young woman. "This is Stephanie Halloran. We feel she'd be the perfect fit for you," he said.

The woman stood up and approached Matt with her hand extended. She was shorter than Matt imagined. Her long, supple legs gave her the appearance of height. The expensive, fitted suit she wore did a poor job of concealing her figure.

"Matthew, this is a pleasure. I've read your work. You write beautifully, and your story is fascinating." Stephanie spoke in low, evenly modulated tones, as she found Matt's eyes. She was selling herself, and Matt was enjoying it.

"It's nice to meet you, Stephanie." Matt shook her hand. Stephanie returned to her seat, standing next to it with her hand on its back. The pose highlighted her figure.

"I reviewed the contract from Baldwin." She asked Milton, "May I?"

"Of course," he nodded.

"It may be all right, considering that you're unpublished, but we can do much better."

"You see, Matt, Baldwin is a fine old house, but they need you desperately. They haven't had a young writer of quality in years. They're living off the fumes of past glories—repackaging old material with new covers." Stephanie moved subtly, assuming an equally flattering stance. "I know we can get you twice, perhaps three times the advance, a higher percentage on net, and I wouldn't sign anything long term—no multi-book deals just yet. Keep them in suspense."

Matt watched, hypnotized, following her subtle movements.

"There's a lot we can write into the contract in terms of paperback and international sales, too. And by the way," she said, staring into Matt's eyes as she showed her flawless smile, "wouldn't Paramount or Twentieth Century love to have the rights to *Satan's Twilight* for the big screen?" She paused, giving Matt time to think about her suggestions. "I don't want to overwhelm you, but I think you get the idea."

Ron looked at her and then at Matt. He grinned. "What did I tell you, Matt? Is she the best?"

"If she isn't, she'll do 'til the best comes along."

Matt was in awe. She was soft-spoken, but her fire and passion inspired confidence. "I'm worried, Stephanie. They gave me an extension, but we only have a few days before their offer runs out," Matt said with concern.

Stephanie gave him a persuasive smile. "Give me your permission, and I'll call Paul as soon as this meeting's over. We'll get best agreement for you, Matt, not Baldwin."

"Just tell me where to sign." Matt stood up and went to shake everyone's hand.

The meeting lasted until eleven forty-five. The others left. Beauty, brains, and the instincts of a hungry shark. God help the people at Baldwin, Matt thought, shaking his head as he thought about Stephanie. As he signed a power of attorney, Matt asked about her.

"Halloran. Why does that sound so familiar?"

Ron handed Matt a business card. Matt studied it. Of course, Benjamin, *Halloran,* and Stein!

"She's your partner's...?" Matt looked at Ron.

"Daughter—his only child. But believe me, she's not riding anyone's coattails. She graduated from high school at sixteen, was a Phi Beta Kappa with a double major at NYU, got an MFA from Columbia while she worked her way up to senior editor at Viking. All in only five years. She's been with Coughlin since '86."

"How old is she?"

"She'll be twenty-six next month." Ron lowered his voice. "But she's a tiger—loves anything competitive. She was an alternate to the '84 Olympic team in one of those riding events—hates to lose. So stay on her good side," he chuckled.

Matt laughed. "I'd love to be on her good side. She's quite a woman." Matt looked at his watch. He didn't want to be late. Stephanie might be beautiful and brilliant, but *his* mind was on Jesse.

It was after noontime when Matt ran out to the street. He was supposed to meet Alice at twelve thirty, and he didn't want to be late. Throughout the morning, he kept wondering why she'd called.

Matt flagged down a cab. After fighting the midday cross-town traffic, the taxi dropped him at the small restaurant. Matt entered the luncheonette and spotted Alice seated in the last booth. She smiled and got up to greet him, coughing as she did.

"Sorry. I have emphysema, Matt." She patted her chest.

"Don't worry, Mrs. Long." He helped her back to her seat.

They ordered soft drinks.

When the waitress left, Alice said, "I don't believe in small talk. When I saw you and Jesse in the park that day, I knew there was something special between you." Matt began to speak. She held up her hand. "I could see you two were fond of each other," she said, looking at him with sad gray eyes. "Was I right?"

He nodded. "Yes, Mrs. Long."

"Please, call me Alice."

The waitress brought their drinks and asked if they wanted to order. Before Matt could answer, Alice waved her away. "Jesse's in love with you, Matt."

Matt sat mute, unsure he'd heard correctly.

"I know she's made it hard, but she needs something badly in her life besides work and training. She needs to enjoy life. I think you can help her. I know calling you was crazy, but I haven't done a lot to help my daughter," she said, shaking her head. "I've been tired, sick, scared"—she paused—"but when she spoke about you a while ago—" Alice leaned toward him. "I knew I just had to do something. It took time to get up the nerve. I hope I did right." She played with the napkin, looking down at the table.

"She said that…about me, Alice?" He didn't know what to think. He hoped she *wasn't* crazy.

"Yes, she did." She coughed. "She'll be at the Conservatory on Huntington Avenue tonight until seven thirty. She has a rehearsal. Then she gets the train home." Alice reached across the table and squeezed his hand. "And Matthew…be gentle with her." As he looked at Alice, tears welled up in her eyes. "She needs that so badly." Without another word, Alice got up, put two dollars on the table and walked out the door.

Chapter Twenty-One

The two men sat across from each other in the rundown diner on lower Massachusetts Avenue. The smaller man handed Mario a sheet of torn notebook paper. As he studied the information, a smile crossed his face.

"This is good, Frank." He nodded. "Just what I wanted."

"Sorry it took so long. But these Sullivans…they're like the poster family for Southie. Clean as a whistle." The man looked around warily. "You're not going to…"

Mario held up his hand. "No." He shook his head. "Nothing like that."

"Good. Regular citizens like this getting taken down. It's not good business."

Mario lit a cigarette and the notebook page, letting it burn in the ashtray as he stood up to leave. They shook hands. "I owe you one."

****

Matt sat in his living room, with the address of New England Conservatory: 295 Huntington Avenue. It should be easy to find *if* he decided to go. He heard the screen door open as Allen headed upstairs. His brother-in-law was on the third step when Matt called him.

"Got a minute, Al?"

"Sure, what can I do for you?" Allen had been a

surrogate older brother, helping Matt through some difficult times. He came back and flopped into a chair. "What's up?"

Matt told Allen about Jesse, finishing the story by describing his lunch with Alice Long. Matt waited, expecting a litany of wisdom. Instead, Allen stood up and patted Matt on the knee.

"Matthew, you're a smart guy. Sometimes too smart. There's no mystery. This isn't a novel. This woman sees her daughter driving herself, working and studying all the time. The girl breaks down and tells her mother she's crazy about you. What's the problem? The woman wants to help. Get your skinny ass over to the Conservatory as fast as you can."

When Allen was done he approached Matt. "Come on," he said, taking Matt's arm as he pulled him up. "*Go!* I'll tell your dad you have a date, *because you do*."

Matt stood, nodding at Allen. As he headed out the door, the phone rang. Allen motioned for him to go and went to answer it.

Chapter Twenty-Two

Approaching the imposing stone facade of 295 Huntington Avenue, Matt realized this wasn't going to be as easy as finding Jesse at Martel's. The New England Conservatory was a big place, and he had no idea where to look for her.

He stopped a group of students, asking where he could find the information desk. They directed him to the administration building across the street, but added that it closed at five p.m. He was too late. They added that most of the class and rehearsal rooms were in 295 Huntington. Matt nodded and headed toward the entrance.

Entering the massive double doors, he heard singing. The voice was amazing—female and more beautiful than any he'd ever heard.

He smiled at the thought of surprising Jesse. His enthusiasm drained when he surveyed the endless corridors. But there was no turning back. She was too important to abandon his search. Alice had mentioned something about a rehearsal. He decided to ask.

Several young women stood listening in front of him, mesmerized by the lush, robust voice giving life to the aria. He walked toward them, hoping they might be able to help him. He could just see the auditorium beyond. It was Jordan Hall, one of the most famous concert halls in the world.

He tiptoed to the doorway as the singer struck a high note, holding it for several measures. The girls smiled in admiration. He was about to question them when he glanced at the stage. For a moment his heart stopped. The young woman with the haunting voice was Jesse.

"Oh, my God," he whispered in awe. The admirers at the door overheard. They nodded in agreement.

"Isn't she wonderful?" one whispered.

As he sneaked inside, the girls gave him a scolding look, mouthing "Shhh" as he passed. He nodded, bent down and sat, listening. Her voice filled every corner of the empty concert hall.

He recognized the music from an undergraduate music class—Puccini he thought—realizing that Jesse's interpretation was better than the recording. When she finished he clapped spontaneously. Everyone on stage looked toward him. He hid behind a seat. From his hiding place he saw that her performance had been the finale. Everyone was packing up.

No wonder she was so driven. Matt began to understand the conflict she felt. He had no idea how much time developing and training a voice like hers must take. And there was her job, her family…what a load she was carrying. Guilt swept over him at misjudging her.

As the performers picked up their briefcases, Jesse spoke to a man seated at the grand piano. She kissed his cheek and he hugged her.

Matt sneaked out of the hall. Leaving the building, he hid behind the granite stairs to wait. Most of the others had left when she came out of the building. She was alone… and she looked wonderful.

She was halfway down the steps, when he had an idea. He began clapping. Jesse stopped, confused. Quickly, she realized where the noise came from, but he was concealed by the steps. When he appeared she stopped, standing speechless as he approached.

"It sounds like you have an admirer." They both turned as someone approached. It was the man Matt had seen on stage. "Or should I say another admirer. As I'm sure you can imagine, it's impossible to hear Jessica and not want to sell your soul for more," the man said, putting his hand on her shoulder.

"My name's John Van Zandt," he offered. "I've had the privilege of being her teacher and vocal coach." He paused. "When Jessica is famous—and she will be—I'll receive some credit. But it will be entirely undeserved. Jesse was born with that wonderful instrument."

Jesse looked confused. She stood frozen as Matt shook John's hand.

"It's a pleasure. I'm Matthew Sullivan. Jesse and I are…old friends. But I'd never heard her sing before. And yes," he said, turning toward her. "She was *amazing*."

"The pleasure is all mine, Matthew," he continued. "Enjoy the evening. Good night, you two." He patted Jesse on the back and headed toward Huntington Avenue.

They were alone. Jesse turned, finding Matt's eyes. As she did, tears filled hers and ran down her cheeks. They stood mute for what seemed an eternity. Jesse broke the silence.

"That was you inside…clapping?" She brushed a tear away as she approached. "I was *so* afraid I'd never see you again." She smiled. "I'm so sorry about what I said that night at Martel's." She searched his eyes, touching the side of his face.

He stood reveling in her scent as his eyes washed over every feature. "Speaking of Martel's, how's Ellen?" It was all that he could think of to say.

She grinned, wiping her enormous eyes. "She's okay. I kept hoping—" She studied the ground then back at him as the tears multiplied, forming rivers on her pale cheeks. "—hoping that somehow, someday you'd call or come back. But after a while, I thought I'd lost you and…"

He touched her lips. "Shhh," he whispered. Putting his hand under her chin, he raised her face to his. "You couldn't lose me if you wanted to." He paused. "And as far as regrets, I have one." He pulled her close. She put her arms around him. "That I let you get away," he whispered as he held her.

She released him and backed away. "How did you know where to find me? Do you just hang around concert halls picking up impressionable young singers?" She laughed, falling into his arms again. Reaching down, she found his hand, weaving their fingers together. At her touch Matt felt electricity flow up his arm as he thought of the moment in the Public Gardens when they'd touched for the first time.

"I just couldn't stay away. I called you. Your mother said you'd be here tonight. I never knew I'd be in for such a treat." He smiled, stroking her thick, lustrous hair. "I hope I did the right thing."

She didn't speak, but pulled him toward her. He had his answer. He closed his eyes, inhaling her fragrance.

"Matt," she asked, "please don't let go of me—not now, not ever."

"Are you all right?" he asked.

"I am now," she whispered. Then she found his lips and kissed him. They turned toward Huntington Avenue. "Can we spend some time, just the two of us, getting to know each other?" she asked as they walked with their arms around each other.

"Sure. I want to know every detail about Jessica Long."

She put her other arm around him tightly, as if afraid he might disappear. "I'm so glad you came. I'm not much of a believer, but you're the answer to a prayer."

She'd let her defenses down. Let him into her life. He wanted her so desperately, but there'd be time for that. He wouldn't spoil this by pushing her into something she wasn't ready for.

They walked along with no destination, blown by the cool, fall breeze. After a few blocks, Jesse stopped at a restaurant, directing Matt inside.

"I come here sometimes when I need a place to crash or a place where I can think about you," she said. "Have you had supper?"

"Why, are you hungry?" he asked.

"Sure." She nodded.

They ordered a pizza and sodas. Their eyes never left each other. Matt felt like a man in a dream, fearing he'd awake and she'd be gone. But this was no dream.

They talked for two hours. Jesse told Matt about her singing and a wonderful woman named Pauline who'd been her savior. Then she told him about her dreams. Jesse glowed when she spoke. Her excitement was infectious. Matt sat, absorbing every detail.

He had his turn, telling her about his family, his hockey career, the accident that ended it, and of course, about his writing. She beamed as he related the events of the past few weeks. When the owner closed at ten thirty, they pried their hands apart and left. Matt hailed a cab. When Jesse protested, he reminded her that he was expecting a big advance. She just looked at him and kissed him softly.

"Money," she laughed. "I knew there was something I liked about you."

He dropped Jesse in front of her building and asked if he could call her to make plans for the weekend. She hesitated briefly but grabbed him and whispered, "Of course. I can't wait," she added as they shared a long passionate kiss good night.

Chapter Twenty-Three

Late October 1988

Jesse and Matt ran up the stairs. She gave her special double knock and opened the door with Matt close behind. They were breathless from laughter.

"Hi, Mom," Jesse gasped as she stumbled into the living room. She collapsed on the couch.

"*Hello*, Alice. How are you?" Matt asked.

"I'm fine." She beamed at them.

"Jesse, were you on your best behavior with Matt's family?"

Matt answered for her. "She was an angel, Alice, an absolute angel." He nodded at Jesse. Her smile softened as her face grew crimson. Alice had never seen her daughter look at anyone that way.

Jesse got up, walked over, and hugged Alice. "They're such a wonderful family, Mom. I cannot wait till you meet them. Matt's sister and husband were *so* nice and their little girls are adorable." She paused to catch her breath. "And Mr. Sullivan is so sweet—" She punched Matt playfully in the stomach. "—just like this son of his."

"Watch out, Matt. I think your father's stealing her heart," Alice teased.

Jesse checked her watch, and her expression changed. Matt didn't notice, but Alice did. Jesse went over and took Matt's hand, pointed him toward the door. His face registered disappointment, but as he approached the door, Ali burst in.

"I saw your car, Matt," she said breathlessly as she ran and hugged his legs. Jesse wasn't the only one who'd fallen under Matt's spell. He picked her up and twirled her around.

"I would never have left without seeing you." He gave her a kiss on the cheek. "What would you say"— he looked at Jesse—"if I asked you to go out for an ice cream?"

"Could we? Is it okay, Mommy?" Alexis begged like she was a bubble about to burst.

Jesse frowned at Matt, nodding, "I guess I can put up with this big lug for a little longer."

"We'll go to that place on the corner. You can ride on my shoulders the whole way. Come on along, Alice," Matt insisted.

"Why not?" She touched his arm.

"Get your jacket, honey, it's getting dark, and they said it might rain." Jesse took Matt's arm, heading out the door. "But we can't stay too long. I have to study some music and get to bed, and Gerry expects me in by six." She rolled her eyes.

Alice followed along. Jesse's actions showed how much she cared for Matt. But she'd been alone for so long, Alice wondered how long it would take before Matt found the place where Jesse kept her darkest secrets. Much of what was hidden there was ugly. But unless she'd misjudged Matt, Alice was sure it wouldn't make any difference.

Chapter Twenty-Four

Late November 1988

Jesse sat on the swing, moving back and forth lazily, Matt pushed as she shivered against the cold. A plastic smile froze on her face.

"Where are you, Jess?" he asked.

"I was thinking about the last time I was on a swing," she answered after a long silence. "I was with my stepfather." Her words were soft and sad. The last one sounded profane.

Matt surveyed the playground. Since it was almost deserted on this gray, Sunday afternoon, he made a sweeping gesture. "There's nobody here. You can tell me."

The big recital was only two days away. Thinking she was nervous, he wanted to help.

Instead, Jesse turned, pulling him to her and kissed him. With tears in her eyes, she pushed him away. "No," she whispered, shaking her head.

He was confused.

"I don't want to tell you about that time on the swing." She shook her head.

He continued watching as she wiped the tears away. The biting wind blew her thick, dark hair in clouds around her face. "Is everything all right?"

"It's just the cold." She shrugged.

"I know there's a lot you haven't told me," he began, touching her cheek. "My life's been pretty good, but—"

Jesse stood up. "Can we go?" she asked, pulling him along.

They headed toward his house. Matt waved to a couple of kids on the jungle gym. "I know things were tough for you."

She put her arms around him as they walked, snuggling into his chest. "There are things I'd like to tell you." She looked at the ground as they walked. "Maybe…when the recital is over and your book tour is finished. I don't know, maybe…"

"Jess." He stopped her. "There's nothing you could ever tell me that would change the way..." He took a deep breath. "…the way I love you." He'd said it. He'd wanted to say it before, but the time was never right. He waited, suspended. He knew how she felt, but he needed the words.

Time stopped as Jesse released him. They faced each other. She found his eyes, her hair falling away. "I love you, too. I had no idea what love was until I met you." She studied him in the soft, special way he dreamt of. "From that first morning, I've thought about you so much. You're part of me."

She grabbed him with unexpected force. Then, she found his lips and kissed him. He was afraid she'd devour him, and he loved it. He kissed her back, feeling the soft, tender warmth of her mouth and tongue as it sought his. Her fragrance surrounded them as his hands slipped inside her jeans, feeling the soft warmth as he caressed her. She followed his lead.

They stopped in unison, breathing heavily as they

clung to each other. Searching desperately for a sanctuary, their eyes fell on the same thing. Parked a block away was Matt's Mustang convertible. He took her hand, but she was already pulling him toward it.

"You're sure…" He never finished. She embraced him. Matt pushed against her, reveling in the feeling. He grabbed her by the jeans, feeling her body again as he pulled her close.

"Yes, Matthew, *yes!*"

They ran toward his car. Matt fumbled for the keys and opened her door. He looked around. She touched his hand, sending strange, new sensations through him. He wanted to touch every inch of her rich body and more than anything he'd ever wanted in his life, he wanted to be with her.

Chapter Twenty-Five

"Damn! This could make it tough for the Jets to catch them." Lawrence Webb shook his head as he sat in the family room of his sister's home in Hingham, an affluent suburb on Boston's South Shore. His nieces and nephews surrounded him, as the waning moments of the football game ticked away. Everyone but Lawrence cheered as the Patriots completed a deep pass, salvaging a late victory. He shook his head, slapping his oldest nephew on the back.

He got up and opened the French doors leading to the generous deck overlooking the harbor. It was dusk and the lights across the icy water on Crow Point twinkled in the crisp November evening. His sister, Elizabeth, came out and stood beside him. He moved closer, putting his arm around her.

"God, Liz, this is the only time I feel like there's a real world out there beyond the footlights, the critics, and the backers," he said with a mixture of satisfaction and sadness. "I envy what you and Terry have here. This beautiful home, your career, the way the kids have grown up—"

"You're full of shit, Larry. I know because I'm the only one you'll let call you Larry anymore." She pushed closer to him and laughed. He joined her. "And about those backers—when was the last time Webb productions needed outside financing?"

Solo

"Okay, you're right. I love it, God help me, I really do love the lights, the excitement, and all of it so much, but I meant what I said about you and your family."

"I know you did," she said, studying the stars as the night took hold. "What would our parents think? Could they imagine you as the most powerful man on Broadway and me with this wonderful life?"

"They were tough, Liz. But it was worse on you than on me. I left after college and came east. You were there when dad got sick, and they lost the farm."

"You came back and helped. Don't be so hard on yourself. You spent time and gave them money."

"But *he* never forgave me. Dad blamed me for losing the farm." Lawrence shook his head and sighed. He pulled out a cigarette. "Do you mind?" he asked.

She shook her head. "I sneak one once in a while, but not around the kids." She let him go. "You did what you had to. They were older, and we were adopted."

"They adopted you. You were such a sweet, beautiful child." He looked at her. "They took me out of pity." His face grew serious as he took his turn studying the sky.

"Nonsense," she scolded. "Now, what's this problem the world's greatest producer can't solve?" Liz asked, putting her hand on his shoulder.

He sighed, putting his hands under his chin as he scanned the distant water. "I've got this wonderful production waiting—on hold. It'll be the best thing I've ever done if I can find the right person for the lead—a young woman with a special voice—someone with serious training. Someone who's fresh and hungry and beautiful…" His enthusiasm grew as he described this imaginary leading lady.

She cut his words short. "You don't want much, do you?"

He chuckled as he turned toward her.

"I'm serious, Liz. This could be the role of a lifetime. I want to give it to someone, but I can't find anyone worthy of it."

"Well, it's funny you should mention that, because I have a very big favor to ask."

He rolled his eyes. This meant she'd promised he'd talk to her book club.

"No, it's really something right up your alley. Honest."

"Okay, anything for my baby sister." He looked at her, doing his best to show a cheerful face.

"Well, Terry and I are new on the committee to help support New England Conservatory. They have a satellite program here in Hingham, and they're having a big Thanksgiving recital. When they found out you were my brother, they begged me to bring you along." She looked at him with that sad puppy-dog look he couldn't resist.

He shook his head. "Sure. It might be fun to hear a couple of kids sing or play the piano. I never get to do that in my day job."

"You never know, they have some pretty talented people. Maybe the super woman you're looking for will be bellowing out some Puccini," she said, poking him in the ribs.

"You're right, Liz." He put out his cigarette as they went inside to join the family for coffee. "You never know."

Chapter Twenty-Six

"Come on, Matt, please…hurry!"

Matt punched the accelerator. The Mustang responded, skidding on the damp leaves. His destination was the parking lot at Castle Island—a South Boston park thrust into the harbor like a finger. As Day Boulevard faded in the mirror, a massive expanse of asphalt came into view. In mid-summer the area was thick with push-carts, residents, and tourists. At dusk on this November evening, he promised Jesse it would be almost empty. It was.

She sat, eyes closed as Matt caressed her thigh. Her excitement was at a fever pitch. "Just park the damn car," she begged, opening her eyes as the car skidded to a stop.

"Let's get in the back seat," he said, touching her face. They scrambled out, yanking off their jackets as they squeezed into the Mustang's tiny rear seat.

"I love you so much…" he whispered as his lips found her neck.

She wanted to tell him how much she loved him, but his mouth was on hers again. His hand worked its way under her sweater and inside her T-shirt. His fingers caressed her breasts. *Yes…yes…please*, she thought as his fingers pressed harder. Jesse sighed breathlessly. Then, his hand was unfastening her bra. As he undid the hooks, he touched the scar tissue that ringed her back. She flinched. Matt hesitated. His hand explored, discovering the ugly reminder of that night five years ago. He stopped.

Jesse protested. "What are you doing?"

"What…what's the matter with your back?"

"It's nothing. *Please,* don't stop!" But he did. The fire born at the playground was dying. The seeds of its destruction had been planted on a damp night in Portland, but it was Matt who extinguished it. "Forget my fucking back….*please!*" When he kissed her, it was weak and without passion. "I'm…sorry," he whispered. "What happened?"

"Who cares? It's nothing," She leaned forward, letting their foreheads touch. She put her arms around his neck. "I had an accident. It left…left scars on my back," she lied. He'd grown up in a world where everyone was your friend and everything was wonderful—a Norman Rockwell magazine cover. How could she explain hers? Suddenly, it struck her. Maybe she never could.

She sighed again, resigned to the fact that what she wanted so much wasn't going to happen, not tonight, perhaps not ever. He put his arms around her. She backed away angrily, avoiding his eyes.

"I need to get some rest. Take me home." It wasn't a request.

"I'm sorry. I know I screwed up. But when I felt…those…scars…"

She stopped him. Jesse was rebuilding the wall that surrounded her.

"I need to get home *now*, Matt." It was an order. Minutes before, she would have traded a dozen recitals just to be with him. Her rational side had regained control.

Jesse pulled her clothes together, reached over the seat and opened the door. She got out, yanking her coat around her as she got into the passenger seat, staring straight ahead. Her jaw was fixed. Matt sat in back, frozen in place.

"I need to go."

"Jesse, I said I was sorry. I got freaked out and—"

She cut him off again. *"I need to go."*

"Jesse…I love you."

"Should I get out and look for a cab?"

Matt groaned and got out of the car, doing his best to assemble his clothes as he slid into the driver's seat. She stole a glance at him. He looked confused and angry. He started the car and put it into gear, speeding away as the tires squealed.

They rode in silence, tension consuming the small space between them. Jesse wondered again if their relationship could stand the reality of what her life had been like. Could she describe the cold, hopeless days that filled her childhood or the cruel scars on her back from the night when Ali was conceived? She swallowed a sob. Matt reached over, searching for her hand. Jesse kept it guarded in her lap.

"Are you nervous about the recital?" he asked. "You shouldn't be. There's no one with your talent."

"Thank you," she answered coldly.

They rounded Columbia Circle, heading north on Dorchester Avenue. Jesse stared out the window. The shabby, brick facade of the D Street projects sped by. The cheerful, glowing signs on Broadway mocked her. Jesse closed her eyes. After a silent journey across the city, they reached Mass Avenue. Approaching her street, Jesse ordered him to stop. Rain had begun to fall, pelting the windows as they slowed.

"It's raining. Let me take you to your door," he pleaded. "I know you're mad and hurt, but it can't end like this." When they stopped on her corner, Jesse opened the door and jumped out. "*Jesse…*" he called as she slammed the door.

She ran, looking back to make sure he didn't follow. The Mustang sat for a long moment then sped away. Jesse slowed, ignoring the cold, soaking rain. Reaching her building, she plodded up the two flights to her apartment.

Water dripped, forming little pools on the floor as she stood outside her door. Jesse heard Ali and a friend laughing inside. Knowing she couldn't stand in the hall all night, she knocked twice and let herself in. Ali rushed over, grabbing Jesse's legs.

"Hi, Mommy." Ali squeezed her. "You're all wet."

"Hi, honey." Jesse put on a cheerful face.

"Where's Matt?" Ali peeked around her mother. "I want Becky to meet him." A little red-haired girl sat on the floor next to a worn Chutes and Ladders game.

"He couldn't come up," Jesse said. "Hi, Becky."

The little girl smiled as Alice came out of her room.

"Hi," she greeted Jesse, "Did you and Matt have…" She paused as her pleasant look evaporated. "…a nice afternoon?" She watched Jesse. "You're soaking. Go put on some dry clothes."

"I'll change. And I have to look over some music before my final run-through tomorrow. If you guys don't mind, I'm going to my room." She glanced at her mother. Alice's face wore a skeptical expression.

"Okay. Becky's mom is due. Then this little whirlwind is going to take a bath." She rubbed her granddaughter's head, continuing to stare at Jesse. "If there's anything you need, something you'd like to talk about, let me know."

Jesse nodded, headed to her room and closed the door. As soon as it shut, she took off her wet clothes and let them fall to the floor. Putting on her robe, she fell on the bed. She thought of him and all the dreams she'd had—dreams that suddenly seemed so silly, so childish. Jesse didn't live in a fairy tale. Her world was hard and cruel and real.

She lay confused and frustrated. Her mother knocked to tell her Matt was on the phone. The clock said nine fifteen. Jesse asked her to take a message. Alice nodded but came right back.

"What's up, Jessica?" she asked. "Matt sounded funny."

"Let it be." Jesse looked at her music. When Alice refused to leave, Jesse added, "We had a fight."

Alice stood her ground. "He sounded really hurt."

"Too bad." Jesse turned. "Ask *him* what happened." She just stared. "Now, I have a lot on my mind. Tuesday night could be the biggest night of my life...of all our lives." She returned to her music. "I'll go kiss Ali good-night." She started to get up.

"Don't bother. She's been in bed for an hour," Alice offered stoically and left.

Jesse began to cry. The hours dragged on, but sleep wouldn't come. What did come were the vivid recollections—cruel images of the lost, terrifying night that would never set her free. No matter how she tried, or what she did, the pain, humiliation, and realization that whoever attacked her would never be brought to justice was a cross Jesse continued to bear. But the gods had given her something…an innocent, beautiful gift as token payment for what they'd allowed her to be subjected to. That gift was Ali.

No, Jesse could never erase the memories that held her captive. Her exhausted mind drifted to Matt and his reaction. Did he *really* love her? Would he ever understand the hell her life had been?

She closed her eyes, pulling the covers around her tightly, grateful that Gerry had given her the day off. It was almost dawn. And finally, as the sun rose above the neighboring buildings, Jesse fell asleep.

Chapter Twenty-Seven

Matt hung up the phone, angry with himself. He'd overreacted and hurt her. He kept reliving that strange fifteen minutes at Castle Island. Something awful must have happened to her—something so frightening that just touching her back brought it back to life. He'd seen the other women at Martel's wearing tank tops on hot, humid days. Jesse always wore a T-shirt. He'd never thought about it before. Those scars must be the reason.

Was she ashamed or embarrassed to tell him about her fears and her nightmares? Did she think so little of him, imagine him so selfish that scars would send him running in horror? *Was he that shallow?* he asked himself. But remembering how he'd reacted, Matt shook his head. Maybe he was.

He thought about her cryptic conversation at the swings—about the things she couldn't tell him and about Donna's question: "How much do you really know about Jesse?" and his answer: "Nothing." He recalled Alice's plea to "Be gentle with my little girl."

Now he was the one frightened. Would she ever share what haunted her? He opened his fourth Budweiser, as he headed onto the front porch. Settling into a rocking chair, he heard Allen and his father.

They approached the porch talking and laughing. Both served on the church council, and their meetings usually adjourned to one of the pubs on Dorchester

Avenue. Hearing their loud boisterous conversation, he assumed that was the case tonight.

"Top of the evening, son. How are things in paradise?" he asked with a grin.

Matt studied the porch floor. "Okay, Dad. How are you?"

"Great, Mattie, just great."

Matt couldn't help but chuckle as they stumbled onto the porch.

"Come on inside, son. You'll catch your death out here."

"Thanks, I'm okay," Matt answered.

"Suit yourself," Daniel chuckled. "Stay out here and freeze." He slapped his son on the back, weaving his way inside. "You've earned the right to make your own decisions."

Allen started upstairs, then stopped, studied Matt, and sat down across from him.

"Okay, sport. You can't bullshit me," Allen began. "Something's not right."

"You can probably see it a block away," Matt answered with a nod. "Something happened between Jesse and me."

"Well, that's what families are for—to give you useless advice." Allen grinned foolishly as he patted Matt on the shoulder. "Come on, what's going on?"

Matt looked at his brother-in-law. "That's the problem."

Allen waited.

"I'd love to tell you, but I just don't know. I was a *fucking jerk*." Matt looked around as he realized what he'd said. "I screwed up, Al, and I don't know how to fix it."

Chapter Twenty-Eight

"Why are you bringing this up now, Jessica?" John Van Zandt sounded angry and confused. He slapped his precious Steinway grand piano. "You could have mentioned it yesterday or last week!" he said, shaking his head. "It's too late. We decided that piece was just too...different. No one's ever heard of it, for God's sake!"

John seldom became animated. Jesse knew that a major change a few hours before the recital was unheard of. But it was something that had come to her the morning after she and Matt had fought. Her dreams were always vivid—often frightening, but this one had been different. She'd seen herself doing the haunting piece she and John had rehearsed in October. It seemed to make no sense, but somehow Jesse knew it would change her life.

"The accompaniment is simple," she pleaded. "You told me you loved it the first time we practiced it. You said it was perfect for my voice and my range. Give me the first note and I'll sing it a cappella if I have to," she continued obstinately.

"We'll do the Puccini we've been rehearsing all fall. We can't make a change this late in the schedule." John hesitated. "It does complement your voice"—he nodded—"but..."

"This piece is so different, John." Jesse implored

him. "Everyone who's heard me sing it says it was made for me—including you!" She was determined. "And that show—*Les Miserables*—is the hottest thing on Broadway. Don't say that no one's ever heard it. And it's not like I'd be singing Elvis or the Bee Gees. 'I Dreamed a Dream' is an extraordinary piece of music filled with emotion. I'm the final performer tonight. After two hours of listening to the same old classical crap…" Jesse looked around self-consciously. "It will blow them away."

"Suppose I agree. What about the committee?" he asked.

She was making progress. "I…I'll do anything you want. I'll tell them I lied to you and told you I had permission from them."

His expression was still skeptical.

Tears formed in her eyes, running down her cheeks.

"You're really serious."

She began to cry.

"It means that much to you?" he asked, shaking his head.

She wiped the tears away. "It's complicated, John. But yes." Her voice trailed off. She avoided his gaze. The lyrics had haunted Jesse since she'd first heard it. The words describing a downtrodden, struggling, young woman with a child who'd been defeated by fate and circumstance held special meaning for her—as if someone had held a mirror to her life.

John studied her then shook his head. "I don't see how this can help your career." He lifted her face, searching her eyes. "But, God help both of us, if it means that much to you." He glanced at the stage. He was weakening. "You know they'll be hell to pay with the recital committee. And they'll never buy the story that you lied to me. We're not supposed to change the program without prior approval. And *I'm* the one who has to apply for it!" He scratched his thinning hair. "All right, dammit," he agreed reluctantly. "But let's go through it a few times at"—he looked at his watch—"—five o'clock. I want it to be perfect—for your sake, and the Conservatory's."

She wiped the tears away again and hugged him. "Thank you, John. Thank you so much. I'll never forget this." She ran off the stage.

The tears stopped as she approached the dressing rooms. She grinned. She'd played John and felt ashamed. But Jesse was a gambler. She wanted to sing something so different, so unique the audience would be blown away. Maybe John was right. Maybe she *was* too tired and too pre-occupied. Because this was the biggest gamble she'd ever taken. In a few hours, she'd have the answer.

Jesse fidgeted, twirling her hair and playing with her lips. Everyone she cared about: Matt, his family, her family, and Mario would be there in six hours. She'd never performed for such a large, friendly audience. He'd called her endlessly since Sunday. Alice finally refused to answer the phone. Jesse refused to talk to him at first. But she finally gave in, accepting his apology. Every time the pragmatist in her would tell her no, leave it, leave him, her emotional side fought back. It was winning, and Jesse was glad. And she had to admit that she'd overreacted to the situation…perhaps more than Matt. She could have trusted him…confided in him. They'd talked for an hour last night.

She loved Matt so much…perhaps too much. She wanted to tell him everything about her life, but then what? She thought he'd accept it, but as time passed the ugly truth would come between them.

What would he think when he saw the repulsive scars on her back and read the word they spelled? How could she explain it? And what about Ali? He adored her and she him. Would he look at her as sweetly when he discovered she was the child of an unknown rapist? And what would her naïve, sheltered Matthew say if he found out about what her stepfather had done to her? Her nightmares would become his. She recalled a picture of a man being pulled apart by two horses—she knew the feeling.

But she couldn't let her ghosts or fears consume her. Not tonight. She had to summon all her strength, experience, and focus on the recital. She'd done it before: let her talent take over, feeling the adrenaline surge through her as she watched the audience listen in wonder. But then, she'd never been in love before.

Chapter Twenty-Nine

"You ready, Matt?" his father called from the living room.

"Yeah, Dad, be right there."

Matt checked himself in the mirror one more time. He wasn't vain about his appearance, but this was Jesse's big night. He wanted to look perfect. As Matt entered the living room, the doorbell rang. Daniel peered through the sheer curtains and opened the door.

"Hello, sir. Is this the Sullivan residence?" the man asked. "I'm here from Broadway Limo. I believe we have four persons going to Jordan Hall."

The driver wore an expensive, navy blue suit and a pleasant smile.

"Hi." Matt nodded. "You've got the right place."

His father looked confused.

"Sorry, Dad. I forgot to tell you. I didn't want to be late, so I ordered a car last week."

"I'll be by the vehicle when you're ready to go. Just let me know," the driver volunteered. "This time of night, it should take about thirty minutes, but to be sure, we should leave by six fifteen." The driver left and assumed a position by the spotless Lincoln Town Car. As the man turned, Matt noticed something familiar in his profile. Matt was sure he seen him before—near Jesse's building. He let the thought pass, chalking it up to coincidence.

Daniel nodded, "Good idea, son. I don't think we could all get into your convertible, especially with Jeannie about to deliver."

They heard Allen and Jeanne coming down the stairs. "The babysitter's here." They looked impressed. "This is definitely a first class operation," Allen said, giving Matt thumbs up. Jeanne stood, resting her hands on her stomach.

"This should be quite a night," Matt's father said. "It isn't often the Sullivans get involved with culture. Now, let's not keep that lady of yours waiting," he said as he headed out the door.

Matt took a deep breath to settle the butterflies in his stomach. "No, let's not." He shut the door as he headed for the limousine, thinking again that the driver looked very familiar.

****

"Thank God!" Lawrence Webb sighed getting into the cab behind Liz and her husband. They'd been at a reception at the Sheraton Boston for NEC patrons.

"That's the price you pay for fame," Liz teased as her husband Terry squeezed in next to her. "All that notoriety and money's such a bitch, isn't it, Lawrence?" She and Terry laughed out loud.

"Oh, fuck you—and you too, Terry," he said, suppressing a smile, enjoying the small intimacy. The life of glamour, wealth, and power looked so attractive, but it could be a cold and lonely one. Lawrence was surrounded by sycophants whose sole purpose was to serve and please him. Intimate moments like these brought out a longing for so many things he'd never known and feared he never would.

"Oh, come on. You loved being fawned over at the

reception," Liz teased again.

He turned, catching her eye. "You'd be surprised, Elizabeth."

Her face grew sad. Lawrence recognized understanding. "Maybe not, brother. Maybe not," she answered, squeezing his hand.

For a moment Lawrence was swept by emotion. His eyes grew moist. Throngs of cars and pedestrians clogged Huntington Avenue on this icy November evening as the taxi pulled up across from Jordan Hall.

"We're here," Terry said. "Will you two be able to restrain yourselves, or will I have to ask you to sit in the corner?" he asked as he paid the cab driver.

"We'll be fine, won't we, Brother?" Liz assured him. She took Lawrence's arm and the three of them headed across the street.

Lawrence and his sister crossed Boston's bustling Huntington Avenue on that frosty, November evening. Neither could imagine what lay ahead. In less than three hours the adopted son of a poor Illinois farmer would meet the daughter of a poor Maine fisherman. That chance meeting would change the lives of so many and the world of music forever…

PART III

Chapter Thirty

"It's almost time, Jessica," John said while Jesse peeked out at the audience. Matt sat between his father and Mario. Next to them sat her mother and Ali, dressed in a pale blue dress, looking like a fairy princess. While she watched, Matt made a funny face. Ali laughed so loudly Alice scolded her. Jesse had conflicting emotions as she thought about how close Matt and Ali had become.

Tears formed in her eyes as John touched her shoulder. "Are you all right?" he asked. She fought back the sobs. John put his arms around her. "It's all right," he whispered. "Let it all out. You'll feel better."

He pulled out a handkerchief. "Thanks." She nodded. "I'll be fine."

He looked at her face. "I know you will. Now fix that make-up."

"About before," Jesse began, "when we talked about the change, I have to..."

He shook his head. "It's fine, Jessica. You were right. It's different and there'll be hell to pay later, but I've never heard anything so beautiful." He gave her a thumbs-up. "I'd wish you luck, but you won't need it."

****

Lawrence sat in the fifth row, fidgeting and

clearing his throat. He should have been accustomed to nights like this, but he wasn't. When he got bored at a theatrical audition, he left the task to one of his associates. Tonight, that wasn't an option.

He checked his watch. It was almost nine thirty. The young woman playing the Rachmaninoff piano concerto finished and stood up to polite applause. According to the program, there was only one performer left.

"Only one more, thank God," he whispered, rolling his eyes.

"Shut up and listen," Liz said under her breath. "Someone told me this last girl is something really special."

"I'm sure," he said. "I can't wait to hear what I'm sure will be a very unique and spirited interpretation of"—he checked the program—"Puccini. Now there's something different. I can't wait."

"Shut up," she scolded.

A young woman approached the microphone, walking confidently. Lawrence felt suddenly alert. She was tall and graceful. Her simple black evening dress hinted at her striking figure while highlighting her alabaster skin. She had short black hair, held in place by a sparkling silver headband. As she approached, Lawrence saw her enormous blue-green eyes. She was stunning.

"Wow," said Liz. "What if she can sing?"

The young woman took the microphone from the stand.

"Good evening. My name is Jessica Long. I'm a vocal performance major at New England Conservatory. I'm in my third year, and I come from

Portland, Maine." Her self-confidence impressed Lawrence. He moved to the edge of his seat, toying with his sister's question. What if she could sing?

"On behalf of New England Conservatory, I want to thank you for your patronage and courtesy this evening," she paused. "For those devotees of Giacomo Puccini, I must apologize. I'll be singing a piece other than the one listed in your program."

A murmur ran through the audience.

"Tonight, I'll be singing 'I Dreamed a Dream,' the signature work from the popular Broadway musical production, *Les Miserables*."

The auditorium buzzed. Lawrence was intrigued but curious. This young woman might be polished and beautiful, but she was poorly advised or mentally ill.

Jessica Long cleared her throat. Lawrence sat, eyes fixed on her. He detected a change in her expression. But whatever she felt, clearing her throat had its effect. The crowd fell silent. He wondered who'd suggested this lunacy. *What are you thinking?* The audience sat in anticipation, waiting like the hungry spectators at a gladiatorial contest. He felt a wave of pity as he realized that this lovely but misguided young woman was about to commit professional suicide.

****

Jesse felt the glare of the blue-white spots. When she'd asked John to reconsider the Puccini, she felt sure she was right. But as the buzz swept through the audience, her stomach churned.

She swallowed hard, breathing deeply and focusing on a spot just above the crowd the way Pauline had taught her. She tried to ignore the shaking heads, knowing they might be right.

Solo

But when she glanced at John, he exuded confidence. Maybe this was going to work. She smiled and nodded as he began the simple eight bar introduction to the haunting theme she'd fallen in love with. The one with the words that held such meaning.

She saw Matt and the others staring, anticipating. Jesse wouldn't disappoint. As the introduction ended, she began to sing. With each passing note she surveyed the audience. Her confidence grew as she gauged their reaction. She *had* been right.

The crowd sat, hypnotized by the beauty of her selection. After the first few notes her adrenaline surged. John played with flair and emotion as his face beamed. As the music called for, his piano went silent a few bars before the final notes. She let them resonate through a silent Jordan Hall. Jesse felt intoxicated, having reached that special world that only she understood—the extraordinary place only her music could take her.

****

Lawrence sat mute, staring at Jessica Long. Her hands dropped to her side. The song was in French and he couldn't understand a word, but her beauty and poise paled when compared with her talent. She smiled demurely at the audience, capturing them, her confidence growing with every note. Lawrence scanned their faces. He knew who'd made the mistake. Singing this simple but melancholy piece was the shrewdest thing this young woman could have done.

****

Matt stood as a wave of applause swept through Jordan Hall. He cheered "Bravo" with the 1100 others who'd witnessed her performance. Jesse bowed a second time, gesturing politely toward John, bowed, and left the stage. For just a second her eyes met his. He nodded. Before the applause died, he was pushing past the others in his row, heading backstage. He wanted to be the first to congratulate her.

****

Lawrence sat, mouth open. If only she could sing. My God. There was no doubt about that. His search was over. She was perfect. He turned toward Liz and Terry. "I…I have to go backstage. Could you give me a few minutes?"

"Sure," Liz said. "We'll solicit some people for the Christmas fund-raiser."

Lawrence excused himself, heading backstage to find his quarry. It was total confusion, packed with performers, well-wishers, and students. Lawrence pushed through the crowd, looking for Jessica Long. Asking where to find her, he was directed toward one of the small dressing rooms.

Outside the small door a group of people waited— friends and family he assumed. A handsome young man held a little girl in his arms, knocking on the door and calling, "Jesse," as Lawrence approached.

He nodded, asking if she was inside. When someone said yes, he pushed through the group, opened the door and went inside, then closed the door. Once inside, he turned around and saw her sitting at a make-up table, head in her hands. Her face was wet. She snatched a Kleenex.

"Who the hell are you, and who said you could come in here?" she asked angrily.

Lawrence studied her. She was even more stunning in person. What incredible eyes. He'd never seen anything quite like them. When she stood up, she was taller than he'd imagined. That was good, very good. Her figure was perfect—slender with subtle curves in all the right places. The costume design team would drool over her. He could already visualize the publicity photos.

"I'm sorry to barge in like this, Jessica, but I loved your performance. I really have to talk with you."

While he was speaking, the door opened. "Is everything all right, Jess?" It was the young man who'd been holding the little girl. He glared at Lawrence.

Lawrence looked at Jesse, his eyebrows raised. "I think you're going to want to hear what I have to say, Miss Long," he promised.

She hesitated for a moment and then looked past him. "Everything's fine, Matt." She waved the young man away. "I'll be out in a minute."

Her guardian looked at Lawrence, then closed the door.

"You made a good choice, Jesse—may I call you Jesse?" he asked, not waiting for an answer. "My name is Lawrence Webb." He handed her a business card. "I produce musicals. And that was one of the most…*spectacular* performances I've ever heard." He shook his head. "You have the most incredible voice—clear, strong, beautiful."

"Thank you." Jesse read his card. "You're *the* Lawrence Webb, the Broadway producer?"

He nodded. "You may have other, more artistically challenging goals in mind, Jesse. But I have a proposition to discuss with you."

"Please, sit down, Mr. Webb." She shook his hand. "I'm all ears."

Chapter Thirty-One

Thanksgiving Day 1988

Alton coughed the way he did when he'd been drinking. Jesse lay huddled on her bed. He was in the next room. She heard him throw her mother against the wall. Ryan tightened his grip on the bat. As he turned, a bead of sweat ran off his forehead and exploded on the floor in slow motion.

"It's okay," Ryan whispered. "Don't worry about—"

"I'm coming to find you little bastards," Alton called.

The hairs on her arms and neck stood at attention. Jesse felt sick. She put her hand over her mouth. Watching Ryan stand guard gave her strength, but Jesse knew he was as scared as she was.

Alton tried the door to her room. It was locked. Tonight, he was drunk enough to be mean, but not drunk enough to pass out. He rattled the doorknob, breathing more heavily with each second. Jesse's felt her terror mount, knowing how angry he'd be when he got in.

"If you don't open this fucking door, you're going to be sorry!" he bellowed.

Jesse put her hands over her ears. She began to cry as he pushed at the thin door.

Then there was silence. Maybe Alton had given up and gone to his room to pass out. Suddenly, the door was shattered, collapsing inward as Alton's sweat-soaked frame fell into her room.

Alton lay on the floor, looking dazed as Jesse curled tighter on her bed. She could smell the foul stink of his breath. He rolled over and saw Ryan, who'd been catapulted across the room by the impact of the collapsing door.

"Isn't this touching?" Alton smirked. "Ryan wants to be a hero." He stumbled to his feet and headed toward Jesse. "Well, I've got my own ideas about that." He reached down and picked up Ryan's bat.

Alton looked at Jesse and then at Ryan. He raised the bat very slowly.

As she turned away, something warm and moist ran down her leg.

*Ryan...Ryan...*Ryan... she screamed. She was awake.

Jesse lay under her damp covers. Shaking, she took deep breaths, trying to calm herself. The clock said five thirty a.m.

She pulled up the curtain, looking at the dim gray. Thanksgiving dawned bleak and cold. Large snowflakes floated down to die on the warm pavement.

Lawrence Webb had invited her to New York on Friday for an audition. She hadn't told anyone. Matt kept calling to congratulate her and talk about Thanksgiving. She'd avoided his calls. Could she explain the audition, knowing what it might mean to them? The hideous painting of the man being torn apart came to mind again. She knew what he felt like. There must be a way, some way they…

Kevin V. Symmons

"Are you all right, Jessica?" asked Alice. "Were you crying?"

"I had a bad dream," Jesse whispered.

"It's early, honey. Go back to sleep. Matt won't be here 'til eleven."

"I'll try."

The door opened a crack. Alice peeked in. "If you want to talk about anything, just knock." She closed the door.

"Thanks, Mom."

Jesse turned, curling up against the cold. She closed her eyes tightly, trying to think of something good. She imagined the faces of the audience when they'd given her a standing ovation. At eight forty-five, she awoke from a fitful sleep.

Jesse wasn't a believer. In Portland, she'd spent too many nights begging God for help. He'd ignored her. But as she headed to the bathroom, she decided to try again. She closed and locked the door, turning on the shower so no one could hear. Kneeling, Jesse put her hands together, looking around despite the locked door as she bowed her head.

"Please…God, if you really are there somewhere, anywhere, I need your help. I love him so much. I don't want to hurt him," she whispered. "But I can give my family everything they deserve and have what I want more than anything in the world…what I've worked for my whole life" She raised her eyes to the stained ceiling. "Please help me."

****

"Yes, Ian, I know what *fucking* time it is," Lawrence whispered, looking around Liz's guest bedroom. Ian DeStefano was skiing in Colorado. "I've

138

been calling you since Tuesday night." Lawrence was so excited he couldn't sound angry.

"I was out of touch," Ian said. "I figured it could wait 'til the weekend and..."

"I've found our Naomi," Lawrence interrupted.

There was silence. He heard muffled sounds as Ian put his hand over the phone.

"Where did this happen? I thought you were visiting Liz for Thanksgiving."

"I went to a recital on Tuesday night and she was there. This girl was incredible. The most amazing voice you've ever heard with the poise and presentation of a pro." Lawrence thought he could anticipate Ian's next question.

"Okay, but what does she look like?"

He knew his Ian.

"She's a vision, Ian—a real beauty, tall with a great figure."

"You're serious." Ian's tone had changed.

"You're not going to believe her. She's everything we've been looking for."

"What's her name and how old is she?"

"Jessica Long. They call her Jesse and she's twenty."

"Jesse. I like that. But twenty? That's a little young."

"Trust me. She's everything you could want. That's the other reason I called. She'll be in the theater for an audition on Friday morning at ten a.m. I want you there."

Ian started to protest, but Lawrence cut him off. "Have a nice Thanksgiving. I'll see you tomorrow."

Chapter Thirty-Two

Matt was at the Long's at eleven o'clock. Jesse kissed him on the lips as he came in to Ali's cries of glee. Sometimes, Jesse wondered who was more in love with Matt.

"That's more like it," he said as he looked into her eyes.

"I'm sorry for being a bitch these last few days. It's just that…"

He put his fingers to her lips. "Shhh. It's all right." Ali had gone to get her grandmother. He pulled Jesse to him. "We talked about this. I'm the one who ruined Sunday night. You can be yourself with me. We're soul mates. I knew it that first morning."

Jesse hugged him and whispered, "So did I," as she kissed him back.

"Ahem." Alice cleared her throat. "Happy Thanksgiving, Matthew."

"You too, Alice," he said blushing.

He picked up Ali.

"Jeanne's been up since six. So have my dad and Allen, 'cause Jeanne's due in a couple of weeks." He carried Ali in his right arm and put his left around Jesse. "Let's get some turkey."

****

It was almost nine p.m. The day had been nice—almost too nice. Matt lounged on the front porch watching as a jet glided toward Logan Airport. A beer bottle hung from his hand. A half empty bottle of Seagram's Seven sat next to his chair.

Allen clomped down the stairs and slumped in a chair. Matt handed his brother-in-law a perspiring Budweiser. He and Allen had been trading stories and discussing the latest in the Matt and Jesse saga.

"Everything okay?" Matt asked.

"Yeah, the girls both told me to give you a kiss for them." Allen blew a kiss in Matt's direction. "But that'll have to do."

Matt grinned. "C'mon, Al, you can do better than that." He stood.

His brother-in-law got up, pushing him back to his chair. "Maybe I can, but I'm not going to. Not tonight." He winked and sat down.

"How's Jeannie?" Matt asked.

"Good, she just wants to get it over with." Allen shook his head. "I can't imagine what it must be like, you know, to go through that. I don't know how they do it. I've been with her when both girls were born and if it were up to me, mankind would be extinct." He paused. "Anyway, I'm glad things are okay between you and Jess."

"Yeah, today was like Sunday night never happened." Matt gazed up at another jet. "You know, it's scary how little I know about her."

"Haven't we had this talk before, sport? I swear to God, it's like you're trying to find something wrong with her."

"I'm not. I love her so much." Matt whispered, looking away, embarrassed.

Allen leaned over, putting his hand on Matt's

shoulder.

"I understand. I married your sister. I know what love's about, Matt." He took a long swallow of beer.

Matt pushed his chair back and drank from the bottle of Seagram's.

Allen looked at him. "We're more than just brothers-in-law, right?"

Matt nodded.

"Then I've got to tell you, I think you've been going at that"—Allen nodded toward the whiskey—"a little heavy. I know you've got a lot on your mind, but you should ease up on the hard stuff."

Matt was about to argue, when he realized Allen was right.

"I know they say guys like Fitzgerald and Hemingway lived in a bottle but…"

Matt stood, holding his hands up. "All right. I'll watch it." He nodded.

"Hell, that was too easy. I think you're blowing smoke up my ass."

"Well, maybe I am." Matt laughed as he picked up the bottle and headed inside. "But I'll still try. All this cheap booze is putting me to sleep."

Allen got up, giving Matt a high five.

"What's up for you guys this weekend?"

"Not sure exactly," Matt answered. "She's got something keeping her busy all day tomorrow, so it's me, the old hockey team, and Faneuil Hall again." Matt turned as he got to the door. "But I'll make every other drink a Diet Coke. Honest, Grandma."

Allen laughed and blew him a kiss as he headed upstairs.

Later, Matt lay in bed, fighting off sleep. He kept

reliving the last few days. She'd been kind, polite—that was the best way to describe it—polite. After kissing him in her apartment, the rest of the day seemed scripted, like she was playing a role.

Then this thing about the weekend. He had nothing until Monday. Last week she couldn't wait until the recital was over so she could spend time with him. But when he'd asked her what she wanted to do Friday, she told him something had come up. When he pursued it, she dodged him like a boxer.

At first, he considered the unthinkable—that she'd found someone else, but it didn't make sense. On Sunday, she'd wanted him as much as he wanted her. There had to be another explanation. He thought about the man who'd forced his way into her dressing room. Jesse downplayed it, saying that his name was Lawrence Webb, and he came from New York. Matt checked on him at the library. He was impressive. Webb was one of the biggest producers on Broadway. He was casting for a show and looking for fresh talent.

He'd asked Stephanie about Webb. "You've never heard of him? He's the biggest theatrical producer in the last fifty years. Why?"

"Because he was in my girlfriend's dressing room after her recital."

"That's great. The man's a star maker. If he's anywhere near Jesse…" Her voice trailed off.

"But she's not that kind of singer. She does classical music."

"I know his reputation. If he liked her she can write her own ticket."

He sat lost in thought.

"Matt…Matthew…"

"Sorry. Yeah, I heard you. I'm just confused."

Was it possible? She had given an incredible performance. She'd gotten serious ink from the Globe's music critic, Ellen Pfeifer. Had Webb been so impressed he'd offered Jesse something? If so, why hadn't she told him?

Jesse said Webb had gone back stage to offer her encouragement. But maybe there was more to his visit than she'd told him. As he drifted off to sleep Matt's last thought was a prayer. As much as he wanted her to be successful, he begged God to let her stay in Boston—for Alice's sake and Ali's and most importantly, for theirs.

Chapter Thirty-Three

Jesse got out at the Broadway address Lawrence Webb had given her. Staring at the massive theater that commanded the block, Jesse couldn't believe she was standing there. Reading the titles on the surrounding marquees, with household names like "Phantom" and "Les Miz" Jesse felt a pang of self-doubt. Her stomach did flips. She took out the expense money she'd been given and offered the driver a generous tip.

Approaching the theater, Jesse took a deep breath and pulled the door handle. Oh God! It was locked. The butterflies in her stomach grew friends. Jesse double-checked the address. There was no mistake. She tried it again. Still no luck.

Afraid she may have misunderstood, she looked around, her heart pounding. Taking out the card Lawrence Webb had given her, she spotted a phone booth. As she turned toward it, she heard a sound from inside the theater and the doors swung open. Thank you! She offered as a tall, slender young man in a Julliard sweatshirt smiled.

"Miss Long?"

She nodded.

"I'm sorry. *Please,* don't tell Mr. Webb. He'll have me drawn and quartered." He looked embarrassed. His speech was precise and suggested training. "I thought the stage crew had opened the door.

"I'm Bernie Stein, Mr. Webb's personal assistant, or at least I will be unless you tell him about this," he said, his eyes pleading.

"Hi, I'm Jesse Long." She shook Bernie's hand. "Don't give it another thought, the locked door never happened."

"Thanks so much." He touched her forearm. "Mr. Webb can be quite the taskmaster. But he's a real class act. One of the last true gentlemen in this business. Let's not stand in the doorway. C'mon, I'll show you around. We're looking forward to hearing you sing. Mr. Webb has told us about you," Bernie whispered, looking around as if confiding a secret. "You're all he's talking about."

"Thanks." Jesse nodded. "I'm a small town girl and this"—she gestured—"is a little intimidating." Jesse surveyed the theater. It dwarfed Jordan Hall.

"What will you be singing for us this morning? If you'll give me your arrangements—" Bernie stopped. "I'll give them to the orchestra." She fumbled through her briefcase. She looked toward the orchestra pit.

She could see a dozen musicians in front of the stage. This was serious. As if to reinforce her thoughts, spotlights went on overhead as people high above called to one another. This wasn't going to be a simple audition with John accompanying her. But of course it wasn't. This was the real deal. *I deserve to be here*, she thought. I've been rehearsing my whole life for this moment. She swallowed, hoping to convince herself.

"I do have some music with me, but I only brought one copy," she said, feeling like an amateur. "Do they know 'Sono Andante' from *La Boheme*?"

She took out the arrangement.

"I'll check." He winked. "I'll have it copied and be right back. Then we'll find Mr. Webb and Mr. DeStefano."

Bernie's friendly conversation had helped, but she wanted to get on with the tryout.

"Bernie, I'd love to see Mr. Webb, but I'm fine. Just tell me what to do and where to go."

"Actually, he's coming to meet you."

Bernie ran back. "Everything's all set," he assured her. As she passed the orchestra pit, Jesse saw the musicians had sheet music in front of them. Just another day at the office for them. But the course of her life could be decided this morning.

"Good morning, Ms. Long," one of the musicians said as he approached her. "I'll be leading this ragtag ensemble this morning." He chuckled as he gestured toward the men and women behind him. He offered his hand. "My name is Dennis Michaels. Bernie gave us copies of the Puccini you requested. Take the lead, and we'll follow you. Any special requests as to the intro, special dynamics…anything you'd like?"

"No, but thanks." She swallowed hard. "It's…it's very nice to meet you, Dennis."

When they reached the top of the stairs, she saw Lawrence Webb coming toward them. He was flanked by a much smaller man. As they approached, Lawrence waved and spoke to his companion. The man looked at Jesse then back at Lawrence, nodding as he studied her.

"Hello, Jesse. I hope Bernie has introduced everyone and explained the program for the morning." He reached out, shaking her hand firmly.

"Yes, Mr. Webb," she began.

"It's Lawrence. We don't stand on formalities."

147

"That's fine...*Lawrence*." She found it difficult to use his first name. "Yes, Bernie's been wonderful, but I have a few questions. How long do you think this will take?" *You idiot*, she cursed herself. This was her big chance and she made it sound like she had something more interesting in the afternoon. She blushed and looked at the floor. When she looked up, Lawrence's face held a look of amusement.

"I'm *so* sorry. That didn't come out the way I...I meant it."

"It's all right, Jesse. If you weren't nervous, you wouldn't be human. Please, try to relax.

"Before we discuss today's program, let me introduce you to Ian DeStefano." The small, wiry man next to Lawrence exuded pent-up energy. He smiled and nodded. His intense scrutiny made her uncomfortable. "You may have heard of him."

Of course she'd heard of him. Everyone in the music world knew him by reputation. He was supposed to be a genius—and an undisputed son of a bitch.

"Of course I have." She smiled, mustering all the charm she could. She held out her hand. "It's a pleasure."

"From what Lawrence has told me, the pleasure will be all mine. Now let's discuss what you're going to be doing this morning. Oh...how was your trip, Jesse? Lawrence tells me you're from Boston. Did you drive down or take the shuttle?"

"I don't drive, Mr. DeStefano," she said, embarrassed. "I took the shuttle."

Jesse resumed her study of the floor then looked up at Lawrence. His eyes were kind. She saw recognition in them. He touched her shoulder gently. "That's all right. I didn't drive 'til I was twenty-two."

Ian told Jesse that after her piece from *La Boheme*, she was going to sing a song from their new production, *Gates of Paradise*. She nodded. Solfège or sight reading—the ability to sing a piece of music she'd never seen before—was one of her strengths. She'd need all her training and experience. Unless her performance was perfect, she'd be on her way back to Boston.

****

Lawrence sat in the third row flanked by Ian, Bernie, and the song-writing team. Jesse breezed through the Puccini aria. As predicted, her performance was smooth, poised, and professional. Lawrence noted the others nod their approval as she performed the classical piece to perfection. Now came the true test—the *Gates of Paradise* signature piece.

"Have you had time to look over the music, Jesse?" Lawrence asked.

She nodded.

"Would you like more time?" Ian offered. "We could take a break?"

Jesse shook her head. "I'm ready."

"What did I tell you?" Lawrence whispered. "She's got more than beauty and talent, she's got balls."

Ian smiled back. "That she has. And she *is* something to look at. All right, Dennis. Let's pick it up from number twelve," he commanded.

Jesse looked at the sheet music, taking a deep breath as she put it on a stand. The orchestra played the four-bar introduction. Ian nodded and she began to sing. For the next four minutes she gave life to an unknown piece of music in a way Lawrence had seldom heard—

the way she had on the night of the recital. He couldn't resist smiling as he looked at the others. They stared in awe.

When she finished, there was a brief silence. Then, Oliver Donnelly stood and began applauding. He was joined by his partner Jacob Weisman; Bernie, the orchestra leader; and everyone else. Lawrence glanced at Ian. His director sat stunned.

"*Jee-sus*," he stammered, as he got up to join the others. A grin spread across his face. "Maybe she can't drive, but damn it, she can sing." He slapped Lawrence on the back.

Lawrence spoke first. "That was just wonderful, Jesse. Give us a few minutes?"

She nodded.

"Bernie can get you a soda or coffee and you can relax while we talk." He gestured toward Bernie, adding, "You were incredible." He looked around for support and the others nodded. "Don't worry, my dear. We just have a few things to discuss." Lawrence couldn't take his eyes off her. There was something about this young woman, something charismatic and mysterious—a je ne sais quoi that went far beyond her talent.

"Thank you, Lawrence," she said, waiting for Bernie to take her backstage.

The group headed to the stage manager's office.

"Does she have an agent yet?" Ian asked once they sat around a small conference table flanked by Lawrence, the writing team, and members of the production staff. Lawrence would solicit everyone's opinion, but it was acknowledged that he and Ian would make the final decision.

"I'm sure she doesn't. Let's get her someone really top notch," Lawrence suggested. They all looked at him. "Someone from William Morris if they'll take her."

"Wait a minute," protested Carmen Crane, one of the associate producers. "You want us to connect her with the best talent agency in the world when she'd probably sign for $10,000 and a small per diem. I like her too, Lawrence, but are *we* auditioning for Naomi or playing Santa Claus?" She looked stunned.

"Have you read what our publicists are pumping out about how we're turning a corner with *Gates of Paradise*—using this as a vehicle to give the audience something more artistically satisfying? You know the line, creating a hybrid between musical theater and opera?"

Carmen nodded.

"With what you heard from that young woman this morning and the other new talent we've got lined up, I'm sure we'll succeed. Suppose we low-ball her and six months into production, she gets upset and tells the Times or Variety we screwed her, paying her peanuts, because she was a poor little country girl. How would that play in the press?"

"Not very well, I suppose," Carmen answered after hesitating.

"On the other hand when she's the best thing on the street and they do a personal story about her, and Jesse tells them how we helped her, nurtured her, and treated her kindly, like a human being, how will *that* play?"

"Point taken," Carmen agreed. "All right. Let's get her an agent."

Lawrence surveyed the room.

"Anything else?"

Oliver Donnelly still looked confused. "How'd she do that?"

His partner shrugged.

"Hardly looked at the music, but sang it perfectly. Every inflection, every crescendo. I've never seen anything like it, and I've seen the best."

"Do we offer her the role of Naomi?" Lawrence asked.

"I want to meet the asshole who'd vote no on this one." Ian grinned, shaking his head.

"Let's make it unanimous," said Paul Hamilton, another associate producer. He raised his hand. Everyone followed suit.

Solo

Chapter Thirty-Four

By six p.m. Jesse was on the Delta shuttle to Boston. In just a few hours, her life had taken an amazing turn. She sat beaming as the stewardess took her ticket. "Well, it looks like you had a pleasant time today, miss." The flight was only a third full, and Jesse had a row to herself.

"You can't imagine," she said, shaking her head. "You really can't."

"That's nice to hear. Can I get you something to help celebrate? There's not much time, but there's enough for one drink. Soda, coffee or—"

"Do you have any champagne?" Jesse interrupted.

The flight attendant studied her skeptically, then nodded. "Sure. I'll see what I've got back there." She returned with a half bottle of sparkling wine. It wasn't champagne, but it tasted fine to Jesse.

"Would you like some?" Jesse asked. "I'm not much of a drinker."

"Thanks. I'd love some. It's been a long day. Six turnarounds." The woman rolled her eyes. "But I can't." She looked at Jesse. "You look really happy. If it's not a secret, what's the big news?"

"Well," Jesse looked around and lowered her voice. "I've been offered the lead in a Broadway musical."

"Really?" The flight attendant stared in

153

amazement. "That really is big news." She turned and walked away. "Wow," she repeated, her voice trailing off as she left.

Yes, Jesse thought, that's really big news.

When they deplaned at Logan Airport, Jesse thanked the flight attendant again.

"Good luck," the woman offered. "I'll expect to be reading about you. What's the name of your show?"

"*Gates of Paradise*," Jesse answered.

Scanning the half-empty terminal, the enormity of what lay ahead suddenly descended on her. Lawrence and Ian wanted her available by the following Friday. They'd given her the name of several agents at the William Morris Agency. They also said they'd arrange for an apartment, a trainer, dance coach…and a dozen other things. Her head swam.

Before the weekend was over, she'd have to tell her mother and Ali they were going to be alone again— until she got settled. The upside was that they'd have more than enough money. She'd have to tell the Conservatory she needed a leave of absence, break the news to John, but the most painful and difficult task would be telling Matt. She wanted a future with him, but she had doubts that her good fortune would help that. She'd avoided thinking about it for most of the day. But once back in Boston, she couldn't. Riding home in the taxi, Jesse couldn't get his face out of her mind. She got out at the corner and walked the short distance to her house.

As she headed up the stairs, Mario came out the door.

"Hello, Jessica. That was an incredible performance the other evening," he offered. "I felt privileged to be there."

She nodded.

"Thanks. I'm glad you could come. You've been so kind."

He waved his hand dismissively. "It's wonderful seeing your success. But be careful, Jessica, it's easy to get lost in the big city." He looked at her. She smiled and nodded politely, accepting his advice when it struck her.

Success, be careful, Jessica, it's easy to get lost in the big city?

How did Mario know about her success or that she was *in* the big city? No one did. She turned, but he'd vanished. How many times had he asked her about something he had no business knowing? And for that matter who were the men who always seemed to be lurking in the next doorway or around the corner. Jesse had wondered about this before, but her life had been so full she'd always put it aside. She felt the hairs on her neck stand up as she speculated on who Mario might really be and how he knew about everything in her life.

Before Jesse could give it another thought, Ali opened the door to the building and greeted her with a big hug, "Hi, Mommy. I missed you." Jesse picked her up, whirling her around and grinning as she kissed her forehead.

Alice was at the stove making something for their supper. Suddenly, Jesse realized she hadn't eaten all day.

Her mother asked her if she was hungry, adding, "How was the trip?"

"The trip was great. I can't wait to tell you. And yes, Mom, I'm starved." Alice looked at the floor. She explained that there wasn't anything in the cupboard to go with the main course except a can of cat food. "I'm sorry. I don't do a very good job of managing the money you give us. I need some…"

"Screw it, Mom." Her mother stopped. Jesse never talked that way in front of her or Ali, but tonight she didn't care. "What's the name of that fancy place on Mass Ave? Call 'em and order three steaks, all the fixings and I'll go down and get us some champagne." Jesse grinned.

Her mother stared at her.

"Ladies, today I hit the jackpot." She pranced around the apartment as Ali looked on, giggling. Jesse took out a roll of bills Lawrence had given her for expenses and put it in her mother's hands. "There's plenty more where that came from."

"But, Jessica," Alice began.

"Please, Mom, just do it."

Alice headed for the phone.

"I am gonna tell you a story that will make you believe in miracles." Jesse picked Ali up and squeezed her until her daughter squealed.

"All right, honey. Oh, there are some messages for you. There's one from John. I guess there was a problem with what you did on Tuesday. You changed the program? His words were serious fallout." Jesse shook her head, knowing it didn't matter any more. "There's another from Roger about playing tomorrow night. Then of course, Matt called three times, maybe four. He asked me where you were and what you were doing, but I told him I didn't know and I still don't." She looked at Jesse curiously. "He was going out with friends tonight but said he'd call later."

With the mention of Matt's name, Jesse deflated like a balloon hitting a sharp stick. She kept up a positive front for Ali and her mother. "Well, go call and order something delicious for dinner, and I'll answer all your questions," she added.

Alice headed to phone as Jesse went to her bedroom.

"But first, if you don't mind, I'm going to lie down for a minute. It's been a very long day," she said, thinking about Matt. "I love you, Ali," Jesse said as she blew her daughter a kiss.

"I love you, too, Mommy." Ali smiled and headed toward the TV.

"Thanks, honey."

As soon as her head found the pillow, Jesse was asleep.

He was in her room. She smelled the cinnamon incense. The room was bathed in the flicker of a dozen candles. He lay on the bed next to her, looking through her, searching her soul.

Gently, he pulled her to him and kissed her. He pressed his lips to hers as his tongue found hers. Passion consumed her, bringing excitement and fear. She felt his chest hair as it tickled her. Jesse's excitement grew as Matt pushed against her.

Drawn to him, she reached down as she felt the moisture between her legs. With a knowledge born of desire, she directed him toward her. She cried with surprise and joy as his rhythmic movements gave her pleasure.

His mouth teased her nipples. As he moved to her ear he whispered, "I love you so much, Jesse. If I ever lost you, I couldn't go on."

"I love you too," she whispered. "Don't worry. I'll never leave you."

He caressed her back and for a moment she froze. But the scars were gone. He groaned with pleasure. Gently withdrawing, he lay next to her, smiling contentedly.

"You promise?" he asked, kissing her.

She gave him a curious look.

"I mean about leaving me," he explained, laying back and closing his eyes.

Her joy was gone. She turned away, filled by sadness at what she was about to do, unable to repeat her lie.

Chapter Thirty-Five

The taxi dropped Matt at Salem Street—the noisy, fragrant gateway to Boston's Italian North End. He was meeting his friends at a small restaurant where they'd eat before descending on Faneuil Hall.

Evan Lassiter, the old teammate who'd left in July was back in town, and Matt's hockey buddies wanted to repeat their midsummer revelries. Matt's mind was elsewhere. He hoped things were fine with Jesse, wanted to believe it was the recital that made her act so strangely. But she'd been so secretive. He couldn't help wondering.

He pushed through the weekend crowd, inhaling the fragrance of sausage, marinara, and fine wine. As he turned the corner, he felt a hard slap on his back. The force propelled him toward an older, well-dressed couple who barely avoided him.

"Man, are you out of shape. I could never have done that to you a couple of years ago!" It was Evan's husky baritone. "Dave tells me you're one of the literati."

Matt turned. Dave Jenkins was with Evan. He wasn't sure whether Evan was serious. Suddenly his friend's large, ruddy face grew a wide grin as he hugged Matt.

"Come here, you lucky bastard. Congratulations. I hear you're going to be a celebrity." He squeezed Matt so hard he couldn't breathe. "Who would have figured those crummy notebooks you were always scribbling in would lead to this?"

"Feels like they're keeping you in shape in the AHL," Matt said as he escaped his burly friend's grasp.

"Damn straight." He put his hands on either side of Matt's face and smiled broadly. "Seriously, I couldn't be happier. I felt like shit after you blew your knee out. It's great—just great."

"If you think the book stuff is great, you should see the woman he's hooked up with. She's gorgeous and can sing like a bird, or so lover boy tells me." Dave smiled.

"I'll bet you can make her sing," Evan agreed. "You always had a way with the women."

****

It was almost ten p.m. when they got to Clarke's, an upscale bar frequented by athletes, celebrities, and Boston's professional crowd. Inside the clientele stood like sardines packed shoulder to shoulder. The odor of beer, whiskey, and good cigars permeated the room as Matt squinted through the smoke. He headed straight for the payphone, abandoning his friends while they bullied their way toward the bar.

As he stood waiting, he felt a hand on his back. It felt soft, tender, almost like a caress. He turned around, looking straight into Donna's velvet brown eyes.

"Hey there, cowboy," she said, studying him with the eyes of someone who's had a little too much to drink. He returned her look. She still looked amazing. Her radiant auburn hair framed her face with that alluring smile, and her pale silky skin showed just a hint of freckles.

"Hi, Donna. What're you doing here?" He searched the smoky haze for her boyfriend.

"Just out for a night with the girls." She nodded toward a table of young women who gave him a long look. They giggled as they whispered and pointed at him.

"What are you up to these days?" he asked.

"I'm a social worker." She shook her head. "It's a tough job, but it needs to be done, and I love doing it. Once in a while, we do something that really helps people," she slurred with obvious pride.

"That's great. Where's your goalie?" he asked.

"Oh, out with his buddies somewhere." She frowned. His impression had been right. She'd had a lot to drink. She tilted her head and gave him a delicious smile. "Don't—worry—about—him." Donna squeezed his arm. "How 'bout I buy *you* a drink." Her friends were watching them. "You know…for ole time's sake."

"Look, I'd love to." He shook his head. "But I have something to do."

Donna looked deflated. "Oh…ah, okay." She turned toward her friends, then back toward him. "I understand. S'fine." She smiled as she turned.

He took her arm. "I'd really like to, Donna. I just have this thing going on…"

"S'okay, Matt." Donna weaved her way back to the table and sat down. Her friends patted her on the back.

His friends kept waving him over. But Matt waited patiently for the two people in front of him to finish their calls. He wanted to talk to Jesse, but found himself looking in Donna's direction. Dave and Evan brought him a twenty-four-ounce Budweiser.

"Man, this woman's really got you whipped," Evan

teased.

"You haven't seen her." David slapped Matt on the back. "And who was that little number? Wow!" David nodded toward Donna. "Must be the writer thing! This guy's beating 'em off with a club," he chuckled.

"Just an old friend from the neighborhood," Matt said.

As he stood waiting, Donna and her friends got up and left. She smiled weakly and waved, but she still wore the look of disappointment. One of her girlfriends gave him a nasty look as she blew him a kiss.

Chapter Thirty-Six

Watching Donna leave, Matt felt a wave of ambivalence. She was a special woman, and every time he'd seen her lately, they seemed to ignite that old spark, but despite all her quirks and mysteries he loved Jesse.

Evan motioned for him to join them at the bar.

"I'll be over in a minute," Matt mouthed a promise to his friends through the smoky haze. He thought about Allen's warning, vowing to stay moderately sober, but it was difficult in the company of his hard-drinking friends.

The phone was free. He stepped into the booth, shut the door and waved good-bye. They took the hint and left, prompted by a cheer from the crowd. He placed his change next to the beer, put in a quarter and dialed her number.

The phone rang three times, then four. Matt was afraid Jesse wasn't home. He didn't want to wake Alice or Ali. He was just about to hang up when she answered.

"It better be you." Her voice had a low, sexy tone.

"It is."

"I pulled the phone into my room so it wouldn't wake anyone when you called."

"You're pretty cocky," he teased. "How'd you know I was gonna call?"

For a minute she didn't answer. He heard her slow, heavy breathing.

"Jess…"

"Because you love me *almost* as much as I love you," she whispered.

"Jess, have you been drinking?"

"Could be, Matthew. Have you?" She giggled.

"A little. But what about you?" he asked again.

"Yes…yes…yes…" she said stifling a laugh. "Because the most wonderful thing happened to me today—" She stopped in mid-sentence. "No, that isn't true. The *most* wonderful thing that ever happened to me was on June 17th, the morning I met you."

She had been drinking. She sounded adorable and *so sexy*. This was a different Jesse. Matt was instantly aroused.

"Well this isn't that good, but it's close. That's why I'm celebrating."

"That's great. Are you going to tell me what this wonderful thing is?"

She didn't answer.

"Matthew, dear."

"Yes."

"Do you know what I'm wearing right *now*?"

"No, but I hope you're going to tell me." This was a different Jesse, one he'd never seen. She was playing with him, teasing him. He reveled in it.

"Actually, I'm not wearing anything at all."

"Jesse…"

"I don't think you believe me."

He had no idea where this was going, but he couldn't wait to find out. She was quiet for a minute.

He took the bait. "No, you're right, I don't believe

you."

"Well, what—can—we do about that?"

Was she suggesting what he thought she was?

"You're going to have to prove it to me," he said, hoping that was the answer.

"I think you're right." She paused then whispered into the receiver. "I think you should get your cute little ass over here and see whether I'm telling the truth."

"I'll be there in ten minutes."

"Come to the back door. Ali and my mother are sleeping, so I'll let you in." She kissed the receiver loudly, adding, "Oh God, I love you. *Hurry!*" and hung up the phone.

"That will be an additional charge of forty-five cents," the operator said. He deposited the change, taking a long swallow of beer.

Matt looked toward the bar as one of his friends waved to him. He nodded and waved back, pointing to the men's room, walking right by it and out into the crisp night. If she could stay awake long enough for him to get there, tonight could be the most incredible night of his life.

He hailed a cab and jumped in.

"Where to, pal?"

"Corner of Mass Ave and West Springfield. If we get there in ten minutes, there's an extra ten in it."

"No sweat, buddy." The driver hit the accelerator. "We're already halfway there."

Chapter Thirty-Seven

Jesse waited in the back hallway, listening, clad in her underwear, an NEC T-shirt and a bathrobe. It was spitting snow outside. She heard the sound of a car and a voice. A cold gust tore through the worn flannel of her robe. She shivered, fighting to keep the door open. In a few seconds, she heard footsteps as Matt came down the alley.

"Pssst. Hey, Matt, up here," she called.

He ran toward her, jumping the stairs two at a time. In seconds his strong arms surrounded her. He looked at the way she was dressed, laughing.

"God, you look great." He grinned. "I smell champagne."

"Is that okay?" she asked hesitantly, putting her hand over her mouth.

"You smell delicious. I just hope you're going to tell me this great secret. You're celebrating something and if you're this happy, I want to share it." He released her. "Great outfit, by the way. I'm not sure whether it's the bathrobe or the T-shirt that's the bigger turn-on. I can't keep my hands off you."

As another gust icy blew down the alley, he pushed her inside. "Is this for real, Jess?" he asked.

She searched his eyes. Then taking his hands, she nodded, smiling with all the tenderness and affection she could summon. Jesse felt happy, sexy, and *very* drunk. They turned, heading into the back hall. Jesse led him down a dimly lit corridor to her bedroom.

She realized he'd never been there before. She'd bought four candles at the corner store that sat perched atop small plates. They didn't have the bouquet of the ones from her dream, but their flickering gave the room a cozy, romantic feeling.

"Nice touch," he said.

Jesse was a bundle of pent-up emotion and nervous energy. Tonight she wanted it to be the two of them. No interruptions. No inhibitions. And in spite of the champagne in her system, she was also terrified. She'd never made love with a man she cared for. It had to be perfect.

"The back door's an emergency exit. When I saw it, I thought of you. Ali and my mother are sound asleep. I don't think my mother's had champagne since her wedding day. I even gave Ali a couple of sips when I hatched this plan." She grinned. "Can we finally put Sunday night behind us? I want to be with you so much." She kissed him.

What began gently grew stronger. In a matter of seconds they found each other as their hands moved with feverish determination.

"It wasn't you," Matt whispered, holding her close. "I was stupid."

"No…I overreacted," she managed.

He kissed her softly at first—on the forehead, then on her eyes, finishing with a long kiss on her lips. His lips moved slowly and deliciously over every inch of her face…her eyes, her cheeks, her nose. When their lips joined again their tongues worked impatiently and tantalizingly over and around each other. Jesse had never been so aroused. She could feel Matt's throbbing erection as he pressed against her.

Jesse took his hand and led him to her bed. She pulled off her T-shirt and lay down, beckoning him. He lay next to her. As she felt him beside her, she thought about her dream, hoping that what she was about to experience would be half as wonderful...

It wasn't like her dream. It was better—much better. Matt was experienced. He had an easy, confident way of teasing and arousing her. She knew he wanted her, but he was caring in the way he made love, caressing her gently at first, then stimulating her in ways she could never have imagined. Afterward, Jesse reveled in her ecstasy, cradled in his arms, feeling safe and satisfied for the first time in her life. But she hungered for more of him. As she lay next to him, Jesse knew no one could hurt her. She luxuriated in the feeling.

"That was wonderful. You were wonderful," she said softly, kissing him.

"No, we were wonderful." He tickled her. She noticed that even in their most passionate moments, he managed to avoid touching her scars.

He pulled himself up, looking into her eyes. "Now, are you going to tell me what's going on? I mean champagne and sex. What else do you have planned?"

He grinned and she poked him in the ribs. "The champagne was about the good news. The other was me." She grabbed him around the waist and squeezed. "I know your mother and brother died when you were young, but tell me more about your life." She had to know everything about him.

"What's this all about?"

"I don't know. I just want to know more about you," she whispered, kissing his ear, teasing it with her tongue.

"The queen of secrets wants to know more about me?" He chuckled. "Well if you must know, Miss Long, I did have a broken heart once."

"Really?" She propped herself onto her elbow. "This I have to hear."

"It's the reason Donna and I broke up."

"So you two *were* more than friends?"

He nodded. "Yeah, we were a couple in high school." He paused. His eyes grew sad and distant. "But when I was a freshman on the BU hockey team, there was a girl who used to skate after the hockey team. She was a wonderful figure skater—I mean really good. And adorable." Jesse was about to kick him, but she saw he was serious. She took his hand. "Well, she used to and watch me at practice. I started hanging around afterward. We went out, got to be friends, you know. It wasn't long before it grew into something serious. By Christmas, we were a couple. She said she loved me."

He looked away and blushed.

"Its okay, Matt. I asked you."

"Well, she was really good. She made the American national team and went off to skate. She took silver, I think."

"Didn't you go with her?"

"I wanted to, but the hockey team was fighting for a national championship. After a couple of months, I got a postcard telling me she was with some hotshot from Germany." He shook his head.

"I'm so sorry," she said.

"It's okay, because I've got you." He ran his

fingers through her hair, resting his hand on her neck. "I can't describe how I feel about you."

She lay back and squeezed his hand, thinking about what he'd said. That girl left him for success and broken his heart. Was she about to do the same thing?

"So come on. What are we celebrating?"

After his story, she couldn't bring herself to tell him—at least not now. Instead, she turned and kissed him as passionately as she could. He followed her lead, and they made love a second time. By the time they were done, the alcohol had taken its effect. They were exhausted. Matt lay with his arms around her. He was asleep in minutes, snoring softly with a big grin on his face.

She watched him, knowing he was everything she ever wanted. Jesse had a difficult choice to make. But she knew there was no choice. She was consumed by a passion for her music and the hungry way she felt when she stood in front of an audience. Money and fame would be wonderful, but they didn't drive her. Only she understood that.

When he awoke, she'd tell him about *Gates of Paradise,* Lawrence Webb, and the chance that might never come again. She loved Matt, but this opportunity was too much to sacrifice—even for him.

Chapter Thirty-Eight

Matt felt Jesse's slow, rhythmic breathing. He lay next to her, reveling in the comfort of her slender body. He raised himself to see the small clock next to her bed. It was almost five thirty. The candles had died while they slept, and the sun wouldn't be up for another hour.

Laying there in the dark, Matt wanted to shout. He'd spent the night making love to the most extraordinary woman, had an exciting new career, and the most wonderful family a man could ask for. He could see them married with a family. A smile crept across his face as he envisioned a pregnant Jesse, two beautiful children in tow, coming down the stairs on Sunday morning as they headed to church.

But watching her, Matt wondered if his scene was one Jesse would choose. He lay back, staring at the ceiling as the first hint of dawn filtered into her room. Was the role of wife and mother Jesse's fantasy or his? He kept thinking about Donna's question: "What do you really know about Jesse?" The answer always came back, "Nothing." And she was so guarded. Her life revolved around the Conservatory and her family. Whenever he asked her about Portland, she got defensive or changed the subject.

She turned, reaching for him in her sleep. As he watched her thick, lustrous hair cascade across her face, he put his doubts on hold. Of course he had questions

Kevin V. Symmons

but they could wait. Matt realized he hadn't heard her good news, but she'd tell him later, when they re-lived their amazing night. They had all the time in the world.

He checked the time again. 5:50. Damn, he thought, remembering his nine a.m. appointment with Stephanie. As adroitly as possible, he slipped from under Jesse's arm and retrieved his clothes. She smiled in her sleep, letting out a soft moan. Matt hoped she was dreaming about their night together. He'd barely slept, but he'd never felt so alive.

Seeing a notebook on her dresser, he decided to write something clever. Picking it up, he saw the back cover was blank. He sat down in the chair next to her bed and began to write—telling her how much he loved her, apologizing for his story about Gretchen and asking her to come meet his friends that night. He finished and got up, touching the thick black hair that covered her pillow in unruly waves. He bent and kissed her cheek.

He walked to the door, propping the notebook on the dresser so she couldn't miss it. But as he opened the door, Jesse stirred, calling his name in her sleep. He turned. As he did his jacket knocked the notebook on the floor. As he picked it up, he turned it over and saw it wasn't a notebook at all. It was a music folio. Matt saw the name on the cover: Webb Productions—the name of the man who'd forced his way into Jesse's dressing room at the recital. The man who could do magical things for her career Stephanie told him.

He recognized the name on the cover: *Gates of Paradise*, the name of Webb's new production. Jesse laughed about Webb's visit, saying he just wanted to give her encouragement. But as he put the music on her

172

dresser, a sick, hollow feeling knotted his stomach. A piece of paper had fallen from the music folio. It was a plane ticket from New York City.

A big surprise. Something wonderful, she'd said. Yes, it was something wonderful—for her, not for them. He turned, feeling sick as his dreams were suddenly wrenched away. Jesse slept on peacefully. She was leaving, just like Gretchen had. But Jesse had lied. She'd had every chance to tell him about this, but kept it a secret. It was the biggest thing in her life, and she hadn't trusted him enough to share it. What was she afraid of? He wondered what other secrets she'd kept hidden. What he did know was that she didn't have enough faith in him to be honest about this opportunity. "What do you really know about Jesse?" The question echoed again as he searched the room for answers. He wanted to wake her up, shake her, and confront her, but that would serve no purpose. She'd only tell him another lie. How could he have been so wrong? Matt picked up the music, ripped off his note and stuffed it in his pocket, scribbling another on the cover:

Jesse,

Seeing this, I now know what your wonderful news is. I hope it's a big part, something worthy of your talent. After hearing my story last night, you understand that I've been here before. I wish you'd been honest with me.

Good luck,

Matt

He left the music with his note on the bed, looked at her once more and went out the door, feeling sick. Matt reached the bottom of the stairs and headed for Mass Avenue. He had to go home and clean up for his meeting with Stephanie.

****

Jesse sat on the edge of the bed, biting her nails. The clock said seven forty-five a.m. She let the phone ring. C'mon, Matthew, pick up. She had to talk to him. Where could he be at this hour on a Saturday morning?

Frustrated, she hung up. Jesse had to think. She should have been honest with him, told him about the tryout; she knew that now. As she sat looking down at his note, she came to a sad realization. The fame, the money, and everything that went with it meant nothing without him. Damn her selfishness and ambition. Why did this have to happen before I realized what I really wanted? she asked herself, hoping desperately it wasn't too late.

She grabbed some clothes and burst out of her bedroom, past a sleeping Alexis and into the bathroom. Emerging five minutes later, Jesse made too much noise. Alexis asked where she was going.

"I have something important to do, honey." She ran over to kiss Alexis. "Tell Grandma I'll call." She did her best to smile as she rushed out the door, down the stairs and onto West Springfield Street.

She ran the two blocks to Mass Avenue, searching the busy street for a taxi. She hailed one and jumped in. "Take me to the corner of West Broadway and M Street in South Boston," Jesse said curtly.

The driver nodded, smiling as he eyed her in the mirror. "Will do, honey." He made a U-turn and headed south.

Moments later, Jesse threw a ten-dollar bill on the seat as she left the cab, heading for the Sullivan house. It was 8:35. She ran up the stairs and rang the bell.

Someone moved inside. The door opened slowly. Her heart sank. It was Matt's father, smiling and inviting her in.

"Hello, Jesse," he said casually, unaware of her desperation. Jesse peered behind him, searching for some sign of Matt.

"Hi, is Matt here? It's really important I talk to him."

"No, 'fraid not." He turned and looked toward his son's bedroom. "He must have left while I was out for my walk." He went to the dining room table. Since she'd sat there for Thanksgiving dinner two days ago, so much had changed. "He left a note saying he has an appointment with his agent at nine."

"Thanks," Jesse said as she ran out the door. "Oh," she yelled back inside, "if he comes back, please tell him that I came by…and tell him I have to talk to him."

He yelled something after her, but she was gone, running down the stairs, heading for Broadway to hail another taxi.

She had to see him.

****

"Jesse, I'm glad to see you." John invited her to sit down. "There's been some serious fallout about the recital the other night, but I'm sure we can weather the—"

"I'm sorry, John. But I didn't come to talk about the recital. I came to say good-bye."

Her mentor looked up, eyes fixed on her. "I beg your pardon," he stammered. "Did I hear you correctly?" He paused. "I know how hard you've been working. If this is about money, I may be able to work something out. I have some savings and rather than lose someone with your talent…"

A wave of sadness covered her. John was such a good man. He'd helped her through the endless struggle that had been her life. Jesse vowed she'd never forget him.

"That's very kind, John, but it's not about money. It's about opportunity."

She related the events since the recital on Tuesday.

"I have nothing against Broadway or musical theater," he began, "but you know that if you leave here and begin that kind of work schedule your voice will never reach its full potential."

She avoided his eyes. "I know the risks, but I can't afford to pass up this chance."

He stood, taking her gently in his arms as he gave her a kiss on the cheek. He backed away and held out his hand. Jesse took it. "Good luck, Jessica. I hope they know what they're getting."

"Thank you for everything," she said, as tears covered her cheeks. "You've been a teacher and a friend, John…" Her voice failed her.

"The feeling is mutual." He hugged her again. "I'll expect to be reading about you. What's the name of your show?"

"*Gates of Paradise.* It's a musical about the Mormon Church."

"Well, if Lawrence Webb is producing it and you're going to have the lead, it can't miss."

Jesse headed for the door. Turning, she looked one last time at the man who'd changed her life.

John raised his hand offering her the theatrical wish for good luck. "Break a leg, Jessica."

She shut the door behind her, choking, as the tears

streamed down her face. She ran down the stairs, stopping to tap the statue of Beethoven one last time as she went outside. She ran onto Huntington Avenue to get another cab.

Chapter Thirty-Nine

Matt was late. Very late. But after the mind-numbing revelations at Jesse's his mind was far from *Satan's Twilight* and the publishing world.

He checked his watch—9:27. Despite being late, he trudged up the stairs to Stephanie's Commonwealth Avenue apartment and knocked.

"Matt?" she answered immediately.

"Yeah," he mumbled.

"C'mon in. You're late. Is everything okay?" When he stood mute, she added, "Did you have a nice Thanksgiving?"

"Yep," he answered in a monotone as he followed her into the office. The small room was austere but light and had the benefit of facing on the narrow park that extended the length of the avenue. "You?" Matt asked.

She ignored his question, repeating, "Is everything all right?"

"Sure," he whispered. He shuffled to the couch and opened his notebook.

"All right, we've had this talk before," Stephanie began.

Matt knew his literary agent and sensed the standard launch—her lecture on staying focused and living up to his potential was on tap. Instead, her expression softened. She'd apparently thought better of it and shelved the speech on how to succeed in publishing.

Stephanie crossed the room and stood in front of him. "What happened?" she asked softly, focusing her enormous green eyes on his.

"Nothing. Let's get to work." He shrugged.

Tilting her head to one side, Stephanie bent to get his attention. When he finally lifted his chin she extended her hand, finding his. He resisted at first, but when she took his firmly, he accepted the intimacy.

"Remember a couple of days ago when we talked about that producer, Lawrence Webb?" Matt asked. "The one you told me was a star maker."

She nodded.

"You were right. He gave Jesse a tryout. He's offered her a role in his new musical—"

"Okay, so what?"

"She'll be leaving."

"It's only an hour by plane for God's sake, Matt. She can't work all the time. You can still see her," she said, wearing a neutral expression.

"Sounds good, but I've never known a long-distance relationship that worked." He paused, shaking his head. "Besides, I'm guessing that prepping for a big-time Broadway production isn't a nine to five job."

"Matthew…grow up," Stephanie chided. "If you really love her, want to be with—"

"It's not just what she did. It's the way she did it!" Matt explained.

Stephanie sat down, his hand still in hers. "Get it all out. You'll feel better."

"She kept it a secret—lied about it, sneaking around behind my back. I found out by accident."

Stephanie's face showed kindness,

compassion...but for just an instant Matt read something else. Satisfaction? Whatever the reaction it was gone in a flash.

"You're right. That doesn't sound good," she agreed, leaving her hand on his. "I know how you feel about her, but look on the bright side. Its better you found out now what she's really like."

He managed to give her a weak smile. "Thanks. You're a good friend, Steph. You've done so much, helped me in so many ways." He squeezed her hand.

"I'd like to think we've become good friends," she whispered. "I'll do whatever I can to help—you know that." Her voice faded to a whisper as she worked her fingers into his.

"You're sure you're okay?" she asked softly.

Matt nodded.

Stephanie stood, her face flushed. "Good. Let's get to work. I want to go over the galleys for the last few chapters." She put her hand on his shoulder. "We've got a best seller to finish."

****

Matt rode home, torn by conflict. It was almost noon. Stephanie and Baldwin had finalized his book tour arrangements. She'd given him the schedule at their meeting. And after learning about Jesse's plans, the sooner he left the better. He needed time to get his mind around everything. Three weeks in Chicago, Cleveland, New York, and Philadelphia should help get his perspective back. At least he hoped it would. Stephanie had been wonderful—supportive, kind, attentive...

The taxi pulled up in front of his house. As he fumbled for the fare, he glanced at the porch. Jesse sat there. *Damn her!* He didn't want to face the scene he knew awaited, but she'd seen him. When Matt got out and headed up the walk, she moved to meet him. It was cold, and she was shivering.

Despite his anger, he couldn't take his eyes off her. She wore faded jeans and no make-up, but she was still so special, so beautiful. She caught his stare and showed him a tentative smile.

He refused to return it.

"You should have waited inside. You'll catch cold and you have big plans."

"I'm fine," she said. "Please Matthew, I *have* to talk to you."

"About what?"

"What do you think, for God's sake?" she threw at him.

"We're through, Jesse."

They faced each other in silence. Jesse hung her head as he walked up the stairs. When he reached the top, she put her hand on his chest. He sidestepped and got to the door.

"Matt, please. Don't let it…don't let us end like this. I love you too much." Tears filled her eyes as she choked on the words. "Please—I wasn't trying to hide this from you. It just happened. I was going to tell you last night." Her eyes overflowed onto her pale flushed cheeks.

He looked at her, trying to ignore what he was feeling. He wanted to fold his arms around her and tell her everything was all right. He couldn't.

"You were right that night at Martel's," he said, knowing those sad, beautiful eyes could melt his conviction. "There's no place for me in your life."

"That's not true. If you asked me to, I'd give up the show. Please believe me."

"Maybe you would, Jess. But you'd regret it. And you'd spend the rest of your life resenting me. I've thought about it all morning." He faced her. "It just won't work."

"So that's it? Some silly girl ran away from you, and you think I'll do the same." She paused, looking away. "Life's about taking chances and making tradeoffs." She wiped the tears with her sleeve. "You know where I learned that? From you, Matt. Before I met you I didn't give a damn about anyone or anything. Now, my whole life has changed—for the better. We'd only be an hour apart."

He wanted to believe her, but he knew that no matter what they both wanted, it would never work.

"So you can go off and spend your time on your book tour for weeks, but I don't have the right to pursue what I've been working for my whole life. I'm supposed to trash my career because it might mean that we won't we see each other every night." She shook her head violently. "You selfish bastard! What the hell's the matter with you? Are you really that spoiled?"

He opened the door. "Good-bye, Jesse. Good luck with your show and your life."

"You're a little boy who has to have his own way!" She stood eyes fixed on him, tears spilling off her cheeks.

Matt turned and went to his bedroom. He felt sick. He loved her so much. He flopped down on his bed, her image haunting him. After a few minutes, he got up and ran out, hoping she'd be there. She was gone.

He searched the street, angry with himself. He

went inside, picked up the phone and dialed her number. It rang three times and Ali picked up. He cradled the receiver and looked toward the door.

"Good-bye, Jesse," he whispered. He went back to his room. For the first time since his mother had died, Matt felt tears run down his cheeks.

****

For the rest of the weekend Jesse tried to forget—about Friday night, the following morning and Matt. It was hopeless of course. She said good-bye to the small collection of people who'd miss her: Gerry and Ellen, Mario, and the people at the Conservatory. She arranged to pay for her mother and Ali, explaining that they could join her when *Gates of Paradise* opened in New York. She hated leaving them again, but Jesse knew with the work that lay ahead, she'd have no time for them.

Everywhere she went, she saw something that reminded her of Matt. She continued blaming herself for the way she'd handled the news of her audition. But the damage was done. She dialed his number more than once, losing her nerve when Mr. Sullivan answered. She suspected he was screening Matt's calls.

On Monday morning, suitcase in hand, she waited with Ali, her mother, and Mario.

"Where's Matt?" Ali asked.

"Matt's busy, honey." It was all she could say. Alice looked at the sidewalk as Ali stood mute, looking as if she might cry. "I'm sorry. I know how much you liked him. You'll see him again." Jesse was afraid that another minute might bring *her* to tears. She turned away, just as the taxi pulled up. Jesse composed herself and as a somber Ali, Alice, and Mario waved good-bye

183

she directed the driver to Logan Airport.

She left, feeling a terrible ambivalence. As she rode toward her future in silence, Mario's words haunted her.

"Good luck, Jessica," he offered as she got into the taxi. "Remember, when the gods want to punish us, they let our dreams come true."

Chapter Forty

Late winter 1989

Her apartment was small, but comfortable. It was up-town, not far from Central Park. It came with decent if somewhat sterile furnishings. But remembering her barren home in Munjoy Hill, Jesse had no complaints. Two large windows let in a generous amount of sunlight, helping to cheer its impersonal interior. Between the endless rehearsals and the acting and dancing lessons, Jesse saw little of her new home.

The nicest thing about her apartment wasn't the location or the furniture. It was her next door neighbor. Daniela Amato or Dani was an older divorcee who adopted Jesse the day she moved in. Dani had come to America in the mid-80s from her native Italy. She told her young neighbor that her ex lived in Boston.

Despite her youth and talent, perhaps because of it, breaking into the cliques on the *Gates of Paradise* set was difficult. The other performers were helpful, even kind, but their contact with her ended when they walked through the stage door. Daniela was the perfect solution.

Jesse had few friends. She'd never had time for them. Matt still felt like a wound that wouldn't heal. His face and voice haunted her dark, lonely hours. But he was a sad, bitter memory. Jesse had always been a realist and knew that he was no longer part of her life.

But despite the difference in ages and backgrounds, Dani and Jesse found an instant rapport. They spent the little free time Jesse stole from her busy schedule going out to dinner, a movie or shopping. Between Dani's constant attention and Lawrence's interest in her, Jesse began to feel some comfort in her new surroundings.

But on this bleak Sunday morning in late February, Jesse lay in her bed, tired, sick, and confused. She'd felt like this for six weeks and a few days ago a doctor had confirmed her fears. Jesse had always been healthy. But since arriving, she seemed beset by ailments and injuries. It began her first week in New York; she'd come down with the flu. It kept her from rehearsals for a week. Dani was always there, hovering over her with a homespun cure or a bowl of soup. After three months, she was the best friend Jesse ever had.

But the obstetrician's unwelcome news could jeopardize her whole future. Jesse lay staring blankly as the gray dawn filtered through the sheer curtains into her bedroom. Entering the second trimester of another unexpected and unwanted pregnancy was a dismal prospect. Matt was the father, and she knew what he'd say. He was a devout Catholic and despite their bitter breakup, she thought he still loved her. He'd probably accept her news and assume the role of devoted father.

That would be nice—a dream come true for many girls. Find a handsome, successful man who loved you, forget or sublimate your desires and dreams to his and die a painfully slow death while he pursued *his* career. But damn him and his child, that wasn't what she'd spent her life slaving for. Of course, to pursue her dream, she'd have to do something she didn't want to think about.

She remembered the days after Ali was born—days when she'd wished, prayed that her beautiful daughter would miraculously disappear. She also thought of how she felt about her little girl now—how her feelings had grown and changed. Tears of anger and frustration filled her eyes.

She curled up, finally dozing for a few precious minutes on this one day of refuge from her endless work regimen. Awaking to the sound of Dani's familiar knock, Jesse dragged herself to the hallway to answer.

"Hi," Dani began. "I know it's early, hon, but do you want to get dressed and head over to the breakfast buffet at the Warwick?"

Just the thought made Jesse queasy. She let Dani in, excused herself and ran to the bathroom.

"You all right, Jess?" she asked when Jesse returned. Dani was always the soul of tact, but as they went to the living room, Jesse saw her friend scanning the clutter.

"Sorry, I know the place is a mess. It's just that I can't seem to find the time—" Jesse stopped in mid-sentence, feeling nauseous again. She excused herself and ran for the bathroom a second time.

When she returned, Dani wore a knowing smile.

"When are you due?" she asked sympathetically, studying her young friend. "Or aren't you going to have it?"

Jesse looked at her incredulously, slowly shaking her head. "H-how did you know?"

"This is New York City, Jessica. It's filled with pretty, unmarried young women all trying to get ahead any way they can. Sometimes, they don't take the precaut—"

Jesse held up her hand. "It's not like that," she said. "Th-this happened before I left Boston."

"With your boyfriend back home—what was his name, the writer, Matt?"

Jesse nodded, feeling a little better.

"Let me get you some juice…"

Jesse didn't hear the rest. A strange sensation crept over as she realized she'd never mentioned that Matt was a writer.

"Dani," Jesse began, "how did you know he was a writer?"

Daniela had been heading toward the kitchen. She stopped and gave a nervous laugh as the color drained from her face. "Why, you must have told me, hon. I mean how else would I have known?"

Jesse shook her head. "I don't know. I don't remember talking about it." Jesse wanted to pursue it, but she had no stomach for confrontation. She put on a smile and shook it off.

When Dani came back, she gave Jesse some juice and patted her leg. "I don't want to be pushy, but would you like to talk about it?"

They spent the next hour discussing her options.

After talking about what this could mean to her career, Dani asked her friend *the* question, "Do you still love him?"

Jesse stood up, walked to the window and pulled aside the sheer curtain, looking toward the park. When she turned toward her friend again, her eyes held tears.

"More than you could imagine. I hoped in coming here that I'd start a new life and forget him." She shook her head sadly. "It hasn't worked." Jesse laughed bitterly.

Dani crossed the room and took Jesse in her arms. She stroked her hair, whispering, "It's all right. It's all right."

Jesse broke away and stared at her. "But it isn't. No matter what I do, someone's going to lose. If I tell him and have the baby, he'll insist on doing the right thing. He'll want me to come home, marry him, make more babies and spend my time in the St. Bridgid's women's auxiliary. I know him. That's how he sees life."

"Would that be so bad?" Dani asked.

"Maybe not for everyone, but Dani, I've spent my whole life training, studying and sacrificing to get here—so yes, for me it would be." Jesse wiped her eyes and turned away. "Then I think about Matt and the way I feel about him—the way I hope he still feels about me, and I wonder…" She paused, shaking her head. "I just don't know."

Dani smiled. "But Jessica, could you really take the life of that baby. His baby?"

Jesse shrugged. She was quiet for a long time.

Dani raised her eyebrows.

"I really don't know," Jesse whispered. "He was the one who sent me away. I begged him to give it a chance, to give us a chance, but he was too damn stubborn and spoiled. Because we made a mistake one night, should I give up everything I've spent my life working for just to make him feel warm and fuzzy?"

"Should you talk to Lawrence Webb?" Dani asked. "There may be other options. You've told me he's very fond of you, and he has a big ego. How will he react when you tell him you're having another man's baby?"

"I'm not sure," Jesse said, managing a smile. "But I've got a few weeks to show him I'm indispensable."

"You really think you can do that?"

Jesse sniffed and wiped her eyes again. "You're talking to Jessica Long. I can do anything." She laughed. "Let me get dressed. I'm feeling better. I think I can handle some breakfast now."

****

On Monday evening Jesse returned to the obstetrician's office. The doctor was blunt. "Jessica, you have some trauma resulting from the violent episodes you described when you were a teenager. It's vital that you get plenty of rest. You may have been lucky with your daughter. This time, you need to be very careful, at least until the middle of the second trimester."

"I'd love to, but I'm in a Broadway musical. I can't sit at home reading *Lady's Home Journal* and eating bonbons."

The obstetrician shook his head. "I understand. This is New York City."

Jesse was sick of hearing that.

"I can't change your anatomy, Jessica. Keep up a strenuous routine and there's a possibility you could have a serious problem, even a miscarriage." He put his hand on her shoulder. "Do you want this baby?"

She sat contemplating his question.

"Jesse?"

"I-I really don't know," she whispered.

It was the doctor's turn to be quiet. He held up his hands. "Well, keep up the heavy work load and exercise schedule and the decision may be taken out of your hands."

Solo

****

"What did he tell you?" Dani was at Jesse's door before she got the key in the lock.

"He said I have to be very careful, especially during the first five months."

"So you're going to quit the show?"

"Are you serious?" Jesse asked incredulously. "I'll cut back on the lessons, get more rest and eat better, but I'm going to keep rehearsing until the show opens in Boston. That's eight weeks away. Matt will be there when I get back. I need to talk to him face to face—to find out if he wants the baby and me. I've thought about it and I think I owe him that. I think he still loves me. So if he decides he wants me and his child, I'll have a choice to make. I'll try to work something out with Lawrence," she shrugged. "But I'm not the only performer who ever got pregnant."

"I think you're taking a big risk—*too* big a risk with your baby's life," Dani warned.

"I appreciate your concern, Dani." Jesse shook her head, thinking again that Dani had an unusual, almost maternal interest in her life. "You can't imagine some of the shit I've gone through. This is a piece of cake."

Three days later while rehearsing a difficult routine, Jesse doubled over. She sat down as a dark stain grew on her leotard. She tried to stand, laughing it off, but as she walked back to her mark, she felt faint and collapsed.

"Jesse, are you okay?" Paul Hamilton ran to her.

She shook her head.

"Quick, someone call a doctor," he yelled.

Lawrence appeared, picking her up. "Get a blanket or something to wrap her in and get my car—*quickly!*"

In minutes they were on their way to the Hospital. Jesse curled up against the side of the back seat while Lawrence held her hand.

By early evening, it was over. Lawrence stood at the foot of her bed, watching her as she lay with eyes closed as the hot tears burned down her cheeks.

"Jesse," Lawrence began with a soothing voice. "The doctor said you knew about the pregnancy and the fact that it was high risk."

She nodded.

"Why didn't you tell someone? Why didn't you tell me, for God's sakes? I could have taken care of you."

She looked up at him, doing her best to brush the tears away. "I-I was so afraid you'd let me go." She shook her head. "This is such a big chance," she sobbed. "I may never get another. I couldn't pass it up."

"We could have worked something out. I would never have let you go. You...you must know that. You mean too much to..." He stopped, letting his words die.

"It doesn't make any difference now." Her words hung in the space between them. If she and Matt had any chance, it had died with their baby.

"Is there someone I can call, someone you'd—"

"No. It's too late," she said softly closing her eyes.

"You're in great shape. The doctors say that with the proper rest, you can be back on stage in two weeks. We'll work the rehearsal schedule around you. I've already told Ian."

She managed a hesitant smile. "I'm sure he was thrilled about that."

"I don't care. Right now, your health is more important." He came close. "This must have been terrible for you. I wish you'd taken me into your confidence."

She searched for his hand. Finding it, she took it. "Thank you. Thank you so much for everything." He was so kind, so caring. Jesse wanted to thank him. "The day I came for the tryout, Bernie told me you were one of the last true gentlemen in this business." She paused, squeezing his hand. "He was right." She closed her eyes, letting the medication pull her away.

When she awoke, Lawrence was asleep by her bedside with her hand in his.

Chapter Forty-One

It was two days before St. Patrick's Day. Matt sat in the Lakeside Cafe at Chicago's Drake Hotel, turning his Scotch as he stared through it at the lights glittering in the mirror behind the bar. Every so often he glanced at the Bulls-Lakers game. He didn't really care about the score; it was just something to do. Something like the scotch he'd been nursing slowly since dinner, something to take his mind off the scene he'd never been able to erase—Jesse cold and shivering on his front porch, waiting to explain, to make him understand things that his stubbornness and arrogance refused to let him.

He felt a light touch on his shoulder.

"Here's a surprise. America's newest literary light sitting at a bar doing his Hemingway impression." Stephanie sat on the stool beside him. She wore a fitted black dress. It was stylish and offered a tempting suggestion of what lay beneath. "Jack on the rocks," she said to the bartender with the delicious look Matt knew would get her anything she wanted.

The man nodded in her direction. She turned her breathtaking green eyes toward Matt, leaning on her elbow. As she faced him, the seductive look she'd shown to the bartender disappeared.

"What are you doing here?" he asked, wondering whether her presence was a good sign or a bad one.

"You checking up on me, Steph?"

"I should be. You've got the biggest bar tabs of any client I've ever worked with." She shook her head. "Coughlin and Baldwin are all over me. You've drunk the wet bars dry in every hotel you've stayed in. Thank God your signings are overflowing and the stores can't keep your book on the shelves." She shook her head. "You know, I've seen some pretty sad cases, Sullivan, but I swear you're the worst." She gave him a disgusted look, checking out the rest of the bar. "Maybe there's someone here who doesn't want to drink themselves into oblivion for—what is it, Matt—the twelfth straight night?"

He ignored her. She was beautiful, sexy, and knew everything about the publishing business, but after three months crisscrossing the country, he was tired of her nagging and phone calls. Now she was here in person.

"I thought an agent was supposed to help you— build your confidence, say nice things to you. Why don't you take up with one of the ten guys in here who are drooling just looking at you? Leave me in peace." He paused. "And you still haven't told me why you're here."

"Because I think you're the sexiest hunk in the publishing business," she said as she put her hand on his chest, tapping her fingers gently. "You're also my biggest client and the best damn writer I've ever worked with." He turned. Stephanie's face grew serious. "You know, maybe you believe all that shit about guys like Fitzgerald and Hemingway being better because they were drunk 90% of the time. Trust me, it's a crock."

Matt drained his scotch.

"Another Johnny Black, please," he said, motioning to the bartender. The man smiled at Stephanie and brought their drinks over.

Stephanie took a sip of her whiskey.

"No, Matt, I'm not here to ride herd on you. I'm here because I care about you. It doesn't have to be like this." Her tone softened as she searched his eyes. "I could show you a great time." She put her hand on his shoulder, squeezing it gently. "Jesus, forget about *her* and stop wasting your fucking life." She found the glittering antique mirror behind the bar.

"I just need a little more time."

"Time…more time!*"* She faced him, whispering through clenched teeth. "When was it that you two had your big fight, Thanksgiving weekend?" She put her hand on his back. "Matthew, you're young, talented and the biggest hunk in publishing. Please! Get over it. Get over her."

He took a long sip of his drink, shook his head, and called the bartender over. "What do I owe you?"

The man went to get his check.

Matt threw a twenty on the bar. Stephanie picked up the money and gave it back to Matt. She threw another bill in its place.

"I've got it." She told him. "Well, since you're determined to waste the rest of your life lost in memories of Miss Portland, I'll leave you alone, but I've got two pieces of information before you go up to assault the mini-bar."

He got off the stool, feeling the effects of the alcohol. "What?" He held up his hands.

"Do you want the good news or the bad?"

"I don't care. Just tell me so I can leave."

"All right. The good news is you've broken into the top ten—number seven on the *New York Times* best seller list." She applauded quietly.

"And?"

She took a newspaper clipping from her purse, putting it in front of him. It was from the *New York Times* art's section. The headline said it all: Lawrence Webb to preview *Gates of Paradise* in Boston before taking it to Broadway.

"The article says they'll be opening in mid-April. She's coming home and you'll be there just in time to meet her." Stephanie got up. "I guess I thought that maybe we could…" she stopped, giving him a look of surrender. "But I was wrong. I wasted a plane ticket." She sighed, touching his shoulder again as she headed for the door.

Matt turned, watching her walk away. She was an incredible woman. She wanted him. And he was so tired of being alone with nothing but bitter memories.

"Stephanie," he called after her. "Wait."

She turned, eyebrows raised. "What? Can I do something for you?"

Suddenly, he wanted her too—very much.

He ran after her, nodded, and put his arm around her. She looked up at him. "Yes," he answered. "Thanks for coming. You didn't waste that plane ticket after all."

Chapter Forty-Two

Mid-April 1989

"Anybody home?" Jesse asked from outside.

Ali opened the door. "Mommy," she cried breathlessly, wrapping her arms around Jesse's legs.

"It's so good to see you, honey." Jesse picked Ali up and twirled her around as they both erupted in laughter. She put Ali down and crossed to where Alice stood hugging her mother so tightly Alice gasped.

"It's good to be home," Jesse said as she looked around, nodding at the improvements the money she'd sent had purchased. "Nice furniture and rugs," she said casually. "Too bad they'll be going to waste."

Alice looked at her daughter; the trace of a smile crossed her face. "Does that mean what I think it does?"

Jesse nodded. "It does. I've got a great apartment for all three of us on West 58th Street. It's a doorman building, and I've even talked to some people about nursery school for you in the fall, my friend." She turned and tickled Ali.

Jesse looked at Alice.

"So it's going that well?"

"Yup," Jesse nodded.

"That's wonderful." Alice said.

"Mommy, there are pictures of Matt in the paper." Alice put her hand to her lips, telling her granddaughter to be quiet.

Jesse's pleasant look evaporated. "We don't get the same newspapers in New York, Ali," she said quietly.

"Why don't you go get the pictures you made for your mother?" Alice suggested.

"It's okay." Jesse looked at her mother. "We don't live in a vacuum. He's entitled to his day in the sun."

"Here, see what I drew?" Ali handed her a big picture. "See, Mommy, it's the swan boats."

Jesse tried to look pleased and surprised, despite the memories the pictures dredged up.

"It's beautiful, honey," Jesse said, hiding any trace of sadness. "I love it."

Ali ran back to the bedroom she'd occupied since Jesse's departure.

"It must be hard," Alice said.

"Hard? What do you mean?"

"I think you know what I mean," Alice offered.

Jesse sighed and closed the small distance between them, putting her head on Alice's shoulder and hugging her tightly.

"Yes it is, sometimes," Jesse whispered. "Well, what's it going to be tonight"—she recovered quickly—"Italian or seafood? This meal's on Lawrence."

They took a taxi to Jimmy's Harborside, a waterfront restaurant famous for its seafood and its well-known patrons. Jesse told them stories about being in a Broadway musical, describing her dancing and acting lessons and how hard she was working.

"I couldn't believe how little I knew about any of that and how important it is." She shook her head. "At the Conservatory we concentrated on developing our voices, but in this production, I really have to act. There are a couple of scenes when I even have to cry on cue." She faked a sob and tickled Ali, reveling in her mother's presence.

Jesse knew Ali had no idea what she was talking about, but her daughter shook her head and beamed as Jesse related the details surrounding her new life.

"How are the other people?" Alice asked.

"Actually, they're not too bad. I expected some resistance and resentment. What with me being an unknown."

"You call the big producer Lawrence?" Alice asked with amazement.

"I do." Jesse nodded. "He's a very nice man. Nothing like the stereotypes you see in the movies. And he's been *very* nice to me."

Alice and Jesse ate the surf and turf and Ali had the spaghetti from the children's menu. With stomachs bursting after three dishes of chocolate mousse and extra whipped cream, they left. By nine thirty, they were back at West Springfield Street. Who was there to greet them but Mario?

"Welcome home for a few weeks, Jessica."

"Thanks Mario, it's good to be back."

They exchanged a few more words about the show, Jesse repeating what she'd told Alice and Ali—that it was exciting but more work than she'd ever imagined.

"Well, I'm coming to see you next week. I already have my tickets."

Jesse shook her head. "You shouldn't have done that. I could have gotten you seats."

"Don't be silly. Mr. Webb can use the money. Maybe he'll give you a raise." He chuckled. "Are you feeling… all right, my dear?" He looked concerned.

"I'm fine, thanks for asking." Jesse stopped, studying him.

"Can we go inside, I've got to pee," Ali broke in.

"Sure—sure we can," Jesse answered as Mario disappeared into the night.

When Ali was tucked in bed for the night, Alice went to her daughter and held her as Jesse cried quietly. When she stopped, Jesse told her mother about the baby that would have been hers and Matt's.

Chapter Forty-Three

Jesse ran off the stage to applause and shouts of BRAVO! It hadn't been a perfect performance, but it was close.

"What an opening night!" Lawrence called from the wings. He ran to greet her, embracing her tightly for just a moment. "You were wonderful, Jessica, *absolutely wonderful.*"

"Great job, Jess," one of the other performers said as he ran by.

"Way to go, Jess," added a second.

"Thanks. You too, Ross," she called back.

Jesse headed backstage to change. Lawrence had planned a cast party at the elegant Copley Plaza. As she threaded the labyrinth leading to her dressing room, he fell into step beside her. She didn't mind. Jesse had grown very fond of Lawrence. He wasn't young, but he was a commanding figure, tall and handsome in a distinguished way, with an infectious charm and warmth that she found appealing. He had a wonderful sense of humor, always saying something clever or witty when she needed it most. And he'd been so kind after the miscarriage. Her time with him was a welcome relief from the dark moments when she'd despair over Matt or guilt about the miscarriage consumed her.

And she needed his support more than ever. Dani had disappeared shortly after it happened. Jesse had knocked on her door one night and she wasn't home. Her friend had disappeared with no word and no forwarding address. Jesse was mystified and hurt. But, with the show opening in Boston, she would have had little time for Dani.

As Lawrence and Jesse headed down the narrow walkway, well wishers continued to congratulate them both.

"Does it seem possible that six months ago you were at Jordan Hall, singing that beautiful song?" he asked when they reached her dressing room.

"No," she answered, feeling giddy and faint. "It doesn't. It's like a dream. I keep thinking I'm going to wake up." she turned, opening the door as emotion swept over her. "I second-guessed myself so many times when I walked out on stage that night, thinking I'd make a fool of myself."

Lawrence took her hand, squeezing it for a moment. "It was the most incredible performance I've ever seen. So many things could have gone wrong. You took an incredible risk, and it paid off."

"It did, didn't it?" she agreed, part of her still in disbelief at her incredible good fortune. "I should get changed." Jesse added, slowly taking her hand from his.

"Get changed. I'll have the car at the stage door. Don't keep your admirers waiting." He headed toward the exit. There was something in the way he carried himself. Jesse followed him with her eyes, a smile working its way across her face. She knew he'd become infatuated with her. She didn't mind because she felt the same way about him.

****

He watched her at the cast party, moving gracefully

through the suite. She seemed to float, stopping and greeting each small group as if she were the hostess. That was fine. Lawrence welcomed the idea.

He remembered the difficult days when she'd arrived, plagued by one thing after another. But tonight, he wanted her to enjoy her success, to revel in it. No one had worked harder to master her craft. In four short months, despite all the setbacks and the physical problems, she'd become the consummate professional. As he turned to find Liz, he felt a tap on his shoulder.

"Lawrence, I'd like you to meet my mother, Alice, and my daughter, Alexis."

"Mom, Ali, this is Lawrence Webb."

He and Alice shook hands. Lawrence bent his tall frame to speak to Ali. "Why this is a pleasure, Alexis. May I call you Ali?" Ali stood mute, smiling and nodding. "I'm so very glad to meet you. Your mother has told me so much about you. She's always talking about how smart you are and what a good girl you are."

Ali slid behind her grandmother's leg, but she beamed as she peeked out from behind Alice's skirt.

"Mr. Webb, I don't know where to begin. How can I ever thank you for having faith in my girl? You've given her—all of us—a whole new life." Alice extended her hand and pumped his again.

"I didn't do anything, Mrs. Long. Jesse deserves the credit. She worked day and night to become the performer you saw tonight."

Jesse blushed.

"Don't believe a word of it. If he hadn't taken a chance on me, I'd still be doing nightclub gigs and scales in front of John's piano," she said, putting her hand on his shoulder, squeezing it gently..

After a few more accolades, Lawrence excused himself and went to find his sister. He'd invited her and Terry as a thank-you for introducing him to his Naomi.

He found her across the room.

"Well, brother, this is quite a spread. If tonight's any indication, I think you've got another hit on your hands."

"I owe it all to her," he nodded in Jesse's direction, "and to you. Her drive and talent has elevated this whole production."

Liz nodded. "You're right. How did the other cast members take to having a young unknown thrown into their midst?"

"All right—after they saw what she could do. With the exception of Ian, of course. But he's always been a pain in the ass. If I paraded in Sarah Brightman or Liza Minnelli, he'd still find something wrong. I can keep him in check and he's a brilliant director." Lawrence nodded at Ian, who was subtly fondling one of the chorus girls. "He deserves a lot of credit."

"My God, Larry." Liz smiled at Jesse. "If you wrote this in a novel, nobody'd believe it."

He nodded. "I'm sorry Terry couldn't come."

"Me too. He's got some malpractice thing that's been consuming twenty hours a day."

"Well, *Lawrence*." Liz patted him on the back as she headed for the door. "This old girl has had enough champagne for one night." She gave him a quick peck on the cheek. "I'll call you tomorrow and congratulations again!"

"Sounds good." He gave her a wave.

It was after two a.m. The crowd of well-wishers and cast members had dwindled. Ian waved good night, his hand strategically placed on the attractive dancer he'd been pursuing.

"Goodnight, Ian." Lawrence smiled.

He felt a gentle touch on his shoulder.

"It looks like we're alone," Jesse said looking at her watch. "And it's very late."

"It's all right. I know the producer. You can be late for rehearsal. You were quite the hostess."

She smiled at his compliment.

"You've come a long way in a few months, Jessica."

"Thanks. I owe it all to you." She reached up as she pulled him to her, kissing him on the cheek. "And could you call me Jesse. Jessica sounds so formal. I think we're beyond that, aren't we?" she asked, looking at him with those beautiful blue-green eyes.

He had the irresistible urge to do what he'd wanted to for months—take her in his arms and kiss her till she was breathless. He resisted, knowing what that would mean.

"Of course…Jesse." He touched her shoulder. "I think I've had too much champagne. This old soldier had better go home."

"I don't think you're a soldier and you're certainly not that old."

He felt himself blushing.

She smiled, looking at him in a soft, special way. There was affection and admiration, but there was more in that look and he was glad.

"Share a cab?" she asked. "I've got a great job. I'll even pay."

They laughed.

It had been a magical night. As they left the suite,

Jesse took his arm, putting her head on his shoulder. When she did, Lawrence stopped. He'd had his share of beautiful women, but this was different. It wasn't just that she was very young and incredibly talented. He knew she'd been through her own private hell. Jesse had never told him about her life. She didn't have to. He'd read it in her face in brief unguarded moments. No, this would be no casual fling, but he didn't care. He'd found someone very special, the someone he'd been searching for.

Jesse looked up at him, embarrassed and unsure. "What's wrong?" She put her hand over her mouth.

"Absolutely nothing." He took her arm and she relaxed. It wasn't the excitement of opening night, or the flush of champagne. Adrenaline and alcohol had no part in this. Lawrence needed something—someone, and he'd found her. That someone was Jessica Long.

****

At the intersection of Arlington and Boylston Streets, Matt sat in a taxi with Dave Jenkins after a night of bar hopping, trying to forget what *else* was happening in Boston that night.

He turned, staring absently out his window. He'd had too many Scotches chased by too many beers. Another lost night. Maybe Allen and Stephanie were right about his drinking. He thought of their time at the Drake Hotel. Maybe life wasn't so bad after all. He wanted to call and tell Stephanie he missed her.

"Hey, Matt," David pointed. "Whoa. Check out the babe coming out of the Plaza. Jeez, what a piece of—" He choked on his words, realizing the beautiful woman was no stranger. Matt followed his eyes.

"Damn," Matt whispered. "Hey, driver, pull up

over there," he ordered, pointing to the cab stand in front of the Plaza. The man complied.

Matt pushed open his door before the cab stopped, throwing a ten dollar bill at the driver. He got out just in time to see Jesse getting into a cab with a tall, distinguished man he recognized. As the man bent down to get in, he saw her smile, kissing the man as she pulled him inside.

"Son of a bitch. Hey...hey, you...wait!" he called after them as the taxi pulled away, its passengers happily ignorant of his pleas from the sidewalk.

David exited the cab, too. Matt heard him running to catch up. He stopped and put his arm around Matt.

"Hey, buddy, you okay?" he asked.

Matt watched the taxi cross Boylston. It was at St. James, slowly moving out of sight as it took a right and headed toward Mass Avenue. Son of a bitch, Matt thought. He's taking her home.

"Yeah, Dave, I'm fine. Just fucking fine." He forced a laugh.

"Wasn't that...*her*?"

"Yeah." He followed the taxi with his eyes hoping his thoughts might bring her back to him. "Yeah, Dave, that was her."

PART IV

Chapter Forty-Four

Five Years Later, February 1994

The weathermen predicted the Maine coast would suffer the fury of a strong nor'easter. But on that Wednesday afternoon as Matt and Mario passed through Kennebunkport on the way to Alice Long's funeral, the sky had a hazy, buttermilk quality. They pulled into the gravel driveway that worked its way up to the lodge. It sat stark and lonely, perched atop a rocky cliff, conjuring up images of an Agatha Christie novel.

Matt looked at Mario, sitting in the passenger seat. He wasn't sure how or when they'd become friends. It just happened.

Matt had visited Alice and Ali after Jesse left. He thought they were as lost and lonely as he was, maybe more so. During Jesse's first few months in New York, Mario had looked after Alice and Ali. Matt admired him for it. And somehow, when Alice and Ali left, he and Mario kept in touch.

When Jeanne and Allen had moved to the suburbs, despite the difference in their ages and backgrounds, Mario filled his brother-in-law's role as confidant and advisor.

It was Mario who'd asked him to come to Alice's funeral. But Matt never fooled himself. He came because it would give him a chance to see Jesse, even if only as a spectator. He suspected that was why Mario had invited him.

"You say that all the hotels in Kennebunkport are filled?" Matt asked, hiding a yawn.

"Matthew, you've asked me a dozen times. Yes!" Mario shook his head.

"But there must be another place we could have stayed. I thought I saw vacancy signs when we drove through town." Matt looked out from under the visor. The Ford Explorer kicked up gravel, climbing the steep slope to the bed and breakfast. "You know the situation," he said, frowning. "With everyone in such close quarters here, it could get a little…*sticky*."

"Alice always thought the world of you. Stop acting like a spoiled child for once and make the best of it," Mario scolded.

"Yeah, it'll be great. Me, Jesse, and her producer boyfriend. I can tell I'm going to have a great time. I should have brought Stephanie."

"That woman's not right for—"

Matt stopped him. "We've had this conversation before. Let it go."

"Fine," Mario agreed. "Maybe you and Jessica could talk in a civilized way. You kids loved each other once." He shook his head. "It's a shame."

Matt couldn't stand any more. "Enough! You're like a *damn broken record*." He looked away, seeking solace in the Atlantic. "It was over years ago."

"Fine."

Matt pulled the SUV into the parking area. They

got out, glaring at each other.

"If it wasn't for the weather, we could have come up and back the same day," Matt said, surveying the grounds. "Why is it that people always die at the most inconvenient time?"

Mario stopped in his tracks.

"Okay, okay, I'm sorry." Matt held up his hands. "I'm just uncomfortable." He shook his head. "I-I won't know what to say to her." He opened the tailgate, pulling out his suitcase. Mario followed him.

"Maybe you could start with hello," he offered.

Matt was relieved that theirs was the only car in the parking lot. At least I won't see her until I've had a couple of drinks, he thought.

He walked up the stairs, stopping to survey the unseasonably hazy sky and the ocean one more time, thinking that the weathermen were crazy.

****

The Maine Turnpike was half an hour behind them. Lawrence shot a look at Jesse, sensing that with each passing minute, she was more uneasy.

"Can you please... *stop*...making that annoying sound?" Jesse snapped as Ali looked out the window, humming her favorite song.

"Sure, sorry, Mom," Ali said, catching Lawrence's eye in the mirror as if to ask, what did I do?

Lawrence winked at her. "Gee, I thought it was kind of nice."

Despite everything she'd been through, he thought, Ali was turning out to be a great kid.

"How much longer?" Jesse bit her lip as the Town Car negotiated the narrow roads approaching Kennebunkport. "Until we get there, I mean."

"Probably ten to fifteen minutes, depending on traffic." He smiled. "With any luck, we'll be there by four."

She looked at her watch.

"I can't wait to see Matt again," Ali offered from the back seat. "Can you?"

Jesse looked at Lawrence. "No, I just can't wait," she answered, picking her nails.

"Calm down, Jess, I've never seen you like this. You eat audiences for breakfast. This is just a guy you had a crush on."

She shot him an angry glance.

"I'm sorry. It was more than that." He reached out to touch her hand. "It'll be fine."

"I've read stories about him. He drinks a lot. I just hope there are no ugly scenes," she said, looking straight ahead. "I don't even know why he's coming."

"I assume he's come out of respect for your mother. Maybe you could give him the benefit of the doubt."

Lawrence checked the rearview mirror, uncomfortable about having this discussion with Ali as a spectator. Though Jesse had never confirmed it, Lawrence was almost certain that Matt was the father of Jesse's baby. He suspected it was part of the reason for her attack of nerves.

"Maybe you're right." She smiled weakly. She turned to Ali. "Sorry I snapped at you. Go ahead. Hum all you want."

"No sweat, Mom."

Lawrence slowed as he saw the sign for their destination. He turned into the long, steep driveway, gravel spitting as he headed to the main house. He parked next to an Explorer with Massachusetts plates. He looked at Jesse and squeezed her hand.

"We're here."

Jesse looked at him and then toward the lodge. "That's what I was afraid of."

Chapter Forty-Five

"Welcome to the Rocky Point Inn," the man behind the desk greeted them.

"Hello, I'm Jessica Long."

"Yes, ma'am, I recognize you," the innkeeper said with a distinctive Maine twang. "Me and my missus saw you a couple a years ago."

Jesse looked around. Seeing no signs of Matt, she felt relieved. She put on a smile. "How'd you like the show?"

"It was wonderful, Miss Long." He nodded enthusiastically.

"I'm glad you enjoyed it." Jesse looked around again. "Can we check in?"

"Of course, ma'am." He gave her two index cards to fill out. "That'll be two rooms, right?"

"Yes, one for myself and my daughter." She turned, nodding at Lawrence. "And one for Mr. Webb." She put her hand on his shoulder.

"Yes, Miss Long, we've—" The man stopped in mid-sentence as everyone turned toward the stairway. Jesse got a queasy feeling in the pit of her stomach, because she knew what they were looking at.

Ali grinned and exploded across the room. "Matt—you're here!" She ran to him.

He picked her up, pulling her to him and twirling her around. "It's good to see you again, honey." He put her down and ran his hand through her dark, thick hair. He brought his lips down and kissed it. "I'm so sorry about your grandmother."

His gaze shifted. He put his arm around Ali, closing the distance between him and Lawrence. Jesse's stomach tightened into a massive knot. Matt was notorious for surly behavior. She remembered a Times article describing him as "a literary Goliath, with a talent second only to his ability to get into mischief."

Matt stopped in front of Lawrence. The tension was palpable. Jesse took a step backward. Even the innkeeper had a wary look.

Suddenly, Matt smiled, extending his hand. Lawrence reciprocated. "How do you do, sir? It's a pleasure to meet you. You're a legend."

Jesse let out a sigh as Matt turned to face her, offering her a smile that looked genuine.

The years had been kind. He was a little heavier, but still as handsome. His deep blue eyes had a hint of lines around them. His hair was longer than she remembered. It hung loose over the eyes that still penetrated her soul. She wondered if he could see into her heart and know the longing she felt as she stood a few feet away, wanting to run to him, have him hold her and kiss her until she was breathless. She felt flushed and sucked in a deep breath.

"Hello, Jesse. It's good to see you." He held her eyes with his. She felt hypnotized. He held out his hand. She extended hers and he held it. He pulled her close.

"I'm so sorry about Alice," he whispered. "I thought the world of her."

"And she did of you," she whispered back, clinging

to him. Electricity ran through her as their bodies joined. She closed her eyes and inhaled his fragrance, rubbing his back.

Gently, Matt pushed her away. She opened her eyes, exhaling. She looked at him, studying the face that still haunted her dreams.

"It's good to see you too, Matt," Jesse said, looking around self-consciously. "Thank you for coming. My mother was always very fond of you. She thought of you like…" Her words trailed off as she felt a tear. She put her hand on his arm as she turned away. "It's been a long trip. Could we have those keys? I'd like to lie down."

The innkeeper handed her two keys.

"Can I stay here and talk to Matt, Mom? *Please?*" Ali begged.

Jesse was about to tell her no, when Matt interrupted. "It's fine. I'll bet this young lady has a million stories to share about the Big Apple."

Jesse glanced at Lawrence. He shrugged.

"Okay. But be upstairs in forty-five minutes to get ready for dinner."

She handed Ali one of the keys.

"The room's the second door on the right—on the top floor," the innkeeper told them. Jesse headed toward the stairs, waiting for Lawrence.

"A pleasure to meet you." He nodded in Matt's direction. "If you ever decide to take one of those novels to the stage"—he held out his hand—"give me a call."

Matt took his hand and nodded. "Thanks, I may take you up on that." He took Ali by the hand, heading to the back of the bed and breakfast.

Lawrence headed up the stairs in back of Jesse and stopped at the first room on the second floor. "This is me." He nodded. "I guess they want to guarantee there's no fooling around between us city folk." He smiled. "You're on the next floor. Here, I'll give you a hand."

"I'm sorry about the rooms. I thought, well, just in case some of the relatives dropped by," she stammered. "They're kind of funny up here about appearances."

He touched her arm. "It's all right. Really. I'll see you downstairs."

Jesse stood, drained by her brief reunion with Matt. She shook her head. "Thanks for always being so kind. I'll catch up with you later." She reached up, kissing him quickly on the cheek. "How about six thirty for dinner?"

He smiled and nodded. "Sounds good to me. Get some rest. It's been an emotional day."

You can't imagine, she thought as she headed for the stairs. She needed time to come to grips with her feelings. She still loved him, she always would, but the strength of her emotions had surprised her. She had to do something—anything—to get him out of her head. She had a new script to read. Maybe that would take her mind off Matt.

She trudged up the stairs and opened her door. The room was large and quaint. It was well furnished with a large four-poster bed and two overstuffed, comfortable chairs—just what she needed.

There was a message from the minister, explaining the details of her mother's funeral. She called him back and they talked about the service. She told him that neither she nor her mother were religious, explaining the only reason she was having a ceremony was because Alice wanted to be buried near her family. They discussed contingency plans in case the predicted nor'easter developed. Jesse lay down. She couldn't sleep. She closed her eyes, but all she could think of was his face, his fragrance and the way his body felt pressed against hers…

Jesse gave up on sleep, got up and looked out her window. She decided on a walk to clear her head. She went down the stairs leading outside and opened the door. The wind had picked up, but it was still pleasant. She went onto the large, wrap-around porch and down the stairs, heading toward a bent solitary tree and the rocky spit of land that gave the bed and breakfast its name.

Dusk closed in as she searched the cold gray Atlantic for answers. The smell from the sea, the howling of the wind and the telltale feel of cold mist from the waves below brought back memories of her childhood. She closed her eyes hoping her bittersweet recollections might take away her need to see him, touch him, be near him again.

She thought about the other people who'd be coming to her mother's service. There weren't many, but she should get back inside, phone them and get ready for dinner. Ali would be back by now, probably wondering where she'd gone. She turned with her head down, unable to forget Matt. As she was standing there, darkness had descended and a light snow began to fall.

Unable to see the path, Jesse stumbled. Suddenly, strong hands steadied her. In the dim light she looked up, trying to see her rescuer. But as the wind blew the fragrance of his cologne in her direction, she knew.

She saw his shadow and the trace of a smile. He looked into her eyes and held her arms, keeping her steady. Slowly, he pulled her close. At first she resisted, but she had no choice. She could no more stay away than halt the upcoming nor'easter.

She fell into him. His strong arms locked her in a tight embrace. She raised her face to his, felt his breath and closed her eyes in anticipation of feeling his full, moist lips meet hers…

"Mom…*Mom…wake up.*" It was Ali.

Jesse lay curled on the bed, fighting to return to him. Ali was shaking her. Reluctantly, Jesse awoke. Sitting up, she stared out the window at the gray twilight. Putting her head in her hands, she closed her eyes, haunted by the dream.

"Mom, are you okay?" Ali asked.

Slowly, Jesse returned to the present, leaving him behind. Reaching for her purse she nodded at Ali, giving her a weak smile. She found the phone numbers she needed as Ali turned on the TV, checking to see what the local stations had to offer.

"Can I go back to Matt's room?" Ali asked as Jesse dialed. "It's only down the hall."

Jesse shook her head crossly. "Can't you see I'm on the phone?" After she left a message, she had to ask. "You mean he's on *this* floor?"

"Right—next—door," Ali said with a grin.

"That's nice." Jesse tried to look casual. "I-I had no idea. I've got a couple more calls to make. Why don't you go get ready for dinner?"

"Yep." Ali raised her eyebrows. "He's *right next door*," she repeated and ran into the bathroom, giggling as she closed the door.

Jesse imagined him a few feet away, lying on the bed, wondering what it would feel like to lie next to him. But as she thought about him, reality pulled her back as she thought about what had happened five years ago. She sat on the bed, letting her pocketbook and the phone fall from her hands as tears burned in her eyes and rolled down her cheeks.

She knew that no matter what they might overcome, if they were together, someday, she would have to tell him about that dark February afternoon and about the child he would never know or love. She could never do that. He had let her go, discarded her like a spoiled child would a broken toy. But regret and sorrow about their lost child haunted her. And Jesse knew Matt would never forgive her.

Chapter Forty-Six

The weathermen were right. As dawn filtered into Matt's room on Thursday morning, the wind howled so fiercely it moved the sheer curtains in his window.

He and Mario had eaten the evening before in the small bar. Matt had gone back to his room on the pretext of outlining his ideas for a new novel. But his time was really spent nursing a bottle of scotch while he fantasized about his next-door neighbor.

Despite the alcohol, when he put away his notebook and slid between the sheets, he had a restless night. He stared at the wall, knowing all that separated them was six inches of studding and plaster. The slightest noise from Jesse's room brought images of her lying alone and sad, clad there in something sheer.

He lay there thinking about the relationship between Jesse and Lawrence Webb. What were they to each other? He kept asking himself, hoping that the answer was nothing. He'd talked to Mario about it over dinner.

"Do you think they're a couple?" Matt asked as his old friend turned a beer in his massive hands.

"I don't think so," Mario answered thoughtfully. "They have a useful relationship," he said with a faraway look. "I saw many couples like that in my homeland. They use each other," Mario continued, "giving the world the appearance of a relationship.

People assume that Webb has captured the heart of a talented, young beauty like Jessica. At the same time, potential suitors avoid her because they think she's spoken for by a powerful man. Put in simple terms, she scratches his back, he scratches hers."

Matt nodded. While he understood the logic, he hated the thought of Lawrence anywhere near Jesse's back.

"You're quite the psychologist."

"In my business I have to be," Mario answered.

Matt wondered what being a landlord in the South End had to do with psychology. He remembered Jesse's question the night they'd made love. Why does Mario always seem to know where I've been and what I've done? Matt's writing had made him a good investigator. He'd developed a sense about things like this. And in Mario's case, his instincts warned him: Leave it alone. There were some stones better left unturned.

"I can see why Webb would want that kind of relationship," Matt asked. "But why would Jesse?"

Mario squeezed Matt's forearm. "Matthew. It protects her… because she still loves you."

Matt shook his head. "I'd like to believe you."

He lay there, trying to sleep, Mario's words bouncing around in his head. She still loves you. I'm sure of it. He must have slept, because when he looked at the clock it said six thirty a.m. Matt got up, went into the bathroom and splashed water on his face. Outside the blizzard was louder. The lights flickered. He got back into bed and took out his journal, trying to make sense of his notes. He was just dozing when the phone rang. Matt answered, hearing Mario's deep baritone sounding absurdly cheerful for that hour in the morning. "Jesse just called. The funeral's been postponed. She hopes we can get out by tomorrow."

"Thanks. I'll call you later."

Matt closed his eyes, only to be startled by the phone again. He picked it up, wondering who'd be calling. He hadn't given the name of the bed and breakfast to Stephanie or his family.

"Hi." His heart stopped. It was Jesse's voice, soft and throaty.

Matt cleared his throat. "Morning." He closed his eyes, imagining her at the other end. "Mario called me about the funeral."

There was silence for a moment. "Oh, that's good. I-I wanted to make sure you knew…"

"It's okay. I didn't sleep very well."

There was silence again.

"Me either," she said quietly. "Must have been the wind."

"Must have been," he agreed, searching his mind, trying to think of something, anything to keep her talking. "I know this may sound funny, but, could we meet for breakfast?" Matt heard her breathing rapidly.

"Jess?"

"I'd like to, but I've got Ali and Lawrence," she whispered.

"Sure. I understand." And he did. "Thanks for the call. I guess we'll have a long day watching—"

"I could meet for a cup of coffee? About ten?"

For a minute he couldn't speak. He thought about his conversation with Mario. Was it possible? Could she still love him?

"That'd be great. There's a snack bar in the back

facing the ocean. I'll see you there at ten."

"I'll be there, Matt."

He couldn't believe it. He heard noise in the room next door. He imagined her getting up, hair mussed from sleep, still looking beautiful, just the way she had the morning after they'd made love.

****

Jesse looked in the mirror one last time. Her jeans fit perfectly and a clingy, knit sweater showed off her figure. She blew into her hand, checking her breath for the third time. Why was she going to all this trouble? If Matt knew her secrets, he'd walk away and never look back, she told herself. She walked into the bedroom where Lawrence was playing a board game with Ali.

"You look very nice, Jessica," Lawrence said.

She heard the formality in his voice. He was hurt and angry. "It'll be fine," she reassured him, touching his shoulder. "I'll be back in a little while."

She had to tell him about meeting Matt. She owed it to him. The two of them had found warmth and affection with each other, holding their loneliness and demons at bay. Lawrence was a fine man, so kind and caring. She had given him her body with no regrets. In a way she loved him. But whatever she felt for him, he would never own her soul. That belonged to someone else. It always would. So Jesse lied, telling him it was just a cup of coffee with an old friend. His eyes betrayed he knew better.

Jesse didn't care. Before Matt, she knew nothing of love. She knew desire and want. She'd seen it in their eyes: the men who watched her, leered at her; selfish men who craved her for themselves. Now she knew how they felt—the way she felt when she looked at

Matt. But her feelings for him were so much more than passion. She wanted desperately just to be with him, to lie next to him, hear his voice, to inhale the fragrance of his body. She had to be near him, if only for a few minutes. Jesse took a deep breath and headed downstairs.

He looked around, fidgeting as she approached the table. When he looked up, his eyes confirmed that the preparation wasn't wasted. Matt fumbled with his napkin and stood, smiling as he moved to pull out her chair.

"Hi, Matt."

"Hello," he answered, looking every bit the handsome man she'd fallen in love with. His prominent cleft chin, bright blues eyes and that shock of dark, wavy hair that rested over his right eye looked the same. But he wasn't that man, and she knew it. We've both come such a long way, she thought, far too long.

"You look wonderful," he said.

"Thanks." She nodded. "So do you."

She sat as he pushed her chair in.

"Well, how many best sellers is it now—four?" she said.

He looked away. "I've done all right," he said, dismissing her praise.

"All right?" She grinned. "That's an understatement. You're a legend." She turned her head to one side as a smile worked its way across her face. "And wasn't there something else in there…like a National Book Award?" she asked, feeling more relaxed as her eyes washed over each feature.

"May have been one in there somewhere." His expression softened and a sad look spread across his face. "I owe it to you."

She looked at him, startled and confused. "I'm sorry?"

"If we'd stayed together, I'd have never found the time." He looked into her eyes and then toward the snow making windswept circles on the point.

She looked at him, searching for a sign. Is *that* why he wanted to meet? She always assumed he felt as she did—the longing, the pain, the loneliness. That was what she wanted to believe. Did he want to hurt her again? She looked away. She felt his hand turning her face back toward his. He took her hand.

"I'm so sorry. That was a stupid thing to say. I wanted this to be so perfect."

She sighed deeply. He did feel the same. "That hurt, Matt," she whispered, taking his other hand. "I guess you had to get it off your chest, but don't punish me for something I didn't do."

"Speaking of success"—he dodged the accusation—"you've had what, three Tonys in five years, and *Gates of Paradise* won the Theatrical Guild Award?"

She nodded. Perhaps this hadn't been such a good idea. "Thanks. I guess that's a big deal." It was her turn to study the storm. "At least it was for Lawrence."

She turned toward him again. They stared silently at each other as they had a lifetime ago in a pizza place on Huntington Avenue. Matt squeezed her hands, his eyes never leaving hers.

"I loved your *Music of the Night* CD. You made Sarah Brightman sound like a school kid."

Jesse felt her face flush. "Your books were great."

"I didn't think you were a reader." He looked

surprised.

"I am now." She lowered her eyes. "I've read three so far. I loved *Bloody Lane*. The way you described what happened at Antietam was incredible. I thought I was there."

"Thanks."

They sat quietly again. She wondered where his mind was. Hers was in the Public Garden on that perfect July afternoon, the first time she touched his hand.

"How 'bout if I get *you* a cup of coffee?" he offered.

"Sure," she answered, still lost in things that might have been. Seeing the innkeeper, Jesse let his hands slip from hers. "With cream and two sugars, please."

He excused himself and went to the coffee stand, returning with two steaming cups.

"Thanks." She took a sip. "It's great. Just like Martel's." They laughed softly. "Are you okay, Matt? I've heard some…some things about you."

"People talk. You must know. They exaggerate when you're in the public eye. I was lost for a while when we…split." He turned away.

She put her hand on his. "I did some…things, too," she said, looking at her coffee. "I-I…" She couldn't finish. She squeezed his hand. He pulled it away.

"Jesse, what about you and Lawrence? Are you two together?"

She found his hand again. "It's hard to explain," she said, turning toward him. "What about you and your agent?"

He caressed her wrist. "It's the same. So where does that leave *us*?"

She'd wanted this time with him so much—too much. Jesse stood as the tears began, knowing it *really* had been pointless—a tease, a selfish game that would only torture both of them in the long years ahead.

She got up and put her hand on his shoulder. "Good-bye, Matthew." Jesse couldn't look at him. He'd never understood her before—he wouldn't now. She headed toward the back hallway and the stairs.

She heard him get up and run after her, grabbing her arm. She turned. As their eyes met, Jesse knew it was futile. She fell into his arms. Suddenly his lips were on hers and nothing in the world had ever felt so wonderful. The kiss was warm and passionate but over too quickly. They parted, breathing heavily. He folded her in his arms.

"I've been dreaming about that for five years," she whispered, leaning into his chest.

"I was such a fool. Can you ever forgive me?"

She closed her eyes. "I did, long ago. But it's not that simple."

"We still love each other. What could be simpler?"

"I-I just can't be with you."

"But why? I love you so much. Don't you still love me?"

"Do you need to ask?" She pulled his face to hers, kissing him again. The kiss was long and moist. Memories washed over her—his heady scent, the taste of his lips, the feel of his body pressing against hers. Her tongue found his as their bodies came together. She was aroused; she could feel the same in him.

The kiss seemed endless as the world melted away. She reveled in it. They felt each other feverishly as she pressed against him. His hand was inside her jeans.

"Jesse," he whispered as he touched her ear with his lips.

"No…no, Matt. Don't," she protested, knowing she could no more resist him than stop the relentless fury of the blizzard. "Yes, yes. Oh, God, yes!" She gave in, begging breathlessly as she dug her fingernails into his back, pulling his mouth to hers.

Through the fog of passion she heard a sound, a voice. No, two voices—voices she knew.

She mustered her strength and pushed him away. He resisted and held her tightly. "Please trust me. There are things you don't know. It didn't work then, it won't now. I have to go."

He heard the voices, too, because he released her. Still flushed, they straightened their clothing.

"Is it because of Lawrence?" he asked, looking in the direction of the voices.

"No. It has nothing to do with him. He's been wonderful." She pulled a small envelope from her pocket, quickly stuffing it in his hands. He looked confused.

The voices were only a few steps away.

"Please, I'm begging you. If you love me, don't read this until after you leave." She shook her head violently as she turned. "Leave now…*please!*" She pushed him toward the coffee shop.

"*If…if* I love you," he stammered, staring at her.

"*Go…now!*" she implored desperately.

He ran, glancing back at her. Jesse followed him with her eyes. The voices had grown silent. She turned. Lawrence stood there, his arm around Ali. Her face was still hot and flushed. She looked back as Matt disappeared around the corner. She tried to speak.

Before she could, Lawrence took Ali's hand and headed back up the stairs.

****

As he studied the envelope he felt a reason to hope. He thought about their few minutes together. Whatever the envelope contained, she still loved him. There was no doubt about that. He went back to his room. The bottle of scotch called to him from his dresser. He stared at it. Then he grabbed it and walked into the bathroom. He took a deep breath and poured it down the sink. As he worked on the notes for his new book, his mind drifted back to what she'd said, her grand eyes, the heady bouquet of her perfume. When he and Mario dined that evening he saw Jesse, Lawrence, and Ali. The table seemed quiet and tense. She stole a look in his direction. He smiled at her as he ordered a drink. She smiled back and nodded imperceptibly, seeing that he'd ordered a cup of black coffee.

The weather moderated, and Alice Long's funeral was held on Friday morning. The sky was clear and bright, sparkling above the crisp blanket of fresh snow. Afterward, he and Jesse nodded, but didn't speak.

Matt kept his word about the envelope. When they left, he asked Mario to drive. As his friend threaded the narrow roads back to the turnpike, Matt opened it.

February 21, 1994
Dearest Matthew,

If you think my love for you has changed or diminished, know that it has not and never will. You are the love of my life. From the first day our eyes met, I have never doubted that you are and always will be my soul mate. But despite my love for you, there are things that would hurt you—things you could never understand.

You will be in my heart forever—only a thought away. But I would rather live apart than have you heartbroken. This may be difficult to understand, but I ask you with all my heart to let our love live as a beautiful memory.

I can survive if we're not together, knowing we'll always love each other. I could never bear the thought that I might become the object of your pity or worse.

All My Love, Always,

Jesse

Matt read it twice. Something was haunting her, something she couldn't tell him. Because he'd pushed her away? He had to find out. He turned to face his friend.

"What did she say, Matthew?"

"How do you know so much?" Matt asked.

"Maybe someday I'll tell you," Mario answered. "Well, what did she say?"

"She says she can never see me again."

"Then why are you smiling?"

"Because she still loves me."

Mario wore that "I told you so" look. "So, now what?"

"I'm going to find out what the secrets are—why she can't be with me."

Mario nodded.

"You know something—"

"What?" Mario interrupted.

"If I didn't know better, I'd think you set this

whole thing up."

His friend pulled over, stopping the car.

"Now that you've read your love letter, you can drive." He shrugged. "And I don't know what you're talking about, Matthew. I just came along for the ride."

Chapter Forty-Seven

May. Three endless months had passed since those few days at Rocky Point Inn. Before their rendezvous at that snowbound bed and breakfast, Matt thought Jesse had traded him in for something bigger and better. Now, he knew better. The snow had melted long ago and he was impatient for the chance to discover what dark secrets kept them apart. He saw a window of opportunity, a chance to get away from writing, his readers, and most importantly, from Stephanie.

The thick, warm air held the fragrance of lilacs and forsythia as he and Allen sat on the Sullivans' front porch. Allen nursed a Bud, Matt a Pepsi. Matt thought about his plans. He paused and closed his eyes, pretending for a moment that the intervening years were an illusion. Meeting Jesse was still a month in his future.

"I'm proud of you," Allen intruded. "It took a long time, but I think you've finally grown up. Lucky for you, too, 'cause I'm not here to help run your life anymore," he said with a satisfied look.

Matt turned. "It just took a kick in the ass."

"It was her, wasn't it?"

"Her?"

"Jesse," Allen answered. "Something happened when you saw her in Maine. I ran into Mario. I asked him what happened."

"What is he, the six o'clock news anchor?"

"C'mon, Matthew, since you came back from Alice's funeral, you're a different man. You only drink at communion. You're involved in everything good in this city. Mike Barnacle referred to you as Boston's young literary Messiah." He stared at Matt. "We all knew she was there and wondered. Didn't want to pry. But if it wasn't something between you two that's responsible for this transformation, what is it?"

"I found something I'd lost," Matt acknowledged.

Allen raised his eyebrows.

"Hope," Matt answered. "For the first time since she left, I found hope."

Allen started to speak. Matt interrupted.

"I don't know what it is. I only know we still love each other." He stood up, walking to the railing as he looked at the darkening, cloudless sky. "I was a fool five years ago, Allen. I pushed her out of my life. I can't write again until I can find some answers. Before I punch another keyboard, I have to find out what's keeping us apart."

"Have you asked yourself what happens if she's right?"

Matt's brow wrinkled.

"What if these *things*, her secrets, really are too ugly?" Allen continued.

"Nothing could be that ugly.*"*

They heard Daniel approaching the door.

"My God, Matt. I just figured it out. Maybe Jesse's a Republican." Allen looked at Daniel and then back at Matt, a grin spreading across his face. Daniel opened the door. He came out and sat down.

"What's all the noise about?"

"Nothing important." Allen looked at Matt. "Our boy here is going on a search, a holy quest. He's going to—"

Matt shook his head violently.

"It's nothing, Dad." Allen nodded and got up to leave.

"Did I hear someone say Republican?" Daniel asked as if the word had a bad taste.

"God forbid. Not around these parts." Allen motioned for Matt to follow him. "I've got to get back to Belmont, where we have nothing *but* Republicans. Caitlyn's got a soccer game under the lights." He waved at Daniel. "It's been great. Don't forget. You're both coming over on Memorial Day. Jeannie's already buying the food. And some of the neighbors will be there, Dad, so please no politics."

"All right. I'll be on my best behavior." Daniel scowled.

Matt walked Allen to his car.

"About this quest of yours." Allen began, looking back at Daniel sitting on the porch. "What about your publisher? You're a rising young star, Matt—a household name right now. Can you just leave?" Matt wasn't sure he knew the answer. "And here's the real big one—what about Stephanie? You've been together a long time. How does she feel about this?"

"I haven't told her." Matt knew Allen was right. She was his biggest challenge.

Allen looked into Matt's eyes. "Good hunting." He held out his hand. "I hope you find what you're looking for."

Later on, Matt called his publisher to tell them he needed a leave of absence. The news wasn't well received. He explained he needed some time to settle some personal affairs—which, of course, was true. They reluctantly agreed, but insisted he be back by the fourth of July. His new book was an historical novel about Washington's attack on Trenton. They were using Independence Day to launch it.

Matt should have notified them through his agent, but he hadn't told her yet. He had to admit it—he was afraid of her reaction. He and Stephanie shared an upscale condo on Beacon Hill and there was one subject that never failed to raise the anxiety level in their household—Jesse. The mention of her name flushed his partner's face, sending her into a tirade.

And Jesse was everywhere. Her musicals had served as a springboard. She leveraged her popularity and talent, selling compact discs and tapes by the millions. She quickly became the darling of the talk show hosts. Jesse's poise, charm, and beauty were captivating, especially when coupled with the dramatic, often told story of her meteoric rise from Portland's worst slum. She'd been the host of Saturday Night Live twice and rumor said she was heading to Hollywood to make at least one major motion picture. Matt had no intention of telling Stephanie why he was leaving, but then he didn't have to. She had an uncanny knack for getting at the truth.

"You're doing what? Taking time off to do special research?" Stephanie asked, biting her lip. It was a sure sign she was angry. "Research on what?" It was an accusation, not a question. "How long will you be gone? We have a book tour coming up, a dozen signings and those charity things…"

"*Enough!* They'll have to wait. Let it go," he

demanded.

She bumped his chest with her hand.

"You're not fooling me." She pushed her finger at him. "This is about her, isn't it? It's always about her. You don't think I know where you were in February and why you've been moping around like a lovesick puppy ever since? Well, I do, my sweet."

He grabbed her wrist, bending it back roughly. She flinched but refused to back down. He let it go and turned away.

"I knew it." She came around to face him, continuing her assault. "You can't fool me, Matthew. You can smile at me and kiss me and *screw me*, but it's her you think of while you're doing it, isn't it?" she exploded. "*Isn't it? Damn you!*"

"No!" he lied, not wanting to hurt her. "I'm here, aren't I?"

"That's because she sleeps with the biggest producer on Broadway." She turned away, tears running down her cheeks. "If Lawrence Webb was hit by a truck tomorrow, you'd be sniffing around that cocky bitch in a minute. I'm second best. I always have been," she spit the words at him.

He began to protest. She wouldn't let him.

"Okay, you go off and do your research about Miss Portland. Maybe I'll be here when you get back, maybe I won't." She headed for the door, turning as she wiped her eyes. "By the way, find yourself a new agent. I quit." She slammed the door and left.

Chapter Forty-Eight

The three days at the Rocky Point Inn had been bitter for Jesse. She'd lost Alice—her best friend. And even the short time with Matt only teased her—reinforcing how much she still loved him. But her life had been filled with an ugliness and privation he would never understand. And worse she'd been responsible for something he could never forgive.

She sat at her dressing table, staring at the picture. Matt, Ali, and her mother smiled back from a sparkling October day long ago. Damn him! She cursed. The foliage on the Common was the color of fire. She remembered the sky—so blue it had hurt her eyes. God, if you're really there…please, hear me just this once. I'm begging you. Please let me be free of him. She pulled the picture to her chest and closed her eyes, hot tears spilling onto her cheeks. At the sound of a tap on the door, she hurriedly wiped her hand across her eyes, turning the photo face down and covering it with her other hand.

"May I come in?" It was Lawrence. They hadn't slept in the same room since returning from Maine. Lawrence never mentioned her rendezvous with Matt. And Jesse never knew how much he and Ali had seen. But rather than show hurt or anger, he withdrew. Jesse understood it well, because they were so much alike. Instead, he apologized making an excuse that he was having a problem sleeping. Jesse wasn't buying.

"Of course." She managed a smile, catching sight of his reflection in the mirror.

"Here." He put a hand on her shoulder, placing a script on the table in front of her. "It's the screenplay for *Gates of Paradise*. Take some time and look it over. Let me know what you think." She reached up, softly touching his hand and taking it in hers.

"I will." She nodded. "Give me a minute and I'll be right down." He squeezed her shoulder lightly and turned. Jesse followed him with her eyes, biting her lip.

"Lawrence, wait. Please don't go." She couldn't take his patronizing, sterile kindness, "Can't we talk? It's been four months."

"What do you mean? Talk about what?"

"You know what. For God sakes. We sleep in separate rooms, you treat me like a houseguest." She shook her head slowly. "I know I hurt you. I'm sorry, so very sorry."

"Jessica…"

"Don't do that," she pleaded.

"What?" he asked, confused.

"*Don't* call me Jessica." She turned. "It's what Mother called me when she was mad at me as a child," she whispered.

He grabbed her by the shoulders spinning her around.

"*There's nothing wrong!*" he exploded. "Everything's fine. I don't…don't know…what…" He coughed, his face turning crimson. He gripped her tightly, looking down at her, his eyes closed. "Give me a minute," he managed.

Suddenly his face grew pale. Sweat appeared on

his forehead as he released her and stepped backward, collapsing onto a chair. "Lawrence." Jesse reached for him. "Can I get you something?"

He waved her away. "No! No, I'm fine." He rose, moving awkwardly to the bathroom.

"You don't look fine," Jesse protested.

"I just need some water." He closed the door. When he came out, his color had returned. He put his hand on her shoulder lightly. "I'm sorry. I shouldn't have raised my voice."

"No, it's all right." He moved toward the door. She reached out, taking his arm. "We didn't settle anything. Please."

"Everything's all right, Jessica." He smiled weakly. "Don't keep us waiting. Dinner's almost ready." He pulled away from her.

"But…" Her words died in her throat as he closed the door.

****

Matt ran down the stairs of the bed and breakfast. He'd decided to stay outside Maine's largest city, afraid his growing celebrity might bring recognition. Wanting to remain anonymous, he took a room on the coast at the Golden Bell. It was well-maintained, reminiscent of Rocky Point Inn. His room was large and comfortable, sporting heavy wooden furniture and a beautifully detailed four-poster bed. Two oversized windows overlooked Casco Bay and the Harbor Islands to the east, warming the room each morning as the dawn crept in.

Matt divided his time between the Public Library in Monument Square, the Cumberland County Registry of Deeds, and the archives of the Portland Press Herald.

So far, his research had yielded almost nothing. He'd found only traces that Jesse and her family ever existed. He learned they lived on Fuller Street, in one of the poorest neighborhoods in an area known as Munjoy Hill. There was a brief story—too brief it seemed to Matt—telling of the death of her stepfather and older brother, Ryan. The deaths were the result of a struggle, but Matt's instincts told him there was more to the story. He found small pieces about Jesse as a performer sprinkled throughout the archives and reference to a woman named Pauline Richards. Jesse had spoken of her.

As he began his third week, he was frustrated, sick of being confined in the public buildings. He wanted do get out and do some leg work. Matt decided to visit the place where Jesse had grown up, hoping someone there might help.

As he asked directions at the Registry of Deeds, the clerk gave him a wary look. "You real sure that's where you want to go, sonny?"

"Is there a problem?" Matt asked.

"Nope. Guess not," she said, surveying him.

"Then why the question?"

"Well, I don't think anybody's still livin' there…and if there is, it's…it's not the kind of place for a nice young fella like you."

"I don't understand," Matt said.

"Maybe you could tell me what you're lookin' for."

"According to your records people there still pay taxes."

"All right," she said, raising her eyebrows. "But don't say you weren't warned."

Maybe she was trying to be helpful. Matt didn't care.

He drove slowly, studying Munjoy Hill. He passed by a park known as the Promenade. Its lush, green grounds and walkway commanded stunning vistas of Casco Bay. As he drove, much of what he saw was reminiscent of his South Boston neighborhood. The small homes and multi-family houses were clean and well-maintained, many surrounded by small, neat lawns, and flanked by shrubs. But as he moved north and inland, the woman's meaning became clear. The closer he got to his destination, the more squalid and neglected the surroundings became.

The trip took about thirty minutes. When he turned onto Fuller Street, he stopped his SUV and pulled over. A dozen dwellings confronted him, standing like lonely derelicts. Like the road they bordered, most of the homes were in a gloomy state of disrepair. Broken windows, doors swinging in the breeze and peeling paint hanging in strips off dilapidated clapboards were the rule.

Matt looked at his notebook. According to the tax records, someone still lived at numbers twelve and thirty-five. But first, he searched for number twenty-nine. He stopped and got out, guessing that a small, two-story house might be his target.

What had once been a picket fence did little to protect the small front yard and the home it guarded. The rusty hinges on the gate squeaked in protest as he pulled it open and walked the short distance to the porch, dodging debris, hostile weeds and puddles of dirty water.

He stepped up, testing the wooden surface to make

sure it would hold his weight. He crossed to the door, stopping at the mailbox. He ran his finger across a small, tarnished plate. It was barely legible. "Number 29—Long" it read. He pulled the door. It opened reluctantly and he went inside.

Chapter Forty-Nine

As the days passed, Jesse's relationship with Lawrence remained unchanged. She cared for him—very much. She had for a long time. He was a commanding figure she wanted to share her life and her bed with. He'd always been a passionate and willing lover. But now he seemed indifferent.

She was desperate and lonely—forever surrounded by people whose only task was to insulate her from reality, to placate her, to make her happy. Except for Pauline and Dani, she'd never had a real friend. Ali was the joy of her life, but Jesse needed more. She needed warmth and affection from Lawrence.

She sat alone in her bedroom, searching the darkness for the demons that lurked just out of reach. There were times when Jesse feared the voices from the past would swallow and consume her. She shivered, hugging herself tightly as she bit her lip.

Slipping out of bed, Jesse left her room, tiptoeing quickly toward the person who could stay her loneliness and fear. She tapped lightly on his door and opened it. Lawrence lay propped up on several pillows, reading a novel. He looked up, gray eyes heavy. Lawrence had always been so strong, so much in command. Suddenly he looked so fragile, so vulnerable.

He did his best to compose himself. Jesse stopped, fearful that this uncharacteristic display was her fault.

Lawrence cleared his throat, placing the book on the covers.

"Hello," he said awkwardly. His face was sober, almost stern.

"What is it? Lawrence. Please." She begged, kneeling next to him, taking his hand in hers. "We have to settle this. Are you hurt that much? Please don't hate me." She pleaded.

He retrieved his hand and bent, taking her shoulders gently.

"I could never hate you, Jesse. Yes, I was hurt and angry. But...this isn't about anything you did." He sighed.

She caressed his hand. "I don't understand. If it's not about what happened in Maine, then what is it about?" Kneeling there, she spotted prescription bottles on the night table.

"No, my dear, beautiful girl," he whispered, the trace of a smile emerging as his massive hand stroked her hair. "It has nothing to do with you."

"I don't understand, Lawrence," she repeated, searching his strong gray eyes.

She looked at the night table, studying the labels. And suddenly, she knew—why he'd been a stranger to her bed; why he'd been absent from the theater, making vague, silly excuses for his absence; why he no longer smoked those pungent aromatic cigars. Jesse knew. For just a moment, she felt relief as it struck her that she hadn't driven him away. But her relief was short-lived as she realized how sick he must be to abandon large chunks of his life so completely and so suddenly.

"I've been dreading this." He took both her hands in his. "I'm sick, Jesse." He swallowed hard, squeezing her hands. "I have advanced coronary disease."

"You have a bad heart?"

"Actually, I have a good heart." He chuckled warmly. "Why only a few years ago I took an unknown singer from Maine and turned her into a superstar..."

"Stop it," she scolded. "You know what I mean."

He grew serious again. "Yes. I have a bad heart—a very bad heart."

"You stopped smoking, you walk two miles every day, you've turned work over to the associate producers, and you moved out of our bedroom. Oh my God. You're afraid to..." her words trailed off.

He nodded.

"How long have you known?"

"A few months. Since right after Alice's funeral."

"There must be something you can do. No, something *we* can do. An operation, a treatment—something—somewhere." She backed away looking for a glimmer of hope, a smile, anything.

His eyes found hers, sweeping over every feature. "No, afraid not. The doctors use a ten-dollar word that means inoperable," he said, shaking his head slowly as his eyes grew moist. "But don't write me off yet. They can treat it with medication. I can still work and lead a *fairly* normal life. I just have to be careful."

She raised her body, gently pushing him as she lay on the bed, her head on his broad chest. He closed her in his arms, caressing her back with a surprisingly strong touch.

"No marathon this year, I guess." She squeezed him tightly.

He kissed her hair softly. "'Fraid not, my love." Then he lifted her, pulling her toward him, kissing her softly at first, then more passionately. "God, I've missed you," he whispered.

"Lawrence, you have to be..." He put his fingers to her lips.

"Shhh." He turned off the light.

"Oh, Lawrence. I've missed you too. So much," she whispered, realizing that God *had* finally heard her, because at this moment she felt safe and warm. Jesse wasn't alone anymore.

Chapter Fifty

Matt sat in the well-appointed waiting area of the NEMC's intensive care ward. He got up to stretch his legs, glancing impassively at the expensive furnishings, lush plantings, and beautiful watercolors of Boston landmarks. He approached the heavy oak doors that lead to the patient area, hoping for a glimpse of his father. The two days since Jeanne's call bringing him home had been endless—the hurried drive back from Portland, the hours spent at the New England Medical Center…it was a blur. He turned as he heard the doors from the elevator lobby burst open.

"Anything new?" Jeanne asked breathlessly as she hurried to the doors separating them from their father.

"No," Matt answered. "Nothing yet." He took Jeanne's arm, leading her to one of the overstuffed leather chairs bordering the waiting area.

"The doctor downstairs said it may be days before we know the extent of the damage." Matt was consumed by frustration and guilt. "It's a miracle he's still alive. The fact that Dad lay there for hours before Mrs. Kelsey found him…" Matt stood up and went to the window, bringing his fist down on the sill.

The doors opened again. Matt heard Allen's voice, soft and comforting, as his brother-in-law touched his shoulder.

"There was nothing you could have done,

Matthew," Allen paused. "You're *not* responsible for this."

"I guess you're right. But if I hadn't been in Maine playing detective, I might have been there."

"Matt." Allen faced him. "I don't know if I can take you. But if you don't stop this bullshit"—Allen looked around self-consciously—"we're gonna find out."

Matt smiled. "Okay, okay, you're right." He paused and stared toward the private patient area.

"I called Stephanie, Matt," Jeanne volunteered. "I thought you'd want her to know."

"What?" Matt understood Jeanne's reasons but her call only added to his angst. "We're not…" he stammered.

While he was trying to find a way to explain the situation, the door to the elevators flew open, and Stephanie burst in. As soon as she saw Matt, she ran to him, throwing her arms around him tightly.

"Oh, Matthew, Matthew." She pulled him to her, whispering, "I'm so sorry about everything. I'm so glad you asked Jeanne to call me." She pushed him away gently, holding his eyes with hers.

Jeanne stared back innocently, unaware of the tension. He opened his mouth, but Stephanie continued. "I'm here for you. I was such a fool. I promise I'll never leave you again. Can you ever forgive me?"

She turned her face upward. Her large green eyes held tears that ran onto her cheeks. Her smile was so penitent and so warm, Matt melted. After his time in Portland, he needed something or someone. Pulling her close, the lush curves of her body melded into his.

"Of course I can." He kissed her hair as he inhaled

its fragrance.

"What happened?" Stephanie asked.

Matt ushered her to a chair next to Allen and Jeanne. "Dad had a massive stroke two, no, I guess it was three days ago," he explained calmly. "It was hours before one of the neighbors found him." He took Stephanie's hand, squeezing it. "He's lucky to be alive."

"I'm so sorry. But he's a strong man, and he's got all of you." Stephanie nodded at Allen and Jeanne. "I know he'll be all right."

"Thanks. Your being here means a lot," Jeanne said.

Just as they finished speaking, the heavy oak doors to the patient area swung open. A tall, slim man approached them.

"Are you the Sullivan family?" he asked.

"Yes, I'm Mr. Sullivan's son, Matthew, and this is my sister, Jeanne." Matt paused, then introduced Allen and Stephanie.

"I'm Dr. John Stedman, head of neurology." His eyes lingered on Stephanie. "We've stabilized your father, but he's had a difficult time. It's going to be a long, hard struggle." He focused on Matt, then on Jeanne. "There's a chance he may never completely recover. He'll need a lot of your time and love." His expression softened, but his tone remained serious.

Jeanne choked back a sob. Allen put his arm around her.

"I'm sorry," Doctor Stedman continued. "Please understand, I don't want to worry you, but I don't believe in being falsely optimistic." He wore a kind, practiced look as he turned toward Jeanne. "But he's strong, and with the support I can see in your faces, he has a good chance."

"When can we see him?" Matt asked.

"You can look in on him from the hallway, but he's still groggy. He can't speak right now, so I think it would be best to wait before you visit him." He paused. "It would be difficult for all of you—especially your father."

Matt started to protest, when he felt a hand on his shoulder.

"That's fine, doctor," Allen said.

"I'll have a nurse come and get you. It may be a while before we're finished. There's a cafeteria on the second floor. Actually, the food's not bad." He nodded. As he started to leave, he stopped. "Don't you write those historical novels?" he asked Matt.

Before Matt had a chance, Stephanie answered, "Yes, isn't he wonderful? He's so gifted. Everything he writes is so…" Her words died as she looked at Matt.

The doctor turned toward her. "Why yes, yes he is." He stopped, his eyes studying Stephanie. Allen and Jeanne were watching her, too.

"Yes, so *very* gifted and so very special," she repeated in a shrill voice.

Matt turned toward Stephanie, curious why they were staring. Her eyes were fixed on him in a way that made him uncomfortable.

The doctor cleared his throat, "Why, yes…of course," he said, retreating toward the intensive-care ward. "Oh, I'm sorry, miss. Only family members are allowed on this floor."

The sound of the doors closing brought Stephanie out of her trance. She shook her head and took Matt's hand. He stole a look at Allen then at Jeanne. Allen raised his eyebrows and shrugged.

"I can't wait to see your father. He was always so nice." Stephanie smiled broadly, oblivious to her peculiar behavior.

"Didn't you hear the doctor, Steph? You can't be here. I'll take you home," Matt suggested. Stephanie looked at him vacantly. He turned to Jeanne.

She and Allen nodded in agreement. "I think that's a good idea," Allen volunteered.

"Call my cell. I'll be back later," Matt told Allen. He took Stephanie's arm, pushing her firmly through the doors to the elevator.

After taking Stephanie home, Matt returned. He sat huddled under his jacket in one of the plush chairs. It was well past midnight. Allen and Jeanne dozed fitfully on a long couch across from him. Exhausted, he closed his eyes, trying to will himself to sleep, knowing sleep wouldn't come. It hadn't in three days—since he'd seen the woman on Fuller Street. Her pale lean image haunted him. But it was more than the haunting figure that held him captive—it was what she'd said...

"Did you know the Longs? The people who used to live here?" Matt asked when the frail specter of an old woman materialized in the entrance of 29 Fuller Street. She said nothing as she entered timidly, searching the gloomy interior, looking around warily as if someone or something might pounce on her.

The stale smell of decaying wood and mildew filled the ragged remnants of what had been a living room. Water dripped invisibly from somewhere over their heads, the sound of it hitting the floor kept time with the woman's tentative steps.

"I asked if you knew the people who used to live here," he repeated.

She nodded, still searching for the hidden presence she feared might spring. Then the woman stopped.

"I'm not deaf," she said evenly. "I heard you the first time."

"Matt." He awoke as Allen shook him.

"Huh?" Matt looked up, groggy from fatigue. He was back at the NEMC intensive care ward. He must have dozed off. "Yeah, Al." He shook his head. "What's up?"

"Jeanne's asleep, and I've got a big meeting in"— he looked at his watch—"six hours. I'm sorry, but it's something I just can't miss."

"I understand." Matt straightened himself in the chair, rubbing his eyes. "Take Jeannie home. The kids need her. I'll stay and let you know if anything develops. Doctor Stedman said it might be a while."

"Okay." Allen hesitated at first. "Thanks," he nodded as he woke Jeanne. She protested, but they convinced her the children would need her. Matt moved to the large couch across the room. Using his jacket as a pillow, he lay down and closed his eyes…

He was back in the deserted, filthy remnants of the house where Jesse spent her childhood. Matt couldn't imagine how it looked then, but it held no warmth now. He focused on the apparition whose words haunted him.

"What do you want here?" The woman's shrill voice sent shivers through him. "You're another of those souvenir hunters. Come to steal a piece of the house?"

"No, I'm not," he answered.

Her stare penetrated him.

"I'm a friend of Jesse's."

"If you're a friend, why would you want to see this place?" The woman shook her head, surveying the foul, empty shell surrounding them.

"I wanted to see where she grew up." Matt crossed the distance between them, extending his hand. "My name's Matt Sullivan." He forced a smile.

"Burke," the woman volunteered after a long pause. She kept her hand by her side. "Emily Burke. Lived here for almost sixty years."

"If you're a friend of hers, what was her mother's name?"

"Alice," Matt answered.

"And her daughter's?" The woman continued her interrogation. Obviously the house had been visited by others trying to snatch a piece of Jesse's past..

"Ali." He said evenly. "Look, I came here to see where she grew up, not play twenty questions." Matt's patience was running out. He moved toward the door.

"What do you want to know?" the woman asked as he passed.

Matt stopped and turned. "I was hoping to find out something about what her life was like. I've read about the murders and I thought if maybe you could..."

"You read a lot?"

Matt nodded.

"Ever read a really sad story? The kind where it seems like everything bad that could ever happen happened to the person in the story. Things got so bad you just wanted the story to end. You'd put the book down but you couldn't get away from it." The woman paused. She stopped and turned, looking at the stairway

and landing for a long time.

She hung her head, shaking it slowly. "Go home now, sonny."

She turned, trudging toward the door, her head resting on her chest. Matt followed, grabbing her arm.

"But Mrs. Burke, you didn't tell me anything about Jesse and what happened to her."

She took his hand, removing it with surprising force as she looked up at him. The sun filtering through the cloudy, cracked windows, made strange patterns on her sallow face. As he looked at her, she frowned sadly and nodded.

"Yes I did, sonny." She released him and walked away. "Yes, I did."

Chapter Fifty-One

It was the Tuesday before Thanksgiving. Matt's eyes were fixed, looking out the front window of Flour Bakery and Cafe, a South End delicatessen and coffee shop. The atmosphere was thick and sweet. The fragrance of pastries baking, fresh deli meats hanging over the counter, and gourmet coffee battled for control. Mario was late. As Matt looked onto Washington Street snowflakes drifted lazily to the damp pavement.

Returning to the South End evoked vivid memories: taking Ali trick-or-treating; a night in a smoke-filled jazz club watching Jesse tempt him with a seductive rendition of "As Time Goes By"; their one Thanksgiving together. Visions crept in, teasing him—her perfume, the way she kissed him, the warm, soft touch of her hand on his…

"Wake up, my young friend." Mario slapped his back. "Where are you?"

Matt shook his head. "Nowhere special." He got up to shake Mario's hand.

"It's been awhile. Sorry I'm late. I had a dispute to deal with," he said, sitting across from Matt.

"It's been too long." Matt nodded. "I've missed our talks."

"How's your dad doing?"

"Better every day. Thanks. How are you?"

"Can't complain. If I did, no one would listen." He

chuckled. "So, now tell me…" Mario stopped, slapping the worn tabletop as the waitress approached. "The usual, dear." Mario winked. "And for you?" He gestured toward Matt.

"Another Pepsi, thanks."

"So," Mario repeated. "What are you up to?"

"I'm going back on the road now that my dad can get around. I have a nurse coming every day, and Jeanne's there whenever she can be."

"Where's 'the road'?"

"Detroit, Cleveland, Pittsburgh, the garden spots of middle America." Matt paused for a minute, turning from Mario as he focused on the sparse flakes dying on the asphalt. "I really tried, you know."

"Tried?"

"To find out about Jesse, her life, the mystery keeping us apart."

Mario's expression softened as he patted Matt's forearm. "I knew you would." He nodded. "Can you tell me what you found out?"

Matt shrugged and turned back toward his friend. "Just more mystery." Matt raised his eyes to meet Mario's. "Some bad things happened to her—very bad things. Her brother and stepfather died—killed each other, I guess. I met this sad old neighbor who—" Matt stopped.

"Who what, Matthew?" Mario asked quietly.

"I think Jesse's life was a living hell."

"What're you going to do?"

"Between my father and the book tours, I haven't got much time, and I won't for a while. And Stephanie would explode if she knew I was playing detective again."

Mario shook his head.

"I know there's something about her you don't like, but she's been great to me." Matt looked toward the street again. "Look, there's something else."

Mario raised his eyebrows.

"Remember the letter?" Matt asked. "The one she sent after Alice's funeral?"

Mario waited patiently.

"She said that if I found out too much about her my love would turn to hate or pity. That was exactly what she said."

Mario said nothing. He seemed to be studying Matt.

"Well, all these months taking care of my dad, I've had a lot of time to turn this over in my mind and..." Matt's words trailed off.

Mario nodded, touching his friend's forearm again. "You're afraid she might be right."

Chapter Fifty-Two

1997

A bright spring morning promised better things to come. Jesse held her coffee, staring out the study window at the green patchwork on the newly budding trees. The morning mist hovered, creeping slowly through the new grass between the rolling hills of her farm in Southwestern Connecticut.

Heavy footsteps interrupted her thoughts as the sound of riding boots hit the polished hardwood. She turned to see Ali standing in the doorway.

"Well," Jesse asked. "How do you like your birthday present?" She nodded toward the window and corral beyond.

A black Dutch warmblood waited impatiently, saddled and ready for his new mistress. It was Alexis's thirteenth birthday.

Ali didn't answer. She seemed to by studying her mother. "Mom, now that I'm thirteen, can I ask you something?"

"You can ask me anything, honey."

Alexis continued to look at her. She screwed her mouth up, considering how to phrase her question. "Okay." Ali looked around self-consciously. "How come you and Lawrence don't sleep in the same room anymore?" she whispered.

Caught off guard, Jesse protested. "What? Why would you ask that?" she stammered defensively. "I-I don't think it's any of your business where we sleep, Alexis." How could she explain? Lawrence's heart problems were their secret. Only Lawrence, Jesse, and his doctors knew of it. Sadly, lovemaking had disappeared from their relationship.

"Do you love him?" Ali blurted out.

Jesse stared angrily, finally managing, "How can you ask me that? Why of course I-I…"

"Sorry, Mom," Ali said awkwardly, giving her mother a clumsy hug as she turned to leave. "I like Lawrence. He's a great guy." As she reached the door, she turned, adding, "It's okay. I know who you *really* love." Ali said, looking back at her mother. "I still love him, too."

Her love for Matt remained a painful wound that haunted her empty, restless nights. She hadn't heard from him, so she assumed he'd honored her letter, leaving her past in anonymity. Strangely, while that brought her peace, it also brought disappointment.

There was a part of her that hoped he was still the brash young lover, someone who cared so much he'd ignore her warnings, crashing ahead at full speed just to find out what was keeping them apart. Apparently, he hadn't.

Lawrence *had* been so much to her: a mentor, best friend, a father figure, and of course, her lover. But that was over. So Jesse took consolation in Ali—her wonderful way with people, her legion of friends, her intelligence and abilities.

After her own brutal childhood, Jesse did everything possible to guarantee Alexis the perfect, sheltered life. She sent her daughter to the best schools and provided the finest coaches and tutors. Her most extravagant indulgence was the farm where Ali spent endless hours in the saddle. While she excelled at everything, Ali had a special gift for riding. Her coach hinted they should consider the 2000 Olympic tryouts.

But Jesse's devotion to Ali's pastime was not entirely selfless. Expensive thoroughbreds and private riding lessons were things to be flaunted and envied. They signified affluence and status—things Jesse had come to enjoy.

Lawrence counseled her about her extravagance, constantly warning her against buying the best and most expensive. He begged her to save, to invest. She had an enormous salary, revenues from record sales and dozens of endorsements.

"The eight-cylinder Mercedes will get you there as fast as the twelve," he said as they browsed the Mercedes Manhattan showroom on West 41st Street. "For God's sakes, the West Side Highway isn't the Autobahn." She stared at him, unable to explain her compulsive need to have the best.

"You should think about your future—and Ali's. You spend like the world was ending tomorrow." He shook his head. "Do we always have to go to 21 or the Rainbow Room? There *are* places where you don't need a bank loan to pay the check."

But Jesse ignored him. Substantial money flowed in, flowing out just as quickly. Money was meant to spend. Conspicuous consumption had become Jesse's surrogate for passion and love.

Yet, despite the advantages that her mother heaped on her, Ali wasn't spoiled or self-indulged. She

appeared to be what her mother had always hoped for—
the perfect young woman.

Then, one sparkling summer day, the letters
began…

Chapter Fifty-Three

The gray rain clouds looked pregnant, ready to unleash a deluge and relieve the tension in the heavy summer air. Matt stepped into Amrhein's—a German-American restaurant on Dorchester Avenue. Despite the fresh paint and new air handlers, the old restaurant still held the fragrance of one hundred years worth of whiskey and cigarette smoke. Looking around, he saw Allen waving and joined him at a table in the rear. Matt sat down facing the door to wait for the rest of his family.

Allen looked impatient. "I'm getting worried," he said, looking toward the door. "Maybe I should go to the house. This is Dad's big night."

"They'll be fine. The guy from Broadway Limo is taking care of it. He's an old friend of Mario's." As if on cue, his old friend strolled into the restaurant, brushing the rain from his summer suit.

"Speak of the devil," Matt said, shaking his head. "Look who's here."

Allen motioned Mario toward their table. When Mario saw them, a grin spread across his broad face. He approached, holding out his hand.

"Well, well. What a wonderful coincidence. My two favorite young Turks. One," he said, nodding at Allen, "a captain of banking and industry. The other"—his gaze shifted toward Matt—"a renowned practitioner of the arts."

"What are *you* doing here?" Matt asked.

"Matthew, I have friends throughout this glorious city." He chuckled. Mario made a gesture in the direction of two large men at a corner table. Both were middle-aged with dark complexions. One was well groomed and wore an expensive suit. The other had outgrown his cashmere blazer. "I'm meeting a couple of business associates. And you?" he asked, eyebrows raised.

Matt glanced at the men. They nodded. "We're waiting for the rest of the family. It's my father's birthday, and this is his favorite place." Matt craned his neck, finding the door. "But we're going to be thrown out if they don't get here soon."

"That's a coincidence. I just spoke to the man driving them. There was some tie-up on the Broadway Bridge. I'm sure they'll be here in a few minutes. I could speak to the hostess."

"Sometimes I think you run this city." Matt put his hand on Mario's shoulder. "But thanks. I think we'll be okay."

"Suit yourself." Mario shrugged. "You give me too much credit. I'm just a poor immigrant trying to make his way." He paused, shooting a look at the table where his associates waited. Their faces held tension and impatience. Matt noticed Mario giving them a subtle nod.

"Well, it's been a while. Have you given up the crusade?" Mario asked.

"Crusade?" Matt said, watching Allen. He understood the question but felt uncomfortable.

"It's all right, Matthew. Allen and I have no

secrets."

Allen smiled weakly. "Well, somebody's got to watch your back while you're tilting at windmills, Don Quixote."

"I should have known you talked about this," Matt said.

"So, do you still have doubts? You were questioning what to do." Mario studied him. "Is she worth the trouble?"

Matt looked around the crowded restaurant. "Yes," he answered, lowering his voice. "I found out her stepfather was a son of a bitch." He narrowed his eyes. "After he died, she and Alice had *nothing*."

Mario glanced at Allen.

"Next month I'll be in northern New England," Matt continued, "and I'm going to look up her old music teacher's husband. Nothing I've found has scared me off—just made me want to help her." He looked up. "She must have so many terrible memories."

They fell silent for a few seconds. Mario looked toward the door and cleared his throat, "Well, time for me to go." He slapped his thigh. "Your family's here." He rose and waved. Daniel and Jeanne were approaching, flanked by Caitlyn, Theresa, and the newest family member, Patrick.

Mario shook hands and left. Matt saw him take his place across from the men at the other table. As Matt ate, he glanced at them. Their conversation looked serious. While the Sullivans were still on their crab cakes and cheese sticks, Mario and his friends finished their business.

At nine fifteen, Matt and his family left Amrhrein's. When they reached the sidewalk, Matt pulled Allen aside. "So you and Mario are buddies?"

Allen nodded. "Well, he knows how close we are and you know he loves you and Jesse like the kids he never had, so once in a while, we grab a cup of coffee and talk. He gives me some good tips on what's going on in the city, too." Allen studied the sidewalk. "I think he always hoped that you two would...you know—end up together."

Despite his surprise, Matt wasn't angry. "It's all right, Al. I've got no complaints." He waved to his nieces and nephew. "It's nice to be loved. It's funny though. If I didn't know better, I'd swear he planned this, right down to the Broadway Bridge being closed."

"Now that's just plain crazy. How could he have done that?" Allen asked dismissively.

Matt paused. "What'd you make of those guys in the booth with him?" he asked. "They weren't there for the meat loaf and sauerkraut."

Allen pulled Matt aside. "For someone so well connected, I'm surprised you didn't recognize them. They were in the news a lot last summer."

"I thought they looked familiar, but I was barnstorming around the Southwest."

Allen nodded. "Well, one's Salvatore Genovese and the other is Luciano Santorini."

"Yeah?" Matt said, still puzzled.

"Matthew, you just ate dinner two tables away from the two biggest figures in the New England crime syndicate!"

Chapter Fifty-Four

It was a Tuesday when Jesse's life began to come apart.

Ali didn't usually ride at the stables, but that morning the flooring in their indoor arena was being replaced. Jesse had been away promoting the movie version of *Gates of Paradise.* She wanted to spend some time with her daughter. After parking her Lexus SUV, Jesse got out to meet Ali. Jesse loved hear the instructors fawn over her daughter, even if some of it was due to her celebrity.

As they went to the car, Jesse noticed the admiring stares. Even at thirteen, her daughter cut an eye-catching figure in her fitted riding clothes. Ali hopped in the back, pulling off her boots with her mother's help. Jesse got in and swung the Lexus out of the parking lot.

"That's a lot of work, Mom. I'm not sure that I want to go through with this Olympic thing," she said, putting her riding helmet on the seat next to her.

"Do me a favor, honey, throw your stuff in the tote in the back. Being an equestrian may be elegant, but on hot days it just plain stinks."

Ali grinned. "Gotcha, Mom."

Jesse glanced down at the passenger seat and saw a small envelope. She assumed it was a bill from Ali's instructor or the stable. As they rode home, she told Ali that her first stop would be a long shower. It was a hot day, and the unmistakable fragrance of sweat, horses, and the stable filled the SUV.

"Can't I just go for a swim?" Ali pleaded.

"Take your shower. Then you can go swimming."

Ali nodded in the rearview mirror.

When they got back to the farmhouse, Ali took her boots and helmet to the barn and headed inside to take her shower.

"Meet you by the pool in ten minutes," Jesse called after her. Ali smiled and nodded. What a great kid, Jesse thought.

Getting out of the car, Jesse remembered the envelope. Heading inside, she opened it. She was surprised when a small group of pictures fell to the ground. She assumed one of the other parents had taken pictures of Ali at a competition.

But as she picked up the pictures, her heart stopped. They showed Ali and her friends at a pool party. There were several of her daughter without a top. They were taken from a distance, but there was no question who and what they showed. Jesse recognized Ali and her friends.

Inside was a note, typed on plain white paper. It explained that the pictures were taken while Jesse was on tour, adding that there was alcohol and marijuana present. The note suggested the local papers and tabloids would pay the photographer a lot. The writer offered Jesse the chance to outbid them.

Jesse was furious. She ran into the house, where Ali was still in her riding clothes. She slammed her daughter's door shut, throwing the pictures on the bed. Slowly, Ali picked them up. She studied them, letting them fall to her bed as tears formed in her eyes.

"I'm sorry, Mom, it just happened. I mean you and Lawrence aren't here very much. I got lonely and we got talking and it…it just happened."

"Jesus Christ, Ali, you're only thirteen, and you're parading around naked. Whoever took these says there was alcohol and drugs here, too." Jesse shook her head. "Where was Melinda? Wasn't she supposed to be watching you?"

"Don't blame her. I gave her the night off. I told her I was going to a sleepover at Morgan's."

"So, tell me, how many of these *orgies* have you been to?"

Ali's eyes were fixed on the floor.

"C'mon." Jesse stood in front of her, putting her hand on Ali's shoulder.

"This is the first one we had here, but there've been a couple at some of my friend's. Their parents are gone a lot too."

"I want names and dates, and I want them now or your social life is over." What was angering her? Jesse asked herself. The fact that her daughter had violated her trust or the fact that Ali wasn't perfect.

"Mom, please don't ask me." Ali said, sobbing. "I just can't tell on my friends."

"Your loyalty comes with a price." Jesse was firm. "Go take your shower. When you're done with that you can sit in this room until you decide to tell me what's going on."

"But Mom…"

Jesse would hear none of it. "No more social functions, riding or anything else, until you tell me *everything.*" Ignoring her daughter's protests Jesse left the room, taking her phone and slamming the door on the way out.

When Lawrence called later, she explained what had happened. As she'd expected, he took Ali's side.

"Couldn't you come up with something a little softer? You haven't left her many options. She either tells on her friends, destroying her social life or you keep her captive, which has the same effect."

"I can't think of a third alternative."

"A lot of what she says is true, Jess. We're never there anymore. Between the two of us, we've been on the road the entire month of July."

"So, I do what I can, I buy her everything she could possibly want."

"Don't you get it? Ali doesn't want another horse or a bigger TV. She wants to see *you* once in a while. I've been telling you that."

"I knew you'd blame *me* for this," Jesse raised her voice. "Traveling is part of my job, Lawrence. We've got a movie to shoot. That's only going to make it worse."

"I'll be home on Saturday. Can you give her a reprieve so we can talk this out? Let her go riding, see her friends as long as there's adult supervision. She can't always be perfect. She's only thirteen, for God's sake."

"What should I do about the money?"

"It's your choice. If you want those pictures in a tabloid, be stubborn. But you know what it will do to her. What did they ask for?"

"They didn't give me a figure." She shook her head. "But he knows who we are. He'll want plenty."

"That's your call. I can tell you what I'd do. We

can split it if—"

"No, this is my problem." Jesse stopped him. Afraid she'd hurt him, she asked. "What do you think about calling the police?"

"And tell them what? That your thirteen-year-old daughter and her friends are prancing around unsupervised naked, drinking, and doing drugs."

"I see your point."

****

The blackmailer teased Jesse. Just as she was beginning to think it might have been an elaborate prank, one late summer afternoon, she received a call. Jesse was to leave $25,000 in cash at a predetermined location. The muffled voice guaranteed that media people would stand in line for anything to do with America's biggest musical star. They were right.

She tried to explain she didn't have bundles of cash lying around. The person laughed and hung up. There would be no negotiation. The following week she got the money and followed the instructions, hoping it was over.

Jesse agreed to Lawrence's idea and modified Ali's punishment. She rationalized that summer was almost over and the *Gates of Paradise* Company would be leaving for location shooting in Utah. Ali would be back in private school under the watchful eye of housekeepers and tutors. Jesse hoped to leave her daughter's indiscretions in Connecticut.

Two months passed. Jesse thought the blackmail incident was behind her. She and Lawrence had taken a rambling home outside Salt Lake City for the duration of the location shooting in Utah. As Jesse picked up her mail on the set one afternoon, there was an envelope that looked suspiciously familiar. She got a sinking feeling. When she got back to her house, she tore open the envelope. What she saw made her struggle for breath. She collapsed on the couch.

There were no photos of Ali. These were photos of her on the night she'd been raped. "No...No!" she screamed, tearing them into shreds and flinging them across the room. They showed her lying naked and drugged in the dirt. There were several front views and one showing cruel, ugly letters freshly cut into her flesh.

Jesse,

What would your lovely daughter think if she knew she was conceived on this night? Wouldn't the tabloids have a field day with these pictures and the story behind them? Maybe you'll get better attendance at your new movie. The sympathy factor! "Broadway mega-star attacked, left naked and disfigured in the dirt, has illegitimate daughter as a result." What would Ali and all her rich friends think?

Better yet, we could package them with the pictures of Ali—a mother and daughter thing!

Expect to hear from us!
Pleasant dreams.

Chapter Fifty-Five

Though most of Matt's investigations had yielded nothing, he'd learned one valuable piece of information: the name of the Long's one real friend—a woman named Pauline Richards. She was a retired music teacher who'd volunteered in the Portland schools. She'd discovered Jesse. Pauline had died two years earlier, but on an early fall afternoon, her husband had agreed to an interview.

The Richard's house was in a well-maintained neighborhood of capes and small colonials. It overlooked Casco Bay. The houses were guarded by stately poplars and maples flanking the narrow street. Some already wore their fall colors. As Matt approached, he saw Jim Richards standing in front of his home. He was tall—very tall, a trim man who looked extremely fit for his eighty years. He greeted Matt, shaking his hand.

"It was like that poor little girl lit a fire inside Pauline," he told Matt after some casual conversation. "I remember her sitting at dinner the first night she went to teach. Jessica was all she could talk about. She was taken by the contradiction. Jesse was such a shy child with an old, threadbare dress. But when the class began to sing, Pauline said it was like there was someone else inside her." He shook his head, recalling the conversation; then he stopped and studied Matthew.

"Why are you asking, son?"

"I'm doing a feature article for the Boston Globe," Matt lied. "She's going to be starring in the film version of *Gates of Paradise,* and they asked me…"

"Don't you think I know who you are?" Jim said, stopping him. "You're that young writer who's had so many best sellers. I watch TV and read the papers. Now, would you like to tell me why you're really here?"

Matt sighed deeply, embarrassed.

"I think Jesse's in trouble, and she's very special to me. I'm trying to find out anything I can that may help her. I'm sorry," Matt said as he turned toward his car. A strong hand gripped his arm, Matt turned to see Jim Richards smiling.

"Matt, we had four children of our own, but I swear Pauline loved that little girl more than any of 'em." His face took on a far away look. "She was devoted to that child. Jesse became a cause to Pauline." He studied Matt. "Are you a drinking man, son?"

"No, sir, not any more."

"Good, neither am I," he said, gesturing toward the door. "Come inside, I just brewed some fresh coffee. There was a lot of mystery surrounding Jesse and her family, but I'll tell you everything I can. When she came back for Pauline's funeral, I could see she'd changed. Jessica wasn't the same cocky young woman she was when she left. It was like she'd lost something. Something very important." Jim found Matt's eyes. "Maybe that something was you."

Chapter Fifty-Six

It was early October. Outside Salt Lake City on the *Gates of Paradise* set things weren't going as planned. The schedule called for final shooting by November. They were already days behind and the problem was coming from an unexpected source—their star. Jesse was the most popular musical celebrity in America. The story of her meteoric rise from desperation and obscurity captivated the public consciousness. Everyone wanted to see her in the movie.

Jesse had always been a hard working, no-nonsense pro who learned her lines and had ice water in her veins. As one of the producers and her longtime partner, the director asked for a private meeting with Lawrence.

There was a learning curve in the transition between the Broadway stage and a movie set, but based on her work ethic and abilities, everyone expected Jesse to breeze through the shoots. She wasn't. She'd show up late, would disappear into her trailer and reappear with a strange glow that suggested drugs. She stumbled through her lines like a nervous amateur.

"Lawrence, she's your girl," said the director. "We're mystified. We heard she was the consummate professional. Since she's been on my set she's behaving like a bad rock star. We're weeks behind and way over budget. We can't afford this—and neither can you. I want to work with Jesse, but we can't put up with this. Either straighten it out, or we'll have to look at an alternative."

Lawrence promised to talk with his protégée and partner, but he was nervous. He'd noticed the same erratic behavior. He wasn't sure he could resolve whatever was tearing Jesse apart. They'd lost their physical intimacy because of his health, but he hoped that they could still work as a team, helping and caring for each other.

Lawrence knew he'd met the great love in her life. Matt Sullivan was tough competition. He was young, looked like a movie star, had incredible talent, and any fool could see Jesse adored him. From what he'd seen in Maine, he adored her right back. That left a monumental riddle. Why didn't she run to him? What was keeping them apart? He wanted to ask her so often. Now, he'd have to.

Lawrence left the lot, dialing their mountainside home. "Hi, Jess," he said, trying to sound cheerful.

"Hello," she answered.

"I'll be home in half an hour. I need to talk to you. I'll pick up some take out."

"That's good." Her voice sounded tense. "Because...I think it's time I explained some things."

"I agree. You know I love you, but it's time we talked about what's going on." He paused. "Whatever it is, I want to help you get through it."

There was a hollow laugh at the other end. "After you hear what I have to tell you, you may change your mind."

Three hours later they sat on the couch, drained, holding hands and looking out at the purple Wasatch in the dusk. For the first time in her life, Jesse had told someone about every bitter detail from her childhood. The tears had stopped. She sat drinking strong coffee Lawrence had brewed. In some ways the dialogue had been cathartic, in other ways it brought back sad, bitter memories she'd spent years trying to erase.

"So you can't remember everything that bastard Alton did or what happened to him and your brother?"

"No, only bits and pieces," She said, putting her head on his shoulder. "I have terrible nightmares where I re-live parts of that night, but it's like a puzzle with pieces missing."

"I know." He nodded. "I've heard you."

"I've talked to psychologists and counselors," she continued. "They've told me it's unusual to have such realistic dreams. They suggested that my mind's protecting me from something too ugly or frightening to remember. They say that one day it might all come back, but I'm not sure I want that to happen. And now there are these." She pointed to the pictures sent by the blackmailer. "They keep pressuring me."

Lawrence looked at the sickening photos that showed the ugly five-letter word carved in her flesh. "But your back. I never..."

She shook her head.

"By the time you and I got involved, I'd been to a plastic surgeon. He was able to repair most of the damage. There are some telltale signs, but nothing you'd notice."

He managed a smile. "I never would have known." Pulling her close, he stroked her hair. "You know I've loved you since the first time I saw you. It's all right, Jesse. I know your feelings aren't as deep."

She began to speak. He put his hand to her lips "When I saw you and Matt together, I knew they never would be. I know how hard you've tried, even though we can't be as close..." His words trailed off. "But I want to help you. There must be something we can do."

"I've thought about the police. I talked to private detectives. They told me there wasn't a lot I *could* do. Even if we find out who's doing this, all they have to do is put the pictures and the story in the mail, and Ali's life will be ruined." She stood, biting her lip and pacing. "They're threatening to tell the tabloids lies to go with the photos. When people see those pictures, they'll believe anything." She kissed Lawrence on the cheek. "Thank you for always being there—always the voice of reason. Without your strength and support, I couldn't have managed all this."

They held each other for a long time.

"I hate to say it, but I think you're right about the blackmailer. We have to pay. But before you do anything else, you've got to stop the drugs. If we don't make this movie, we'll both lose a lot of money and our reputations."

"You're right. I've behaved like a spoiled child," she acknowledged. "I'll do it for you."

He had to ask. "Jesse." He took her face in his hands. "I saw the way you and Matt were with each other."

She blushed and turned away.

"Please, look at me. I have to know. Why don't you go to him, why—?"

"It's simple," she interrupted. "Because of what happened ten years ago." Tears ran down her cheek. "I'd have to tell him about the baby—our baby. I know he'd never understand what happened—no matter what the reasons."

"So he *was* the father."

Jesse nodded, continuing, "His world was so different—a Norman Rockwell existence where everything was good and everyone was your friend. I know him. He could never forgive the fact that I may have brought on the miscarriage."

"I'm so sorry." Lawrence shook his head. "Do you feel…*guilty* about it?"

She sighed, staring at the dark mountains in the distance. "Guilty?" She shook her head slowly. "I don't know. He pushed me away. I did what I had to so I could survive. I have regrets." She paused, hanging her head. "There's not a day that goes by that I don't ask myself 'what if?'"

He walked across the room and took her in his arms. They held each other for a long time, neither speaking.

Lawrence broke the silence. "How much does the blackmailer want?"

She pushed him away and walked to the glass door that overlooked the blue-gray mountain peaks, now just a dull outline against the darkening sky.

"Twenty-five thousand dollars right away."

"My God."

"They don't care. Whoever is doing this thinks I have all the money in the world. So I pay him, or he ruins Ali's life and probably mine."

"What are you going to do?"

Jesse crossed to the desk, opened the top drawer, and pulled out a cashier's check for twenty-five thousand dollars.

"Pay him for as long as I can, or until I can think of something else."

****

"Hello," Mario said when Dani called. "I met Matt at the bakery, but I couldn't tell him what we've discovered about her stepfather. It would break his heart."

"I know." She paused. "When are you coming down here?" She sounded tired. "I'm sick of living in exile. Debt of honor be damned, I want to be with you." She sounded angry. "I know how you feel about her. But my dearest, there are some things even you can't fix."

"If only I could have helped her." He paused. "But there's more. Someone's blackmailing her. I'm worried. If some of what we know got out, she'd be ruined."

"Do you know who's doing it?" she asked.

"Not yet. But I will. When I find out, I may take care of it the old-fashioned way."

"You promised you'd never do that."

"I don't have the patience of a saint. I've kept my hands clean, but—" He stopped in mid-sentence.

Now she was as frightened as he was.

****

For the fall and on through the winter of 1998, Matt continued his secret quest. He did well at concealing his side trips as he followed up the leads he'd found in Portland. But if his actions were invisible to Stephanie, his associates, and his publisher, so were his results.

When the ice melted on the Charles and the grass peeked through the snow in the Sullivans' back yard, he had nothing to show for his detective work. As another cool, damp spring came to Boston and Matt threw out the first pitch at the Red Sox opener in April, he had to admit defeat. Either Jesse had hidden her trail very well, or what she was hiding left no trail at all. He stood brooding on the balcony of his penthouse, listening to Stephanie singing cheerfully while she made tomato sauce. He shook his head, knowing he'd reached the end of his journey.

Chapter Fifty-Seven

Late April 2000

Matt waited for Stephanie amidst the pungent confusion of the stable area. She was competing at the Rolex Three-Day Equestrian Event, in Lexington, Kentucky. It was Sunday, the final day of the competition. The event that day was show jumping, and Stephanie had finished her ride. Matt craned his neck, looking through the riders and attendants to spot her.

The weather had been unusually warm and the staging area was thick with the fragrance of horses and closely-packed humanity. Since Stephanie was nowhere in sight, Matt headed toward the open viewing area for escape when something stopped him. An announcement. The competitor's name caused him to halt abruptly. The name was Alexis Long. At first he thought he'd made a mistake, but the announcer repeated it. *"Now on the course, Alexis Long from Heavenly Farms in Fairfield, Connecticut, riding Apollo's Promise."*

He pushed through the spectators, finding a place on the fence next to the course. Poised astride a splendid black horse sat a stunning young woman. Beneath her helmet and riding habit, he could plainly see Jesse in Ali's face and figure. Matt stood spellbound as the rider, seemingly joined to her mount, skillfully guided him over the course. He watched as the girl and her horse rose as one, completing the last jump with a fluid grace as he watched, awestruck. The stands erupted as the announcement came that Alexis had completed the course without a fault.

Matt stood for a moment, following Ali as she trotted away, then, shaking his head, headed back to find Stephanie. She'd ridden poorly, and he was worried. In the last few months, she'd become increasingly critical, often showing a nasty, almost cruel side. She'd always been jealous when Jesse's name was mentioned, but this new behavior made him uneasy—more so because it often happened in public. He'd thought of suggesting she see a counselor. Before he found her, he heard her tirade. She was dismounting and swinging her riding crop, hitting the side of her trailer with a loud crack.

She stood, flushed with anger. "Damn this horse. I guided him perfectly, spurred him at just the right time, but he balked. He stumbled through the last obstacle, knocking down two rails."

An attendant approached.

"Can I help you with your mount, Miss Halloran?"

"Get this worthless beast out of here," she yelled, this time striking the horse with her crop. He kicked out violently. Matt grabbed her arm, pulling her aside as riders and spectators looked on in shock.

"For God's sake." He shook his head. "It's not the end of the world."

She pulled away. "You were an athlete. Did you enjoy losing?" she spit through clenched teeth. "This is the Rolex. I was a champion once." She stabbed his chest with her finger.

"I know you were, Steph. Calm down."

She turned away. When she looked back, her expression had morphed into a plastic smile. "You're right. I'm sorry. Who gives a damn?"

"I didn't say that. But as long as you did your best…"

As he spoke, a familiar figure passed. Matt stopped, recognizing the girl as soon as she removed her helmet.

"Very pretty." Stephanie glared at him. "But I think she's too young for you." Stephanie grabbed his arm. "Her braces might hurt your *tongue*."

"Shhh!" Matt said angrily. "I know her."

He pulled free and followed the girl. "Ali? Ali, is that you?"

The girl stopped and turned, a smile growing as she looked at him.

"Matt." She walked toward him. "I recognized your voice right away. What are you doing here?" She opened her arms and hugged him. "It's so good to see you."

"You, too, honey." He paused and backed away. "My God, you're so grown up." And she was. He could see Jesse in her coloring, features—in everything about her. "Is she…" he began.

She anticipated him. "Yes." She nodded. "Come on, I'll take you to her."

"Where are you going?" Stephanie yelled after him.

"To see someone. I'll only be a minute."

They threaded their way through the dizzying maze of trailers, riders, and spectators. Matt asked Ali how she was, what she was doing and of course, about Jesse.

"Why are you here?" she repeated.

He nodded toward Stephanie. "I'm here with a…friend. You're a wonderful rider, by the way."

"Thanks." Ali blushed. She sounded so mature. "I was going to the Olympic trials, but it didn't work out." She shook her head. Matt thought he saw sadness.

"I'm sorry," he sympathized.

"It's okay."

They rounded a corner and Jesse stood with her back to them, talking to another woman. Alexis sneaked up behind her.

"I've got a surprise for you," she whispered in Jesse's ear.

Jesse turned around. When she saw him, her expression changed. Her eyes showed sadness, even regret. They filled with tears.

"Hello," Matt said.

"Hi," she said quietly. Jesse turned toward her friend. "Could you excuse us for a minute, Annabel?" The woman stood, gaping at Matt.

"Aren't you Matthew Sullivan the writer?"

"Yes." Matt nodded.

"I've read *all* your books."

Matt shook her hand. He pulled out a business card, giving it to the woman.

"Send me one. I'd love to sign it."

"*Will do.*" Her eyebrows raised as she nodded at Jesse. "Thanks." She walked away still watching Matt.

"How are you?" he asked Jesse.

"I get by," she said quietly.

Her face was drawn and thin. Dark circles ringed her grand, blue-green eyes and her pale complexion had grown more so.

"Are you sure you're all right?" he asked.

"I think I'll go see how Apollo's Pride is doing," Ali volunteered. She beamed, touching Matt's shoulder as she headed off. "You just *have* to come by and see our farm." She looked back with the eyes she'd inherited from Jesse. "It's awesome. We've got 40 acres, riding trails, our own pond…"

"Sure, honey. I'll get there," he agreed, knowing he never could.

"Great." Ali nodded. "See ya." She waved and was gone.

"What a great girl—so grown up, so beautiful. It must be like looking in the mirror." He wanted to touch her. "You must be so proud of her."

"She has her moments," she said, as Ali disappeared. "Thank you, Matt," Jesse whispered, lowering her eyes.

"For what?"

"For doing what I asked."

"I didn't." He sighed. "But you can rest easy. Whatever your secrets are, they're safe—at least from me."

She lifted her face. For an instant, he saw that soft, special look he could never forget. He wanted to see her smile. She didn't.

"Well," she said, looking away. Her tears overflowed, but she composed herself. "I told you, Matthew. You'll only find heartache. I think you've been hurt enough. We both have." She turned and came close. Touching his arm, Jesse reached up, kissing him softly on the cheek. "Good-bye." She looked behind him as she walked away. "I think someone's looking for you."

He watched her leave, then turned to see Stephanie. He felt a chill as he caught her expression. Matt had never seen such malice. But Stephanie wasn't watching him. Her eyes were following Jesse.

Chapter Fifty-Eight

March 2002

The Academy Awards were their usual mix of fluff, glamour, and hypocrisy. Jesse was nominated for best actress for her role in *Gates of Paradise*. Matt came because Miramax had made *Satan's Twilight* into a movie, and he'd collaborated on the screenplay. Neither walked away a winner.

Like a shy suitor at a high school dance, Matt spotted Jesse at one of the after-parties. She disappeared. He was heading to find her when someone tugged at his sleeve. It was Annabel, Jesse's friend from the riding competition.

"Well, hello," she said. "I hope you got my thank-you for your note. I had it framed." She touched his arm, flashing an expensive smile. "It's the centerpiece of my library." Annabel sounded tipsy.

"I did. It was delightful," he lied. "I'd love to talk, but there's someone I really have to see."

He turned, scanning the room. Still no Jesse.

Matt freed his arm and backed away. The deck, he thought, heading out the nearest door. He emerged onto a large wood and stone structure overlooking the valley. The lights fell away toward the Pacific, offering the perfect backdrop for this gathering of show business elite. Surveying the clusters of guests, he found Jesse at the far end of the deck. She was talking with someone. The woman's back was turned away, but he recognized the gown. It was Stephanie.

Closing the hundred feet between them, Matt got a sinking feeling. He couldn't forget the look on Stephanie's face at the riding competition. She'd always harbored a jealous resentment of Jesse, but since then, whenever Jesse's name was mentioned, Stephanie spewed sarcasm and hostility like a volcano spitting molten lava.

As Matt approached, he watched Jesse. Her face was ashen and taut. Jesse saw him and whispered something to Stephanie, who turned slowly, displaying a broad, drunken grin.

"Well, look who's here, America's latest and greatest literary treasure," Stephanie slurred. Annabel wasn't the only one who'd had too much champagne.

Jesse stood frozen and mute.

"Hi," Matt said, looking at the two women. "Well, this is something I never thought I'd see."

"I was just telling your friend how sorry I was she didn't win." Stephanie smirked. "Her performance was inspired." She paused and faced Jesse. "But then, she has so many talents."

"Yes. Everyone's talking about it. I guess it's because she's not a Hollywood insider—at least that's what I'm hearing." Matt agreed though sure Stephanie's comments were intended as barbs.

He took her by the arm, but she pulled away roughly. "C'mon, Steph, why don't you go inside and get some coffee? I'll be right in."

Stephanie refused to budge, grabbing the thick mahogany railing. She laughed giddily and nodded.

"Why not?" Weaving toward the door, her eyes fixed on Jesse. "Don't be long, Matthew."

"Hi," he said, watching Stephanie zigzag. "Sorry about that." Matt shook his head. "She doesn't mean any harm." Jesse stood, looking the way she had earlier. Not annoyed or angry. Her face wore fear. "What did she say to you?" As long as he'd known Jesse, he'd seen almost every emotion. Never fear.

"Nothing," Jesse whispered, composing herself. "She'd just had too much to drink."

"I know. I'm sorry if she said…"

Jesse shook her head violently, dismissing his comments. She touched his arm. "Please tell me you're not playing detective anymore."

He studied her exquisite face. "Only a fool pursues the impossible. I told you, there was nothing I could—"

"Believe me, Matthew. It's better this way."

Despite the makeup, Jesse looked exhausted. The circles under her eyes had grown and her designer gown hung loosely on her. But she was still the most beautiful woman he'd ever seen. She exhaled deeply, studying the lights in the valley below as the horizon showed pink, hinting at the sunrise.

"Jesse, what is it?" He found her hand as the first pink rays gave color to her cheeks. He found it and their fingers intertwined as she scanned the deck. She spotted something, pulling away quickly.

"Nothing." She shook her head. "I've…I've just been working too hard."

He started to ask about Ali.

"I've got to go. Lawrence will wonder where I am," she said nervously.

"Jesse…" he started to protest, but she turned and

ran into the house.

****

At the hotel, Matt confronted Stephanie. "What did you say to her?"

"Who?" she asked, innocently.

"You know who...*Jesse*." He was sick of Stephanie—her cruelty, her evasiveness. He'd ignored the dark behavior that had come to dominate her life. No more. Not after the look on Jesse's face. Stephanie had said or done something vicious.

"If you must know, I told her she was a stupid bitch to give you up."

He stared at her with contempt. "It's over, Stephanie." He shook his head. *"I've had it!"*

Stephanie shook her head, green eyes flashing. "You see her, you want to dump me. That's always the program, isn't it?" she spit at him. "Well, fuck you, Matt. I'm sick of you, and I'm sick of her. She's been between us—like a ghost I can't exorcise."

"Any chance we had disappeared...long ago."

She slapped him hard across the face. "I'm leaving *you*, Matthew. Now get out so I can pack!" she yelled.

Matt clenched his fists. He raised a hand, but thought better of it, grabbed his key, and headed for the door.

"You'll be sorry—both of you. Sorrier than you can imagine," she continued her outburst as he opened the door. She was grabbing her clothes and heaved them into her suitcase. He heard the drawers slamming as he closed the door. "When I'm done with her, your precious Jesse won't be able to get a job in summer stock in Montana," she yelled as he headed down the hall.

Chapter Fifty-Nine

The next few days dragged by. Stephanie's warning echoing endlessly. What did she know? *How could she possibly hurt Jesse?* Matt asked himself as he met with the Miramax people about another screenplay collaboration.

"You okay, Matt?" his publicist asked.

"Too many parties, I guess."

She nodded but her look held no conviction.

"Where's Stephanie?" she asked as they were leaving.

"She doesn't represent me anymore."

The woman raised her eyebrows. "Okay, Matt, let me know who to contact."

By the weekend, he was back in Boston, worried about what havoc Stephanie might have wrought in his apartment. She had a key and in her state of mind he didn't know what she was capable of.

When he opened the door, he breathed a sigh of relief. Everything looked intact. But Stephanie had been there and taken everything that belonged to her, the glass swans from the bed and breakfast in Vermont, even her Monet prints from the dining room.

He was afraid for Jesse—needed to warn her. But heading for the phone he realized he didn't know her number. It wouldn't be in information, but he had an idea. He searched and dug out the old card for Webb

Productions and called, leaving Lawrence his cell number, adding it was very important they talk. Then he hailed a taxi and headed to see Mario.

Just as the door shut, his cell phone rang.

"Hello, Matt. Did you decide to take me up on that collaboration offer?" Lawrence asked.

"No." Matt hadn't planned what to say. "This is about Jesse."

"I see." Lawrence's tone sounded cautious. "How can I help?"

"Is she all right?" Matt asked.

"What do you mean?"

"Has she been different since the Academy Awards?"

There was a long silence. Lawrence cleared his throat. "Could be. Why?"

"I'm not playing games, Lawrence. I think something happened out there between her and my agent."

"You mean Stephanie Halloran?"

"Stephanie's been acting strangely. I'm worried and need to talk to Jesse."

"I'm not following you."

"I'm afraid Stephanie might do something to hurt her, because Jesse and I used to be…very close."

"Hurt Jesse?" There was a long pause. "You think Stephanie might hurt her? Should I hire someone—a bodyguard?"

Matt sighed. "I don't know. I have no idea what she's capable of, but I think it's more likely Stephanie would do something to hurt Jesse's reputation."

"Look, if you need to talk to her, I understand. But I'm not sure that—"

"If you don't mind, I'd like to talk to her myself."

There was another long silence. Matt heard a sigh. "All right," Lawrence answered coolly. "Here's her cell number."

****

Matt met Mario at Flour, the South End bakery that had become their rendezvous. He told his old friend everything that had happened at the Academy Awards and his conversation with Lawrence. Mario listened quietly.

"I think calling her is a good idea," Mario said, looking at his watch. "Let me know what happens. I have some urgent business to tend to." He excused himself, hurriedly walking away looking lost in thought.

He took a taxi back to his apartment. There was something strange about Mario's behavior. He was so laid-back, so casual. Yet he'd always been so concerned about every detail of Jesse's life. Why the sudden change? Matt was confused.

He wondered what damaging secrets Stephanie could possibly know about Jesse. He'd been searching for years and found nothing.

Matt thought about Mario. Had *he* found out something about her—something that changed his attitude? Was that the reason for his quick, unexplained getaway?

He walked into his apartment. Everything looked the same, but the living room had a distinctive odor. Cigarette smoke. As he went to his desk, he saw a Marlboro crushed on its polished oak finish. The middle drawer was slightly ajar. Inside was an envelope addressed to him in Stephanie's handwriting. His heart pounded as he tore open the envelope.

Matthew,

Have you called her, telling her I'm coming? I'm sure you have. If not, don't worry. She already knows. Go to her and comfort her. She'll need it. I hope you will. You do make such a handsome couple. I've decided to include her lovely daughter in my little game. But relax, take your time. You'll both wait a long time before I keep my promise. Enjoy your summer!

Love and Kisses,

Stephanie

She'd been clever. There was nothing in her note that sounded menacing—unless you knew the source.

He raced through the apartment, checking the bedrooms, the closets, everywhere. She was gone. He ran to the phone. Matt had no choice now. He had to call Jesse. But first, he'd call a locksmith and a security company. He wanted no more surprise visits from Stephanie.

****

Jesse answered on the first ring.

"Hi," he said quietly.

"Hello. Lawrence told me you called. Thanks for worrying about me."

"I found a note from Stephanie threatening you. I don't understand. This is a nightmare."

"It is. But it's not your nightmare. It never has been. I've tried to keep it that way."

"But I feel responsible. What is it, Jess? What's she going to say?"

She sighed. "I'm not sure. She knows things the

tabloids might be interested in. Some bad things happened to me, Matt—things no one knew about." She shook her head. "It doesn't make any difference to me, but they might hurt Ali." Her eyes overflowed onto her cheeks.

"Isn't there something you can do—we can do?" he asked.

"There's nothing," she whispered.

"If I'd known, I—"

"Don't, Matt. You're right. This is a nightmare. I thought I could outrun my past," she said, swallowing a sob. "Some things we just can't escape."

"Jesse, I don't like the sound of that. What do you mean?"

She didn't let him finish.

"Remember what I said in my letter."

"*Jesse...*"

"I love you, Matthew. I always have. I always will." She closed her eyes and her cell phone. All she could do was wait.

Stephanie kept her word. The spring and the early summer passed quietly.

Just when Jesse thought her tormentor had given up, there'd be a cryptic message on her answering machine or cell phone. Stephanie had no intention of giving up.

Jesse talked to her lawyer, the police, and more private detectives. There was nothing they could do. There was nothing in writing, and the phone messages were so vague they sounded meaningless.

To add to the tension, Stephanie had disappeared. Since the week after the Academy Awards, no one had seen her—not Coughlin, not her family, no one.

As July became August, Jesse waited helplessly for the day when Stephanie would let the next shoe drop. By mid-August, the waiting game was having its effect. Jesse wanted it to be over.

PART V

Chapter Sixty

Matt was in a deep sleep. He was exhausted after weeks on the road when the phone rang at six thirty a.m. Suddenly, like someone falling through a trap door, he was about to discover the meaning of Jesse's letter.

"*Matt.*" Hearing the tone in Mario's voice, he knew something had happened.

"Yeah," he managed, trying to wake up.

"Get over here," his friend commanded. "Your search is over."

Matt was there in fifteen minutes. When he knocked, his friend opened the door. His face was pale. Displayed on the kitchen table, were half a dozen tabloids. Jesse and Ali stared back from the front pages.

There were photos of Jesse. She was naked and much younger. The pictures were old and blurred, but there was no doubt about her identity. Next to the pictures of her mother were topless pictures of Ali.

The text varied. The most damning suggested Jesse was an unfit mother who encouraged Ali's promiscuity. They claimed she hosted parties where Ali and her friends engaged in sex while high on drugs.

There were quotes from vague or anonymous sources telling of Jesse's exploits in exquisite detail.

They alluded to sexual liaisons with everyone from her co-stars to her high school music teacher. The papers were careful. Allusion, suggestion, and innuendo were the order of the day. There was no real evidence to support the allegations, but seeing the pictures, Matt was sure no one would care.

There was talk of Ali's birth, suggesting she was the product of a casual one-night stand. The stories alleged that Jesse was at a loss to name Ali's father.

Matt fell into a chair, shaking his head in denial. His eyes were glued to the pictures. *Stop playing detective…you'll only break both our hearts.*

"I never thought it would be this simple." He continued staring. "I thought there would be something deeper, more complex. She was just a—"

Mario grabbed Matt's shoulders, shaking him violently.

"She was nothing of the kind." His words exploded. "I thought you loved her."

Matt recoiled. "I did…I do…"

"So these stories appear, and you believe Jesse was a *whore*." Mario's eyes narrowed. Matt had never seen him this angry.

Mario was right. This wasn't the Jesse he knew. "No, no…of course I don't."

"Here, look at the original," Mario said, handing him a magnifying glass.

Matt stared at him. "Where did you *get* this?" he stammered.

"It's not important," Mario said dismissively. "Look at it."

Looking more closely, Matt caught it right away. Jesse's eyes were closed.

"She was drugged. The man who took that is involved with your friend Stephanie. They've been blackmailing Jesse for years. She paid to protect Ali."

"But," Matt began, trying to grasp everything. "How? Where?"

"Jesse's stepfather did unspeakable things to her. Then she was raped. Her life was a living hell. She was ashamed, afraid you wouldn't understand." Mario turned away.

"She never gave me the chance," Matt said, retreating into denial. "It wouldn't have mattered."

"Really." Mario studied him. "I wonder," he added with a shrug.

Suddenly Matt felt small and very selfish. "Please, I love her so much. I want to help."

"We'll see."

"What about those pictures and the stories?"

"*They mean nothing!* It took a lot of persuasion, but I found people who'd talk." Mario smiled coldly. "After some arm-twisting, one of them gave me this." He handed another photo to Matt.

It was a picture of Jesse naked, lying face down. The word BITCH was carved into her back in ragged letters. "They drugged her, raped her, then did *that* to her. Punishing her because she was beautiful and more talented than they were."

"Oh my God." Matt hung his head, thinking of that Sunday night years before at Castle Island.

"I knew about the blackmail. Stephanie was behind it. Jealousy and hatred are incredible motivators, Matthew. She and the others will pay the price. I swear it. But there's one more thing. She wouldn't tell you, because she was terrified of what you'd think of her."

Mario crossed the room, pulling an envelope from his desk. "In here is everything I've found about her life." He handed it to Matt. "There are some terrible things, Matthew, things you may not want to know. But there's a report from a hospital. It's in an envelope with your name on it.

"Read it. If it's something you can't overlook, there's nothing more to say. But Lawrence Webb isn't well." Mario put his hand on Matt's shoulder. "If something happens to him, I'll be going away. You must look after her and Ali."

"But, who are you really? How did you get all this?" Matt's mind was overloaded. "And why would you be going away?"

"I know you're confused." Mario nodded. "We have a lot to talk about. I've had a debt of honor for sixty years. You can help me repay it."

Matthew stared at the envelope, terrified of what it held.

"I need you to come to my lawyer's office."

"All right. Why?"

"I need you to witness my last will and testament."

****

Lawrence visited the country store when he heard the buzz. People stole furtive glances at him then returned to what they were doing. Everyone knew who he was and who he lived with. When he picked up the tabloids, they were silent. He threw ten dollars on the counter, got into his SUV, and raced back to the farm.

An hour later, Jesse sat in the living room, reading the lies, as tears ran onto the newsprint. She looked at Lawrence, shaking her head. Stephanie's revenge was complete.

Her first concern was Ali. She could fight the accusations, and Lawrence would never leave her. But Ali had to face her friends at the stables, social events, and at Dartmouth, where she'd be a freshman that fall.

She knocked on Ali's door, asking her to come downstairs. Half asleep on this warm Saturday morning, her daughter joined them at the kitchen table. Jesse turned over one of the papers and sat quietly as Ali scanned it. When her daughter looked up, Jesse put her hand on it.

"None of this is true, Alexis," she said, touching her daughter's hand. "I swear I never did any of those things."

Ali stared back and forth between her and Lawrence. Tears formed in her large, blue-green eyes.

"But people will believe you did," Ali whispered. "That's all that matters." She turned over the remaining papers. "That's all they'll care about."

"No, Ali, our real friends won't believe this." Jesse squeezed her hand, only half-believing her words. "When I was a little younger than you, I was drugged and…raped. That's where these pictures came from."

"So who's my real father?" Ali pleaded, trying to make sense of this revelation. "You always told me he was a boy you'd loved in high school. You said he ran away and…"

Jesse looked at Lawrence, then back at her.

"I said that to protect you. I don't know. It was one of the boys…"

"*My father raped you?*" Her words stung and hung in the air. "Didn't the police do a test when they were arrested?"

Her eyes begged Jesse.

"I didn't report it." Jesse turned. "It's complicated. I can't explain what happened." She looked at Lawrence. "If I'd reported them it would have destroyed my chance for a—" Jesse fell silent. There was no way to make her daughter understand that she'd let her assailants go free. Reliving those ugly days Jesse wasn't sure that she understood it now. But accusing Billy Herbert and his rich friends would have detoured her opportunity for a scholarship ending any chance she had to escape her hellish existence.

Ali got up, staring at her mother. It was obvious she couldn't comprehend her mother's words. "I don't understand. " She shook her head violently. "Why not?" she begged, tears running down her cheeks. Jesse sat mute as Ali waited for the answer. When none was forthcoming, she mouthed the word no, then ran to her bedroom and slammed the door. Jesse stood, looking after her.

Lawrence looked at Jesse.

"We've got to call our publicist and put our own spin on this. I'm not judging you, Jesse, but the fact that you never reported it is going to make it very difficult."

The phone rang. They stared at it. The feeding frenzy had begun.

Chapter Sixty-One

By the middle of the week, the Connecticut farm was a fortress. Lawrence hired security to keep the paparazzi at bay. As they'd feared, it was Ali who suffered the most. Her boyfriend said he couldn't see her anymore. By the weekend she'd shut herself away, only sneaking past the hordes of reporters to meet her closest friend.

The publicists for Jesse and Webb Productions issued denials, but without a charge of sexual assault on record they rang false. Jesse's agent called. Several of the scripts she'd been offered had been withdrawn. All she had left was Lawrence's new musical and the sales of her CDs. The show's Boston debut coincided with the opening of the New Opera House.

Lawrence assumed the expenses for the house in Connecticut and the Manhattan Condo where they lived. After her extravagance and years of blackmail, Jesse had little left. But they had always had an independent financial relationship. Despite Lawrence's insistence to help her Jess refused his charity. She'd spent too much of her life living off someone else. Despite his failing health, Lawrence tried to secure a life insurance policy…again Jesse would hear none of it.

As she lay awake tormented, thinking of Ali, she wondered what *he* was thinking. She knew he loved her. She'd always hoped he wanted to solve her mystery, to overcome the obstacles keeping them apart. She wondered if the stories had stifled his enthusiasm. Sometime in the dark, lonely hours she drifted into a fitful sleep.

Just after dawn, Jesse awoke with a sense of foreboding. There was a loud knock on her door. Her housekeeper burst in. "Miss Jesse, Ali was on the phone real early. She had a terrible fight and ran out of her room. She looked kinda crazy—crying and running to the stables. She rode off real fast. I'm worried."

Jesse pushed past her, running down the hall to tell Lawrence. He dressed quickly and summoned their security people. They ran to their SUVs and began searching the farm.

"Lawrence, *you can't go*. Your heart…"

"I have to." He pushed past her, heading toward the lead SUV.

****

Jesse paced nervously on the front porch. Someone approached just before noon. Lawrence jumped out and ran toward her. Seeing no sign of Ali, she ran to meet him. His face told Jesse they'd found her.

"She's on one of the back trails. We've called the State Police, and they're getting a Medivac helicopter. Bob and Leo are there with her. I wanted to tell you in person."

"Take me to her!" Jesse screamed.

"I don't think it would—"

"I said take me to her!"

Lawrence touched his chest. His face wore a pallor. Jesse could see the strain in it. "Are you okay?" She laid her hand on his shoulder. He nodded as they got

305

into the SUV.

"I didn't want you to see her," he said. "She took a bad fall, but I'm sure it's not as bad as it looks."

As the SUV bounced across the rough terrain, a helicopter rumbled overhead. Following it, they came over a rise. Jesse saw her daughter on the ground. Several men surrounded her. Ali lay motionless. Terror shot through Jesse. Rage overcame her at the thought that her daughter might never leave this dusty hillside.

Before the vehicle stopped, Jesse ran to her side. Ali's neck and head were bent backward sharply. She wore no helmet or protective vest and was covered with scrapes and bruises. Pools of dried blood lay in the dirt around her.

Her daughter's beautiful mount, Apollo's Promise, stamped anxiously on a nearby hillside waiting for his mistress to get up and return to the saddle.

"Get him out of here!" Jesse screamed.

"It's not his fault, Jessica." Lawrence took Jesse's arm. "You can't blame him."

"Ms. Long?" The medic looked at her anxiously. Like everyone else he must have seen the photos in the papers.

"Yes," Jesse whispered. "How is she?"

The medic shrugged. "At this point, we can't say, ma'am." He looked back at Ali. "She's had a serious fall."

Jesse broke down. She turned as Lawrence put his arms around her.

"The fact they found her so quickly was a big help," the man said, trying to sound hopeful.

She pushed her face into Lawrence's chest.

"What if she can't walk again?" Jesse whispered.

"We'll airlift her into the city. There's a neurosurgeon on alert. He can answer your questions, but it may be days before they know her condition." The man put his hand on Jesse's arm. "As soon as they know anything, they'll call you...or you could come to the city."

"Yes...yes of course we'll follow you into the city." Jesse looked at the medic and then at Lawrence.

Lawrence seemed to be in pain. His face was covered with sweat..

"Are you all right, sir? You're very pale," the medic asked him.

"I'll be fine." Lawrence nodded. "We've been under a lot of stress this week."

The man headed toward Lawrence, but his partner pulled him toward the helicopter. It took off, hovering momentarily as it threw off a blinding cloud of dust. It disappeared behind the trees, heading southwest. They got into the SUV and headed for the farmhouse. Lawrence put his head back and closed his eyes.

"Are you sure you're all right?" Jesse asked again.

The man was right. He didn't look well.

"Sure. Just tired."

Lawrence closed his eyes for the rough ride back to the farmhouse.

Chapter Sixty-Two

Matt stood in his condo, absently watching the gray clouds and drizzle blanketing Cambridge and the Charles. His thoughts were far away. He recalled Jim Richard's description of Jesse and what John Burke, the retired detective, had found at the Long house. Suddenly, his eyes filled with tears. He thought about the miscarriage. He wanted to erase it from his memory but he couldn't. A child had died. Their child—his child, Matt thought, smashing his hand with his fist.

The phone rang. Matt looked at his watch. He walked to his desk, saw his father's number and pressed Talk.

"Hi, Dad, what's happening?" He sighed. There was silence on the other end. His father cleared his throat.

"You haven't been watching the news?"

"No." Matt picked up the remote and flipped through the stations. He stopped on one with a picture of Jesse.

"For musical superstar Jessica Long, it's been the week from hell," the newsman said.

"What's the latest from the hospital, Jarod?"

"Well, Mike, her daughter's in a coma, having sustained serious injuries in a riding accident. Then a few minutes ago, theatrical

producer Lawrence Webb, Ms. Long's live-in companion of many years suffered an apparent massive coronary. He's in intensive care as well."

"This in addition to the controversial photos and stories that appeared regarding Ms. Long's rise to stardom." The reporter wore a gloomy expression. "Fox 25 News will keep you updated on this story as details become available. Now, turning to the world of sports…"

Matt punched mute.

"Matt?" He heard his father's voice in the background.

"Yeah, I heard." He dropped the remote on the couch, collapsing next to it.

"What are you going to do?"

"What can I do?"

"Couldn't you call her, offer to help?"

"Maybe I will, Dad. Thanks." He paused, knowing exactly who to call and what to do. He hung up the phone.

Mario's phone rang four times.

"I've been expecting your call."

"Things have changed," Matt said.

"Yes. You read that report from the hospital. How do you feel?"

"Hurt, angry, but I still love her more than anything."

"Lawrence isn't going to make it," Mario told him. "He was her rock. She'll need you."

"I know."

"Then we'll proceed with what we talked about?"

Mario asked.

"Yes." Matt felt a lump in his throat. "Then we'll never see you again."

"Never's a long time, Matthew."

"How can I…how can we repay you?"

"Don't thank me yet. We don't know what she may do. Stay ahead of her," his old friend paused, "and Matthew, be kind. She needs it."

"You know I will," he promised his friend. "Mario, how will I know when you've begun?"

"Trust me, you'll know," Mario said. "I'm not going to tell you the details. It's better that way."

Matt was silent for a minute. "You're the best friend either of us ever had," he said quietly. "I love you."

"Thanks, kid. When I heard the news I said a prayer for both of you." Mario hung up the phone.

****

Jesse sat outside intensive care at New York Presbyterian Hospital. The cardiologist had just left, offering his sympathies as he told her they'd done everything possible for Lawrence.

When Jesse explained she wasn't his wife, the doctor asked for his next of kin. Jesse gave him Elizabeth's phone number. She got up and headed to the elevator lobby when her cell phone rang.

"Jesse, this is Liz. I wanted to tell you how sorry I am about what's happened," she paused. "Larry told me everything, and I feel awful. If there's anything I can do, let me know."

"Thanks, Liz. It means a lot."

"You've got so much going on, with Ali and all. How is she, by the way?"

"She's stabilized, but still in a coma. They don't know whether she'll walk again." Jesse's voice shook.

There was a long silence.

"I'm so sorry."

"I know you are, Liz."

"Terry's down there a lot. He'll make the arrangements for the funeral and check with you."

"That would be great. I appreciate it. And Liz, I'm sorry for your loss, too." Jesse paused, trying to hold onto to her emotions. "He-he was very special."

She said good-bye and walked back to watch Ali through the glass partition, relieved that there was one thing she didn't have to worry about. As she stood there watching the electronics attached to her unconscious daughter, it struck Jesse that for the first time in her life she was completely alone.

When the cab left her at the condo she and Lawrence had shared, she walked inside, ignoring the doorman's "Hello." She got on the elevator and headed for the penthouse knowing she had to make changes. She and Lawrence never had any financial arrangements because she was a world-famous star in the prime of her career. How quickly things could change, she thought, remembering her agent telling her about the scripts being withdrawn.

Jesse was about to collapse on the sofa when she spotted the message light flashing. She walked to it and pushed the caller ID button. The message was from Matt. Wanting desperately to hear his voice, she pushed Play:

Hi. I've seen everything in the papers and don't believe any of it. I'm sorry about Lawrence. I know how good he was to you and Ali. Speaking of which, how is she? Please call me. I'll do anything I can to help her or you. Remember, Jessica, things have a way of working out.

Her eyes filled as she listened, wishing there was more. It struck her that Matt had never used her full name before. She played the message three times and pushed the save button. She wanted to call him back, but nothing had changed. Instead, she went to the medicine cabinet, took her drugs and lifted the afghan her mother had knit. She curled into the fetal position on the couch, covering herself as the tears rolled down her cheeks. Jesse played his message again as she fell into a hazy sleep filled with images of a better time.

Chapter Sixty-Three

Matt devoured the papers each day, following the downward spiral of Jesse's life while waiting for a critical piece of information. As Labor Day passed and the college crews trained on the Charles, he grew impatient. He battled frustration, outlining a new novel and thinking of Jesse, alone and desperate at Ali's bedside.

He read about Lawrence's new musical. Its debut would coincide with the opening of the New Opera House. The timing could be perfect if Mario put his plan into action. He threw the paper toward his desk, discouraged by another day without a sign.

He missed his desk and the paper landed on the floor. Picking it up, a small story caught his eye. Somehow he'd missed it.

South End Man Found in Remains of Fiery Crash. Matt was riveted. His stomach did somersaults as he read:

> *Remains of a man identified as Mario Altieri, 79, of 372 West Springfield Street, Boston, were found early yesterday at a fiery crash scene on Rutherford Avenue in Charlestown. While the body was incinerated, neighbors and tenants of Mr. Altieri identified personal items. Altieri was seen leaving his residence by acquaintances.*

Altieri emigrated from Italy in the 1980's and owned an extensive amount of South End real estate.

Matt collapsed on the couch as the walls closed in. It sounded so simple when they'd talked about it, but this wasn't a novel. If they were discovered, the consequences could be devastating. He walked to his desk and opened the drawer, pulling out a picture of Jesse and Ali. They were worth the risk.

****

Jesse sat next to Ali's bed, squeezing her hand, hoping for a sign, anything to tell her that her little girl was all right. She thought of the day she'd brought her daughter home, praying Ali would disappear. She shook her head, catching the attention of a passing nurse.

"Is everything all right, Ms. Long?" she asked. "Any change?"

Like most of the public, the nurses seemed divided. Was Jesse a whore or an innocent victim? This woman seemed to be on her side.

"No, thanks, there's no change," Jesse said. "I was just thinking about a dream I had..." Her words died. The nurse nodded kindly and moved on.

Dream... yes, your great dream, Jessica. Slave, go without, go cold and hungry and end up with what? She swallowed another Valium as images of Matt and Lawrence came and went. *Alone and broke, not knowing if your daughter will ever wake up again. Yes, Jesse, you really planned it well.*

She looked at the clock.

"Shit." She got up and ran to the elevator. She couldn't be late for the meeting with the cast and crew.

It was her first day back, and she was terrified. Ian's in command now, she thought. It's his show. She was dreading the confrontation. They were weeks behind because of her. They had to make up the time if they were going to open on schedule.

****

Chewing her nails, Jesse jumped out of the cab as it slowed in front of the theater. She ran to the stage door, swallowed and closed her eyes as she opened it. The stagehands looked her over, perhaps wondering about what they'd read. The tabloids that printed the original photos continued. Now, even the legitimate press was piling on, reliving every detail of her life. Despite threats from her lawyers nothing stopped the poison.

Sounds came from the stage. She pulled back the curtain. The cast and crew were assembled, facing Ian. He stood, center stage, giving them a speech. Ian liked to pontificate. Her stomach was doing cartwheels, her throat dry. She sighed, pulling back the curtain as she walked onto the stage. She tried to radiate confidence.

Ian stopped in mid-sentence. His words hung in the air as her steps echoed across the quiet stage. She crossed to the back of the group. As they turned toward her, Jesse tried reading their faces. Nothing betrayed their feelings.

Ian had always been jealous of her relationship with Lawrence. Now he pulled the strings. She expected a reprimand as he looked at his watch.

To her surprise, he broke into a grin and motioned for her to join him. "Ladies and gentlemen, I give you the star of *The Ides of March,* the finest performer I've ever worked with, Jessica Long."

Had she taken too many pills? He continued to

motion, applauding as he did. As she walked toward him the applause grew. Smiles of friendship and support appeared on the faces of the cast and crew.

As she got to him, he put his arm around her. He squeezed her tightly, a little too tightly, but she let him. He pulled away and stepped forward. Tears rolled down her cheeks.

"Thank you so much," she managed. "You don't know what this means."

Ian stepped forward, clutching her again. "Jessica, we know what you've been through. The press smearing you with falsehoods, the death of your partner, our beloved producer, and the terrible accident to your lovely daughter."

He was giving a good speech, she thought. Too good. She knew Ian. He wanted something. Then, as she turned, she saw it in his eyes. Jesse was sickened, because suddenly she knew what it was.

Chapter Sixty-Four

Matt was impatient to begin his role. He attended Mario's funeral, playing the grief-stricken friend. He noticed an attractive older woman he'd seen before, and several men who seemed evidence of what Mario had called "his former life."

He was leaving his condo when a loud knock came on the door. Matt peered through the peephole. Two husky men in business suits stood inches from the door. He froze. Matt had seen the men at Mario's funeral.

"Can I help you, gentlemen?" he asked through the door.

"Mr. Sullivan?" one of them asked. "Mr. Matthew Sullivan?"

"Yes. How did you get in?"

"Your doorman let us in when we showed him this." Matt felt a mixture of emotions as the man produced a badge at the peephole. When he'd thought they were mobsters he was frightened. He was still frightened, but for a different reason.

"I'm Detective Sergeant Henry Campbell of the State Police Criminal Investigation Division. May we come in?"

"Sure." Matt fumbled with the chain as he opened the door.

The other officer introduced himself as Matt directed them to his living room. They looked out the window, smiling at the view it offered of the Charles River and Cambridge.

"You're a writer, Mr. Sullivan?" Detective Campbell asked, adding, "You write those historical novels?"

"That's me," Matt said, hiding his concern.

"See, Bud, I told you." He turned, smiling at Matt. "You do a lot for the community."

"Thanks." Matt was wary. He fixed the detective with a stare. "Why are you standing in my living room?"

The man's smile evaporated. "We're from the Organized Crime Task Force." He threw his card on the coffee table. "We'd like to talk to you about Mario Altieri."

Matt held his composure. He'd done nothing wrong. But looking at the detectives, the words "conspiracy" and "fraud" came to mind. "Should I call my lawyer?"

"Your choice, Mr. Sullivan, but we're just here to ask some routine questions concerning your friend's...death."

Matt considered his options. Calling his lawyer might arouse suspicion. He took a chance. "All right. How can I help you?"

They told him things he already knew. Mario came to the US in the 1980's, had been a powerful crime figure in Sicily and was seen associating with known members of the mafia in Boston and other cities.

"That's amazing." Matt tried not to overact.

"You two became friends back in the late 80's." It wasn't a question.

Matt nodded. "We had a mutual friend. A young

woman who lived—"

"We're aware of his longtime interest in Ms. Long."

Matt swallowed hard. His stomach was churning.

"Look, Mr. Sullivan," the detective said. "We've followed Mr. Altieri for years and seen you two together. But it doesn't figure. We assumed he fooled you." The detective looked at his partner. "We'd like to know if you can think of any reason why he'd fake his own death."

"What?" Matt felt perspiration forming. "Why would he do that?"

"A few days before he disappeared, he made a large withdrawal from his investment accounts. We're sent that information automatically. We wondered if he was going to disappear—to take off—so when this accident happened, we were suspicious."

"Why would he do that?" Matt asked. "Has he done something illegal?"

"We can't prove it," Detective Campbell stood and walked to the bookcase. "He made a fortune in real estate and investments." He seemed to be studying the photos, fingering the frames. "He's shrewd. Had a lot of contacts with shady characters, but we can't prove he's broken any laws since he's been here."

"So you came here"—Matt tried to look insulted— "hoping he may have told me something." He shook his head. "I'm sorry. I can't help you."

His indignation was working. The detectives looked at each other. The second detective stood. Matt joined him.

"I've never written a mystery, but I read you found partial remains. What about the forensic evidence?

Couldn't you identify him from that?"

Detective Campbell stopped. He turned, looking at Matt a little too closely. "Funny you should ask, because that puzzled us. There *are* no forensics. Just some dental work, jewelry and lots of witnesses—too many—who'll swear they saw him driving the Town Car too fast. His apartment was so clean you'd think a team from NASA had sterilized the place. Not even a hair in the drain. Believe me, we looked. Outside of the dental stuff, there was no record of any medical work, blood tests, anything. Nothing we could use for comparison."

"That is strange." Matt shook his head as he motioned toward the door. "If you're through, I have an appointment to keep."

The detective was studying Matt. "I guess we'll have to close the file." He nodded. "We took a chance he might have said something...suspicious. It was a long shot." As he was leaving, Detective Campbell turned toward Matt. "You know, Mr. Sullivan, you ought to try a mystery. You seem to know the procedures pretty well."

"Good-bye, gentlemen." Matt showed them to the door.

Detective Campbell nodded. "Good luck. Oh, if you ever want to try that mystery, give me a call."

"Will do." Matt shut the door and sighed. He sat, holding his head in his hands. There were still times when he wanted a drink. This was one of them. He looked at his watch. He was late. He left the building, hailed a cab and headed for Federal Street. He'd never been an executor before. He had to find out what it meant.

Two hours later he was back in his apartment. He read the instructions Mario's lawyer had given him. They were detailed and very unusual. It was his job to contact Mario's beneficiary. He had to hand-deliver a letter. He was to call Mario's investment banker on the tenth of October to get an estimate of his estate. In the envelope containing the instructions was a smaller one. Inside it was a ticket for the October eleventh performance of *The Ides of March*.

Chapter Sixty-Five

Jesse sat in her dressing room. She hung up her cell phone, relieved. Ali would walk again. This was her second piece of good news. Two days before Ali had awoken from her month-long coma. She was confused but in surprisingly good condition. She had no memory of the accident.

There was a light tap on her door. Ian walked in, a smirk on his narrow face. As he came up behind her, Jesse stiffened. He put his hands on her shoulders, squeezing them gently. She saw his smile in the mirror.

"You missed another cue, my dear." He looked around the room, continuing to caress her shoulders. "That's not like you."

"I know, Ian. I'm sorry." She forced a smile. This show was all she had left. For Ali's sake she had to put up with this vile man until she could find something else. "I just have so much on my mind."

"You have nothing to fear from me." He kissed the top of her head. "All I want is to help. And of course, in turn, I hope we can be...*friends*."

"I'd like that very much." She led him on. "It's just that this is such a difficult time. Be patient until after the show opens." She smiled weakly at him in the mirror and touched his hand. "Give me until then."

He released her, giving her arm one last squeeze as he left.

"I understand. Until we open in Boston." He opened the door. "And don't forget those cues."

He grinned and left.

Jesse thought she might be sick. She reached for the Valium and another Percocet, put her hand over her mouth and swallowed, waiting for the mellow feeling to take hold.

****

Jesse spent the evening with Ali. It was almost eleven when the taxi left her at her building. She nodded at the night doorman as she walked to the elevator, dreading the next morning when the whole painful routine would begin again.

She turned the key and entered the living room, throwing the mail on the couch as she reached for the pills in her purse. On the ride home, Jesse realized she could never get close to Ian, no matter what the stakes. Somehow, somewhere, there had to be another answer.

She swallowed another pill, looking at the mail, one of which was an envelope from an insurance company. She remembered the policy Lawrence had taken out a few years ago. It was on her life for ten million dollars.

She paced nervously. Perhaps it was desperation or the drugs. An idea took shape. The more she thought about it, the more it made sense. It was her only way out. At least Ali would have something. There was only one thing left to decide. She thought about Ali's comment on her thirteenth birthday: *I know who you love. I still love him too.*

Jesse studied her pale, drawn reflection in the mirror. With grim sense of purpose she walked to her desk, pulling out a piece of stationery. She wrote, stopping to blot the paper that grew moist from her tears. She'd take the letter to Boston and mail it to him when she was ready. What better place to end her story than where it began.

Chapter Sixty-Six

October 11—Boston's New Opera House

Before the applause died, Matt was up, fighting his way through the crowd. He was worried. He'd come to give her a letter, but after watching Jesse on stage, Matt had a more urgent mission—to make sure she was all right. He saw the vacant look in her eyes, heard the strain in her voice. But if her singing lacked its old strength and beauty, she'd lost none of her ability to connect with an audience. After only a few measures, they stared, hypnotized.

"Aren't you Matt Sullivan?" someone asked as he pressed forward. Matt nodded but refused to stop. He inched along impatiently, finally pushing his way through the crowd. As he climbed the stairs that led backstage, a young security guard put his hand on Matt's chest.

"Sorry, no one's admitted backstage without a pass. Do you have one?" he asked.

"No." Matt was prepared. "But I have this." He handed the man his business card wrapped in a one hundred dollar bill. The young man started to object, but as he studied the card he dropped his hand.

"I'm sorry, Mr. Sullivan." He shook his head. "I didn't recognize you."

"Thanks, Ben," Matt said, reading the man's

nametag.

"And here, sir, you don't need to do this." He pushed the bill toward Matt. "I met you once at a book signing. I was with my girl."

Matt was impatient. He needed to see Jesse.

The guard moved aside. "I'm sorry, Mr. Sullivan, you want to get backstage." Ben pushed the bill again.

"Thanks." Matt nodded, putting his hand on the young man's arm. "Call the number on that card. I'll drop by and autograph the book." Matt rushed off. "And Ben, you keep that bill. Spend it on your girl." When he reached the stage, Matt turned. "Do you love her? *Really* love her?"

Ben nodded.

"Be smart." Matt headed backstage. "Don't ever let her get away."

****

Jesse rushed offstage and changed, leaving her costume on the floor. She ran out the door—right into Ian.

"I was looking for you." He scowled. Jesse knew he was losing his patience.

"That's good, because I was looking for you."

He forced a smile. Jesse wasn't buying it. "We just can't have these lapses on stage, Jessica. Now I know you've been through a lot, but…"

"You're right, Ian." She pushed past him. "We can't. I'll fix that." For the first time in years, she felt completely free.

He continued to stare, waiting. "Well…"

"I quit. Use my understudy. She's a great kid with amazing talent." She looked behind her and ran toward the door. She thought Matt was coming backstage. She had to get away. Seeing him in the audience, Jesse knew she had to finish it tonight. Ian was chasing her, but she stopped at the door and gave her letter to the guard.

"There'll be a man looking for me, Mike." She turned. Ian had almost caught up. "His name is Matt Sullivan. He's tall with black hair and very handsome. Give this to him."

"What if he doesn't show up, Ms. Long?"

"Then drop it in the mail." She smiled. "Thanks."

"You can't quit! You're under contract. *We'll sue you!*" yelled a red faced Ian, approaching.

Go ahead, she thought, in five hours it won't matter. The life insurance policy wasn't a great legacy for Ali, but it was something. Jesse opened the stage door. With the cast and crew watching, she stuck up her middle finger, pointing it in Ian's direction. For a second there was silence. Then, the entire backstage erupted in laughter and applause.

****

Matt weaved through the confusion, asking where the dressing rooms were. He followed the directions, spotted a row of doors and found hers. He knocked. When no one answered, he started to open it.

"That bitch is gone," said a small, well-dressed man with a salt and pepper goatee as he approached. "She just quit."

Matt studied him in disbelief.

"Jesse *quit. She left*?"

The man nodded.

Dammit.

Matt pushed past the man, then turned, returning to where he stood.

"Did you call Jesse a bitch?"

The man nodded again.

Matt pulled back his right arm and punched the man in the face, sending him crashing through the door and into the empty dressing room.

Matt ran to the stage door.

"You're Matt Sullivan?" the man at the door asked.

"Yeah, why?"

"I got somethin' here for you—from Ms. Long."

"Thanks."

Matt went outside. Under the light he tore open her letter and read it. The blood left his face. He cursed as he stuffed it into his pocket. Think, Matthew, think. Where would she go?

He wasn't sure, but he had an idea. It might be his only chance—and hers. Mario had told him to stay ahead of her, but if he guessed wrong…? He had to find her and tell her how much he still loved her—before she destroyed herself.

Chapter Sixty-Seven

It was almost four a.m. when her rented Ford Taurus reached the outskirts of Portland. Rain battered the street, running in small streams down the hill and past her old house. When its dark hulk loomed ahead, Jesse stopped at the gate.

Patting her pocket, Jesse felt the pills. She took a flashlight from the glove compartment. Standing in the rain she thought of all the sad, painful memories this house held hidden. It was a fitting place to end her story. Ignoring the downpour, Jesse climbed the stairs, crossing the small porch and pushing open the old door that hung by a lonely hinge.

Inside, gloom pervaded every corner. It was damp, stinking of mold and mildew. Broken furniture littered the floor. Through the shadows she could just see the old fireplace standing guard over the living room.

Jesse shivered, walking slowly to the landing where it had happened twenty-five years ago. She tried to remember. She needed closure. As she approached the rickety stairway, the rain pounded like Alton's boots on the stairs. Suddenly, it all came flooding back…

Alton pulled Ryan into the hallway and came back to be with her. She lay on her bed in the fetal position.

"Please…don't hurt me again."

"I don't want to hurt you, I just want to..."

Her mother burst in, lunging at Alton with a pair of shears. He dodged, pushing her aside. She fell on the floor, crying out as she did. Alton grabbed Alice by the hair. Her sleeve was bright red. She'd fallen on the shears.

"You son of a bitch," Alice hissed at Alton as he pushed her into the hallway.

He turned toward Jesse again.

"If you go near my sister, I'll call the cops!" Ryan yelled, appearing in the doorway. Jesse looked up. Alton turned toward her brother.

"Your phone's been turned off for weeks." He grunted, shaking his head.

"I'll...I'll go next door to the O'Keefe's and use their phone," Ryan yelled. "I'll tell them what you're doing. Mr. O'Keefe's brother's a cop." Jesse had no idea if he was telling the truth. If it was a bluff, it worked. Alton headed toward the door.

Ryan backed out and raced for the stairway. Alton lunged for him but missed. He must have caught Ryan at the top of the stairs. She heard a struggle. There was a muffled cry, followed by the sound of someone falling down the stairs. Jesse jumped to her feet. She stumbled over Ryan's bat. Picking it up, she ran to the door. Alton was dragging her mother toward the stairs. Alice gasped, seeing Ryan's body lying still on the landing below.

Jesse summoned all her strength and drew the bat back. The stink of Alton's sweat made her gag. His sour breath came in gasps. Her mother was kicking and shouting. Jesse swung the bat. It hit Alton on the neck. He staggered and fell on her mother, stunned. He turned and looked up just as Jesse raised the bat again.

Jesse brought it down once, twice, three times. Bones cracked.

"Jesse...Jesse..." Her mother yanked herself free. She slid the bat from Jesse's hands and hugged her so tightly Jesse couldn't breathe. Jesse felt salty tears on her lips...

"Shhh," Alice comforted her. She gently guided Jesse to her room and laid her on the bed. Her mother ran down the stairs. "No, God... no, please," she cried.

Jesse got off the bed and went to the door to see her mother rocking Ryan's body. She kissed him and whispered something. Jesse couldn't hear, but thought she was telling him she was sorry, because that's what she did when she came back.

"Jesse, we can't tell anyone what happened tonight."

"I understand, Momma," Jesse said, not sure she did.

Jesse watched as her mother struggled, dragging Alton to the top of the stairs and shoved him down. She took the bat, wiped it clean, then put Ryan's hands around it.

"When they ask what happened, tell them Ryan tried to protect us and fell down the stairs with Alton. Okay, honey?" Her mother stroked Jesse's hair. "Oh, Jesse, I'm so sorry."

When she backed away, Jesse realized there was blood on her dress.

"Momma, you're still bleeding."

Her mother squeezed her tightly again and kissed Jesse's hair.

"I'll be all right..."

The rain continued assaulting the metal roof as it

had on that other night. Jesse stared at the landing, feeling the tears on her cheeks. She'd always known the truth. It had been a reflection in an old mirror, too faded and blackened to recognize. Jesse reached into her pocket. Fingering the bottle, she retrieved it. She opened the cap. There was only one thing left to do...

Chapter Sixty-Eight

"Is that where it happened?"

Jesse jumped. As she turned, Matt moved out of the shadows. "Where Alton and Ryan died?"

She reached up, brushing the tears from her eyes as she stuffed the pills back in her pocket. "Matt, what are you doing here? How do you know about Ryan and Alton?"

"I spoke to a Detective Sergeant O'Keefe in Florida."

He came closer. She moved back, tripping on the debris. He steadied her, releasing her when she regained her footing.

"I remember him." She glimpsed the memory. "He was kind."

She fidgeted, trying to compose herself.

"He said there was something strange about the case." Matt craned his neck, looking up the stairs. "The position of the bodies, the bat, the lack of fingerprints." He smiled softly. "But he talked to the neighbors. They told him what they'd heard." He looked around. "The police decided you'd been through enough. He knew your brother didn't kill Eads," he paused. "He thought your mother did it."

Jesse just stared back. "Is that why you came all this way—to gloat? To tell me you've finally discovered one of my secrets."

She held him with her eyes.

"No." He reached into his pocket and pulled out an envelope. "I came to deliver this. You know. I'm a pretty good investigator. You didn't ask me who I thought killed Alton."

"Why should I care what you think? If you have some business, can we get it over with?"

"All right." Matt nodded. "I was sorry to hear about Lawrence. I know how much he meant to you."

"He was wonderful."

"How's Ali?" he asked.

Jesse fought back the tears. "She'll be okay. But it'll be a while before she walks again."

"I'm sorry, Jesse. You know I always loved her. What caused the accident?"

"She was so upset about the stories in the papers. They were all lies." She looked at the floor. "Except for the part about how she was conceived. I was raped."

"I know."

"How could you?"

"The pompous ass at the theater said you quit," he said, dodging her question. "What are you going to do now?"

She sighed, staring at the crumbling ceiling.

"I don't know. I've got no money. I was blackmailed for years and with Ali's medical bills..." She paused. "Why?"

"I came to make sure you're all right and to give you this." He pushed the envelope toward her. "Maybe it will help."

She took it from him, opening it, as she used her flashlight. It was a letter from Mario's lawyer. "My God. It says I'm to receive most of his estate." She looked at Matt. "I don't understand. I didn't know he was sick."

"He wasn't. He died in an auto accident."

Jesse searched his eyes. He was holding something back. Jesse pulled her damp coat around her, wishing Matt would close the gap between them and surround her in his arms.

"Could we sit down?" He motioned to the stairs.

Jesse nodded. He found a rickety chair. She sat on the third step, facing him.

"I hope he didn't suffer."

"He didn't," Matt said with a strange expression. "Do you remember asking me about him?" he continued. "Why he was always around and knew where you were and what you'd been doing?"

Of course she did. It was on the most wonderful night of her life, the night they'd made love.

"Yes," she whispered.

"You were right. Mario wasn't the kindly old landlord he appeared. And he was never in the army."

"But he was so convincing, especially the part about my grandfather saving his life."

"That's because it was true. He was never a soldier—at least not the way we think of, but your grandfather did save his life. He was a mafia chieftain and partisan in Sicily. He fought for the resistance." Matt nodded. "He'd been captured and was going to be hanged. Your grandfather arrived just in time to save him."

Jesse tried to process what he was telling her.

"He and your grandfather fought together and became great friends. All the rest was fabrication. When things got dangerous for him in Italy, he came here. He looked your grandfather up, found out he was dead and that you were very poor. He wanted to help, but he had to keep a low profile. He even pulled the strings to arrange the sale of your home on Fuller Street. There was no urban renewal project. He did it so you could live and go to NEC. Then he went to Boston, because he had friends there. But he followed your life and knew you were coming…"

"But how did my mother get his address?" she interrupted.

Matt smiled.

"He kept tabs on your family. He heard your mother and Ali were moving, so he called, offering to help the family of an old army buddy."

She felt herself smiling. "Incredible."

"He wanted you to call him. When you did he was thrilled. He could finally repay his debt of honor. It was the most important thing in his life."

"So those men that I used to see all the time…"

"Worked for Mario. None of you could go anywhere without your own personal shadow. When you moved to New York, he had friends there, but it was harder. Besides, soon you had another guardian angel, and from all reports, he did a fine job."

She shook her head. "Did you know any of this? I mean how did you…" Her words trailed off.

"No. I knew there was more to him than met the eye. I spent time with him, and we became friends." His smile softened. "You're cold? I'll get the blanket from my car."

"I'm okay. But why did you two spend so much time together? I know you came to my mother's funeral with him, but what did you have in common?"

His eyes showed anger. "My God, are you blind?" He shook his head. "What do think we had in common? *You*, the thing that kept us together was you!" He got up, pushed the chair across the room. "The same reason I drove five hours hoping you'd be all right when I got here. I…." He turned away.

She'd wanted to hear that so badly. She got up, heading toward him. Matt turned, finding her eyes in the dim light. They moved to each other, slowly at first, closing the distance at a run. Jesse fell into his arms and they embraced. His lips were on her face, kissing her eyes and cheeks. As she looked up at him, tasting his lips on hers, thinking of how often she'd dreamt of this moment. Nothing in her life had ever felt so wonderful.

"Oh, Jesse," he whispered, drawing his lips away. She clung to him, feeling safe and warm.

"I've been such a fool." She squeezed him, finding it incredible that she'd doubted him and pushed him away.

"We're together now." He caressed her back.

"But Matt." She pulled away. "I've hurt so many people." The tears ran down her cheeks. "You don't know."

"You mean killing Alton?"

"But how did you…?"

"I watched you relive it from outside. You hit him three times."

She tasted salty tears on her lips. Matt approached her.

"I know all there is to know about you. None of it makes any difference." He held out his hands. She took them in hers. "Do you think I've led a perfect life? I was a drunk for years."

"Because I left you behind."

"No. Because I was a spoiled little boy afraid he'd get hurt again. I turned my back on the most wonderful woman I'd ever known."

"There's something else," she began. "Something you couldn't know."

He approached her, smiling softly. "You mean about our baby?"

Jesse sobbed violently. "Oh God! If I could trade places with that baby."

He put his hands on her shoulders. "Isn't that why you came here tonight?"

"Yes," she whispered as she sniffled. "I thought Ali could have the money from my insurance and…"

"I need you. So does Ali. I don't want to live without you for a moment longer."

"I called you, but I was lonely and sick." She sobbed.

"Shhh," he said, touching her lips. "Thirty-four isn't all *that* old. We can try again."

She looked up.

He smiled softly.

"Are you asking what I think you are?"

"I've loved you from the moment I saw you. My father once told me I had a special destiny. My destiny is simple—loving you."

"I love you too, Matt. More than you'll ever know."

"There's a lot more to tell about the letter I brought and what it means. You're a very wealthy young woman. But we have all the time in the world." He took her in his arms again, stroking her hair. "All the time in the world."

He kissed her softly.

Matt pulled her closer, but Jesse heard something on the porch. She backed away. As she looked at Matt, he turned toward the front door. He'd heard it, too.

The door flew open. Falling off its lone hinge, it crashed to the floor. The damp gray dawn framed a small figure in the doorway. She stepped into the room, shining a powerful light at each of them. Jesse put a hand into her pocket, searching for her flashlight.

"No sudden moves," warned the intruder. "I want your hands where I can see them." The large light tilted slightly, giving them a glimpse of a large, chrome-plated revolver.

The hairs on Jesse's arms came to attention as the woman spoke. She turned toward Matt, seeing the recognition in his face. Jesse had only heard that soft, deliberate voice once, but it was one she could never forget. The person holding the revolver was Stephanie Halloran.

Chapter Sixty-Nine

"This is such a beautiful moment." Stephanie laughed, shining the flashlight on them. "I wish I had my camera. I've been watching from outside, but its getting cold. I hope you don't mind the intrusion."

Matt turned. "Where did you come from?"

He started to approach her, but she waved the revolver.

"Lovely place you have here, Jess. I can see why you'd want to come back to visit."

Matt inched closer.

"*Don't*," Stephanie commanded. "I loved you, Matthew, but—"

"What do you want?" he asked.

"You, of course." She sighed. "I thought I'd taken care of your friend, but it looks like love has triumphed after all." She shined the flashlight in Jesse's face again. "What's the matter? You don't look so good, Jessica. Having a bad day?"

Jesse stepped toward her.

Matt grabbed her arm. "Don't. *She's crazy,*" he whispered.

Stephanie waved her gun toward Jesse. "You do anything, and I'll do *you* right here."

Matt looked around for a diversion.

"This is perfect," Stephanie continued. "A lover's quarrel, a murder suicide. It'll make a great finale to your career, Jess. I may write this story myself." She grinned at Matt. "Of course, that sweet daughter of yours will end up a *tramp* like her mother. Insurance companies don't pay off on suicides. Apparently that little tidbit escaped you."

"Why are you doing this?" Jesse asked.

"I hate to lose," Stephanie spit at her. "Especially to a lounge singer from the wrong side of the tracks.

"Damn you." Jesse clenched her fists.

"Yes, too bad about your daughter," Stephanie pointed the shiny weapon at Jesse. "I'm sure she'll—" She stopped in mid-sentence.

Matt cocked his head. He heard something—footsteps on the porch. He shot a look at Jesse. She nodded.

"Put the gun down, miss," a deep voice yelled. More footsteps creaked on the old wood.

Stephanie glanced over her shoulder but made no attempt to lower her gun. "I don't think so," she said through clenched teeth. "I want to see Jesse's face when I kill you, Matthew."

"Lower your weapon or we'll shoot," the voice commanded again.

A smile crossed Stephanie's face. Her finger tightened around the trigger as two blinding flashes exploded. Jesse threw herself in front of Matt. She screamed. Bullets ripped into her chest as gunshots came from outside. Matt grabbed Jesse. Laying her down gently, he put his raincoat under her head. He shot a look at Stephanie. A trickle of blood ran from her mouth. Her hand fell as her weapon crashed to the floor. Her knees buckled; she collapsed facedown.

He heard talking, Two men, weapons poised,

entered the old house. As the early dawn filled the room Matt recognized the detectives from the Organized Crime Task Force. Half a dozen uniformed officers followed.

Jesse moaned. Blood soaked her raincoat. Her eyes searched for him. "Matt," she whispered, fingers tightening around his arm. "Are you okay?" She coughed deeply, blood trickling from her mouth. "Oh, God. It hurts, Matt…Matt, please. Are you there?" she asked hoarsely, coughing again.

"Of course I am, Jess. I'll never leave you—ever again." Tears filled his eyes. "You stay still. Everything's gonna be fine." Had he found her only to lose her? "Why did you do that?"

"You." She strained, pulling herself up. "Had to-to save you." She coughed, blood dripping from her cheek.

Detective Campbell appeared, hovering above them. Jesse was shaking. He pulled off his raincoat to cover her. "The EMTs are almost here." Campbell squeezed Matt's shoulder.

"Jesse, you're a fighter. You cannot leave me. Not after everything we've been through." Matt looked up. *"Please!"*

When he looked back, her eyes were closed. Detective Campbell searched for a pulse. "She's alive, but she's lost a lot of blood. Don't worry." He grabbed Matt's arm. "They'll be here any second." As if on cue, sirens wailed and lights flashed in the pink dawn.

In seconds, emergency lanterns and gurneys flooded the room as medical people swarmed in. One of them pronounced Stephanie dead, covering her with a blanket as the others rushed to Jesse. Two men expertly lifted her onto a stretcher, checking her vital signs as they did.

Campbell flashed his badge.

"How is she?" Matt asked.

The EMT shook his head. "Alive, but we have to hurry."

Matt looked at the detective.

"Go with her." He nodded. "I'm not sure what happened here, but we'll catch up with you later." He handed Matt a business card. "I hope she's all right. Call me so we can sort this out," adding, "I'm so sorry."

Chapter Seventy

Late October 2002

Once again Matt stood watching the crews training on the Charles River. But on this late October morning he stood in the intensive care ward

The room Jesse occupied was new but cramped, made worse by the array of tubes, monitors, and other electronics. He turned toward the two doctors speaking quietly while they studied the LED displays and her chart.

"Any change?" Matt asked.

"She's stable, Mr. Sullivan," the older man said.

The younger wore a reserved expression. "Ms. Long's lucky to be alive." He walked to Matt's side. "She was abusing pain-killers and tranquillizers and close to complete exhaustion."

Matt looked toward Ali, who sat holding her mother's hand. He took the younger surgeon's arm and guided him toward the door. "I don't want her to hear this."

They went into the hallway. "We've done everything we can, Mr. Sullivan. All we can do now is wait and hope her will to live is strong."

"I understand, Doctor. I won't ask for promises you can't keep."

They shook hands.

"We'll see you tomorrow." The older man nodded at Matt. "If there's any change we'll be notified at once."

Matt took a deep breath and opened the door.

"She looks better, today, don't you think, Matt?" Ali asked, looking up hopefully.

"Definitely much better." He touched her hair softly. "C'mon, I'll buy you lunch. I saw mac and cheese on the menu."

In her three weeks at Mass General, Ali had only missed one night with Jesse. She'd quickly become a favorite of the attending staff. Ali not only possessed her mother's beauty, but a warmth and infectious charm that attracted people.

"Why don't you go? I'll sit here for a while." She looked at Jesse. "Can you bring me something?"

"Absolutely not," Matt said with mock concern. "When she wakes up, I don't want her seeing some scrawny kid. She'll blame me!" He took her arms, gently lifting her up and into the wheelchair she used.

"All right." She shook her head and squeezed Jesse's hand. Matt wheeled her out. "I hope Mom wakes up soon. You're too tough for me, *Dad,*" she said, giving him a scowl that melted into a grin.

****

During her time in the hospital, the media subjected Jesse to the same intense scrutiny that had dogged her since late summer. But the tide had turned. Having risked her life to save Matt, she was a hero.

The truth about Stephanie and Jesse's role as her victim emerged. The media that had crucified her became her champion. Stories appeared about her life, her meteoric rise to stardom and her influence on music. Sales of her CDs skyrocketed; new scripts arrived at her agent's doorstep, and publishers begged for her biography, guaranteeing advances worth millions.

Matt spoke to Detective Campbell.

"I lied," the detective admitted. "We followed you, hoping you'd lead us to Mario." When Matt chased Jesse that Tuesday evening, they chased him—all the way to Maine. Their quarry never materialized, but their presence saved Matt's life.

Boston PD located Stephanie's Back Bay hideout. It contained addresses, photos, and notes that led to Billy Herbert. Weak and ashamed, he confessed his complicity in the extortion scheme, claiming to be a victim himself. He broke down under questioning, admitting to Jesse's sexual assault.

Perhaps the strangest event surrounding the incidents in Maine occurred when Billy and the two high school friends who'd assaulted Jesse disappeared. The statute of limitations had expired, and none were named publicly until *after* their puzzling disappearance. No one could understand it—except Matt. He knew who to thank for this overdue application of justice.

The tragedy of these revelations was that Jesse would never hear them. The two bullets from the .40 caliber Smith and Wesson had done too much damage.

Like Ali, Matt remained devoted, refusing to leave Jesse's side. On the final night, Alexis passed her time curled up in a recliner near her mother's bed. Matt had been dozing restlessly, awakening in time to see Jesse open her eyes. She smiled sweetly and mouthed the words, "I love you." He looked down. Her hand, which had gripped his so tightly, went limp. When he looked up again, her eyes were closed. Jessica Alice Long died peacefully in the company of those who loved her, just after midnight on November second, three months before her thirty-fifth birthday.

Epilogue

The cemetery was a dozen miles north of Portland—the same place they'd buried Alice nine years earlier. Matt searched the white-flecked Atlantic for answers. Finding none, he turned and walked back toward Ali. She brushed tears from her face and reached for his hand, her long delicate fingers surrounding his. They watched the hearse threading its way through the cemetery.

"This is where she'd want to be"—he touched Ali's hair—"near the ocean, next to your grandmother."

"I know, Matt." Ali had borne her mother's death so well. Matt nodded at the Lincoln Town Car parked anonymously under a grove of distant oaks, wondering what his old friend must be thinking. Seeing the group gathering, he turned Ali's wheelchair and headed toward them.

A massive security team surrounded the gravesite. Matt had vowed that the final act of Jesse's life would be a private one. The parasites that helped destroy her would never benefit from her death.

The weather had been mild for November, but a cold wind blew in off the Atlantic. As they reached the graveside, Matt bent to tuck the blanket around Ali.

"I'm fine," she scolded, pushing his hand away. "I'm almost nineteen. I can take care of myself."

"You're right." He knelt, finding the large blue-green eyes that mirrored her mother's.

They were all there: Liz and Terry; John Van Zandt; Jim Richards, supported by a cane; members of her theater company; Allen and Jeanne; his father and…Donna? She stood, staring at the casket. He thought about that perfect afternoon when she and Jesse had met.

After the blessing, Ali gave the eulogy. Matt held her hand, amazed at her composure. Listening, it struck him that she and Jesse had been more like sisters. Their journey had been a long and difficult one. They shared it, making the difficult and often painful passage with no compass to guide them.

The service ended, and the tiny crowd began to leave. As his family approached, Matt saw Donna walking away. "Would you excuse me for a minute? There's someone I have to see."

"Sure, Matt," Allen said, drying his eyes. "She insisted on coming. We didn't think you'd mind."

"I don't." He ran after her. "Donna! Please wait."

She stopped, facing away from him. "It's been a long time." He took her arm. "Thank you for coming."

She turned, tears falling onto her woolen coat. "I hope you're not angry." She looked away. "I wanted to come…Had to."

"I'm not. It was kind of you."

"Thanks," she managed. "I'm not here out of kindness. I wanted to tell you something, but I lost my nerve."

"It's all right. I understand. I heard you got married."

Donna looked down, wiping the tears away. "We're not together anymore, Matt."

"Sorry. The neighborhood grapevine missed that one."

"They couldn't have known. We did it quietly—no fault." She shook her head. "What a strange name for divorce—no fault—like an auto accident. Frank was a good man." She found Matt's eyes. "I was the one to blame."

"Remember the first time you met Jesse—that day at the swan boats?" he asked, wondering why she'd made this long pilgrimage.

She nodded. "Yes. That's what I came to tell you."

"You warned me to be careful, asked what I knew about her."

"I have to fix that." Donna's eyes filled again, but she pushed the tears aside.

Matt was confused. "What do you mean? Fix what?"

She studied the grass. "I thought you were wrong about her, that I was giving you good advice, but I was the one who was wrong—about her, about you, about so many things."

He touched her face. "It's all right, Donna. You were trying to help."

"Please don't be kind, Matt. I don't deserve it." She pulled away. "I've read about Jesse and the kind of life she had. But in spite of everything she went through, she still loved you so much, she gave her life for you." Donna stopped and touched his face. "I couldn't have been more wrong."

"Thanks for the kind words about my mother." They turned. Ali wheeled closer and stopped, holding out her hand. "I'm Alexis Long, Jesse's daughter."

"I know. I'm Donna Flaherty." She shook Ali's

hand.

"I remember you." A faint smile crossed Ali's face. "We met when I was very young—at the swan boats."

Donna nodded. "You have a good memory, Alexis."

"It was nice of you to come." Ali squeezed Donna's arm and turned. "Don't be too long, Matt."

"My God." Donna watched Ali leave. "She's so beautiful, Matt, and so mature. So much like her mother."

Matt followed Ali with his eyes. "Yes." He turned toward Donna. "I appreciate the kind words." He sighed, taking her hands in his. "I've got to go now. Thanks to an old friend, Ali's a very rich young lady. I want to help her make good decisions."

Donna nodded, sniffled, and took a deep breath. "Working on a new book?"

He nodded. "I'm going to write Jesse's biography. It's a story people need to know." He looked toward her grave. "John Van Zandt suggested a title."

"Well?" She asked.

"What do you think of *Jesse's Song?*"

"It's wonderful. I think she'd like it."

"I have to go, too. Good-bye, Matthew. I'm sorry about…everything." She pulled him close, kissing his cheek. "Good luck. Ali's very lucky to have someone like you."

As she turned, Matt called to her. "You still doing social work?"

She nodded. "Head of the Regional Domestic Violence Task Force. It's not glamorous, but needs to be done."

"So I've found out," he said, looking back toward

Jesse's grave. "Maybe I'll see you around the old neighborhood."

She looked back at him. "I'd like that." She paused. "I'm glad I came. It was worth the trip." When she got to her car, Donna waved. Rejoining his family, he said his good-byes.

He knelt. "Good night, my love, my life," he whispered, placing a rose on Jesse's grave. He got up and began pushing Ali toward the car. The wind was picking up, so he moved faster.

"Matt, I know how I'd like to spend some of the money Uncle Mario left us," Ali said when they reached the car.

"How?" he asked.

"I'd like to help people like Mom. People who have tough lives."

"Well, maybe we could help by building shelters." He looked at Donna's car as it left the cemetery. "I think I know someone who might be able to give us some ideas." He looked toward the graves. "I think your mother and grandma would like that."

"I'd like it, too," she said, looking up at him. "Matt?"

"Yes, Ali."

"Do you really think there's a heaven? I mean *really*?"

"With all my heart," he whispered.

"Do you think God heard Mom when she prayed?"

"Jesse prayed?"

"A lot. She was so tired and scared sometimes. I'd hear her crying and..."

"Ali, if she prayed, God heard her." He put his hand on her shoulder.

Matt noticed her expression. "What are you thinking?"

"I'm glad," she said.

"Why?"

"Because I believe you." Ali pushed herself up. She took a tentative step, then a second with more confidence. "If God answered her prayers," she said, holding Matt for support, "she'll never have bad dreams…ever again."

A word about the author...

Kevin Symmons is a successful author, college faculty member, and president of one of the Northeast's most respected writing organizations.

His paranormal novel, *RITE OF PASSAGE*, was a 2013 RomCon Reader's Crown Award finalist and has been an Amazon Best Seller. His latest release, *OUT OF THE STORM*, a contemporary romantic thriller set on Cape Cod, is already gathering five-star reviews and will keep you turning pages late into the night.

His novel *SOLO* is a sweeping women's fiction work that exposes the tragedy of domestic violence in America, released by his award-winning publisher, the Wild Rose Press, Inc., in 2014.

Kevin has collaborated with award-winning Boston screenwriter and playwright Barry Brodsky in adapting one of his story ideas for the screen. He is a sought-after public speaker who has appeared across New England.

Visit Kevin and like his Facebook Author Page, @KevinSymmons on Twitter, at Goodreads, Amazon, and at his website, www.ksymmons.com

~*~

Other Kevin Symmons titles
available from The Wild Rose Press, Inc.

RITE OF PASSAGE
OUT OF THE STORM